THE ROAD TO MANY A WONDER

by David Wagoner

★ NOVELS

The Man in the Middle

Money Money Money

Rock

The Escape Artist

Baby, Come On Inside

Where Is My Wandering Boy Tonight?

The Road to Many a Wonder

★ POEMS

Dry Sun, Dry Wind

A Place to Stand

The Nesting Ground

Staying Alive

New and Selected Poems

Riverbed

★ EDITED

Straw for the Fire: From the Notebooks
of Theodore Roethke 1943–1963

THE ROAD
TO MANY A
WONDER ☆

A novel by David Wagoner

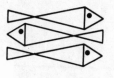

F A R R A R

S T R A U S

G I R O U X

New York

PS
3545
A345
R63x

Third Printing, 1974
Library of Congress catalog card number: 73-87690
ISBN 0-374-25127-4
Printed in the United States of America
Published simultaneously in Canada by Doubleday Canada Ltd., Toronto
Designed by Kay Lee

★ FOR PATT AND CLANCY,
WITH LOVE AND OATS

"A man hasn't got but one chance in life, if that."

—JOSH BILLINGS

THE ROAD TO MANY A WONDER

Chapter One ★★★★★★★★★★★★★★★★★

☞ I'd probably have went Pikes-Peak-or-Busting without no extra help or discouragement, but what made it certain sure was my old man cussing our farm. We'd been scratching to hang on to it for five years, but I could tell there wasn't going to be no sixth when he stood there that early March in 1859, up to his shoe tops in Cass County mud (some of the slimiest west of Plattsmouth, Nebraska Territory, where they know how to make it), and commenced laying his extra-special, Sunday-miss-the-meeting curse on it.

When he got to going, he didn't like to stop for no momentary interruptions like me or Ma or suppertime or sheet lightning. He just kept jawing and ripping and not repeating hisself unless he happened to think up a new one he liked and wanted to run it through the wringer twice so's he could keep it in mind for next time. If mud could burn, he would of burnt our back thirty acres down to bedrock that dim, rainy evening—if there was any bedrock around there, which I never found out, but doubt it.

Pa was little and loud and mean too, if you got upwind of him too long, but I knew how to keep on his good side, which was behind him. I'd had nineteen years of practice since I could walk, so I just waited till he'd had his say and worked it off before telling him supper was fixed.

"Dirt!" he says, like it was the rawest swearword he could think up. "Dirt!" he says. "You ain't nothing but buffalo pies, cow plop, mule apples, and water. Goddamn it, if I couldn't think up something better'n dirt to put underfoot, I'd quit." (Which I guess he meant God had better go find a new job and leave my old man to do the brain work.) "And to think I paid out good hard cash money for you, you rootless, bung-clogging, bone-busting muck, you." (Which I guess he meant that $1.25-per-acre tax he'd been talking about for two years and not paying but one tenth of, while we tried to keep squattering on bad land, getting as poor as Injuns.) "May I rot on a tree if I turn you upside down again with ever a plow or spade." (And I hadn't noticed him using no tools but a knife and fork as long as me and my brother Kit—who run off to the Kansas Territory gold fields last summer—was around to do it all wrong for him.)

Tell the truth, the farm didn't look like much even with the sun up and the crick down. You could stand in the middle of it, and far as you could see, even past our markers, you was the biggest thing growing on it. Whenever there was lightning, like now, it must of had to hunt hard for something to hit. And I didn't like standing outside giving it target practice, but Pa wasn't done yet.

He says, "You won't grow nothing or do nothing but blow off or freeze solid or wash away." (Which was about true because last week that same mud running off into the crick had been snow crust.)

Commencing to holler, he says, "I'm sick of eating you, and I'll be a double-ruptured Show Me sonofabunch if I'm going to kneel down on you no more." (Which I hadn't seen him do but twice in the last year: once when he dropped a nickel and never did find it—oh, what a raking the dirt took that day!—and once when Jess Foley didn't hold him up good enough on the way home from the Wagonwheel.) "And I sure as hell ain't going to crawl under you yet, so you can just go on and wash off down the crick and down the river and out to sea for all I care." (Which was what it was doing anyway without his say-so.)

Raising his arms like a medicine man, he says, "May every stinking square inch of you that stays behind wind up a town dump." (Which was what it was starting to look like already because Pa didn't pay no attention to bottles and lard cans and busted wagon parts and such like—not that he *saved* them: he flung them away all right, he just never flung them very far.) "May you be spat on and shat on and left for trash and nothing green come out of you but scum and mildew," he says. (Which was a pretty good description of the place right as it lay there in front of him, so whoever he was talking to, God or Devil, wouldn't have no trouble making *that* one come true.)

And on and on like that, slow and hard with me keeping quiet and knowing for sure what I'd half-figured out that morning from something Ma said: he'd found somebody dumb enough and sold the place out from under us for back taxes and a little cash to move with. I'd seen it coming after a bad harvest and a hard winter and us eating our own seed corn the last week and a half.

He told the farm how plumb lousy and miserable it looked and smelt, and he picked some up and tried to throw it down, but it mostly stuck to his hand, and he had to wipe it off on his jeans. Then he noticed me standing there and squinted at me to make good and sure I wasn't making no fun of him, which I wasn't, not being stark crazy yet. He pushed his slouchy hat up off his crinkled red forehead and says, "Ike, take a good look at it because you won't be looking at it much more, and you better remember what something really rotten looks like." (Which is what he should of told hisself when he settled us down here and said how grand it was going to be.)

But I done like he told me, my head already working somewhere else, working its way into a different Future. *My* Future. Yet all I says out loud was "Suppertime."

The wind come up and hit us in the face with a gust of rain we didn't happen to need no more of, and he slogged off toward the house ahead of me. "Five years!" he hollers toward the blackest part of the sky. "Each one worse than the last!" He walked hard, kicking mud loose as he went, as if he'd like to gouge off six inches of topsoil, which is about the deepest it run, and get it started in some of the directions he'd been advising it to go—up, sideways, or to blazes.

Over supper he had it all laid out for us, all fixed and figured: we'd load up the wagon with what was worth carrying and just go back to Missouri—and to monumental Damnation with the rest of it. And it come out he'd already sold the plow and one of the two oxen, and since we was all three setting there at the table with our mouth half full of the last of the seed corn, the farming was over for sure.

Ma didn't say nothing, but just shrunk up a little smaller, her skin going loose and leathery around her mouth and one eye getting bigger than the other, the way it does when she's trying to clutch on to herself. Her straw-and-gray hair sprung loose from her bun all by itself.

Mild and kind of sweet, Pa says to me, "I hear you been digging holes."

It was cold in the house, though the stove was going better than usual, and it seemed like it turned even colder then. The roof was leaking in three places since the thaw, and I listened to the drip on the plank floor and to Ma munching her corn for a few seconds, wondering what to say and finally not saying nothing.

"Digging holes with a pickax and shovel," he says soft and easy. "Where did you happen to get a pickax and shovel?"

"I borrowed them," I says, which was the truth as far as it went and didn't get me in no deeper trouble.

"Holes in the *ground*," he says, like it was some kind of unnatural wonder. "Now what was a son of mine doing digging holes in the ground and not getting paid for it? You going to set yourself up in the graveyard business?"

"No, sir," I says. "I just thought I'd dig some holes. For fun." I tried to smile, but I knew it wasn't coming out on my face right. Besides, he didn't know nothing about fun.

"Deep holes," he says. "What was you looking for?"

"I wasn't looking for nothing," I says, which was a fact.

"Just breaking your back for the mere pleasure of it," he says. "If you was so anxious to dig holes, why didn't you dig us a new privy while you was at it?"

"I'd of drownded," I says. "I had to get up on dry land."

"Want some more to eat?" Ma says, trying like always to shovel food on top of talk to keep it nice. Pa passed his empty dish and she scraped the last spoonful of corn for him, adding what was left of her own and even taking a look at mine, which I et up as quick as I could so's I'd have something to choke on in case he thought up some bad questions.

"And Frank Patterson says he seen you sleeping out on the prairie three mornings ago," Pa says. "On the bare ground. We never knew you was out of the house, did we, Ma? Nor out of your mind neither."

"No," she says.

But I could see by the jerky, slantwise look she give me it wasn't true. She must of heard me sneaking out after bedtime these last ten nights and been scairt to say anything. She'd spent her life being quiet and scairt, and maybe if I hadn't had her bad example setting right there in front of me, I would of just kept still and been swallered forever.

Pa says, "Why'd you want to sleep outdoors when you got a perfectly good bed indoors?"

I didn't have no such a thing but didn't figure on saying so.

"The family of Jed Bender don't sleep out on the ground like bagheads and bushwhackers," he says. "And I hear you dug a well for Tom Slaughter last week."

"I just helped," I says.

"How much did he pay you?"

"He didn't pay me nothing." Which wasn't strictly true but near enough.

"You done it just for fun?" Pa says, going very still and dead-faced.

"A man had ought to know how to dig a well, I reckon."

"So you done it for practice?" Pa says. "Why didn't you practice digging one here on your own farm?"

I wanted to say it wasn't my farm nor his neither, but instead I says, "We already got a well."

"So did Tom Slaughter," Pa says. "And now he's got two. Got a mighty pretty daughter too, don't he?"

"She ain't but fifteen years old," I says.

"Well, that's old enough for *me*," he says.

When he seen I wasn't going to answer, he reached in his pocket and took out a piece of newspaper all folded up, and I reckonized it from the creases and cracks where it had been slept on and rained on for the last two weeks since I'd found it. My stomach sank or maybe it was my heart landing on top of my liver: he'd been into my gear, which meant he must of clumb up the ladder into my cubbyhole loft when I was gone, the most work I'd known him to do since the fire out at the Pawnee cider press when it was Come one, come all, and all the squeezings you could cart off free. Now there was no telling what kind of hell there'd be to pay.

He spread it out flat and careful at the foot of the candlestick and begun to read it out loud and, him not being much for reading, it come out real slow, each word separate. First he says the big print at the top: " 'Who Should Go to Pikes Peak?' " His eyes sank back a half inch in his head, and when he looked at me, I wouldn't of known they was green if I hadn't had the misfortune of looking in there before. Flat and cold, he says, "Ike, we're going to St. Louie and get us a couple jobs on the docks."

I didn't say nothing, so he begun spelling out the story. " 'We often hear young men, who never did any hard work in their lives'—well, that's *you* all right—'talk about going to Pikes Peak.' " He snatched a look at me again, singeing his hair a little in the candle flame. "You poor goddamn idjit." But he said it real quiet, then went on reading. " 'We ask such young men what kind of work they think gold digging is.' " He glared at me and says, "Well, I'll just tell you and this here paper what kind of work it is: fool work!"

He'd been awful riled when Kit run off, mainly because I couldn't do all the hoeing and weeding and hauling by myself, and that meant he had to turn out and do something besides give orders for a change. He'd been tongue-lashing gold for six months. I kept still.

He went on reading, going a little faster now. " 'Let them turn out at home and get themselves into practice by digging wells, cellars, coal, quarrying rocks, mauling rails, and rolling saw logs, and eat dry bread and wash it down with water, and sleep on the ground in fair weather and foul, and then form an opinion about the work of digging gold.' "

"I guess I better rench off these here dishes," Ma says, getting up and starting to fuss.

"How much gold you found so far, digger?" Pa says.

"None," I says.

"And that's just exactly how much you're going to find no matter where you roam, so start using the little brains you got. We're going to quit dirt farming. We got to get off this goddamn dirt. It drives people crazy. You start *thinking* like dirt and looking like it. We're getting our shoe leather back on some cobblestones. There's nothing in dirt, least of all gold. Just show me some gold."

"Haven't got none," I says, which wasn't strictly true.

"Neither's anybody else," he says. "There ain't no such a thing for poor folks. Now you just start packing the wagon. You been getting plenty of exercise away from home lately. Now you can start using some of them new muscles for the family." He stood up and stared down at me, almost knocking his stool over backwards. He liked to catch me setting down because I was five inches taller than him now and still going.

"Tom Slaughter must of paid you *some*thing," he says. "Turn out your pockets."

"Don't ask me to do that, Pa," I says, feeling like my face was going to catch fire.

"I ain't asking, I'm dye-*rec*ting you," he says.

"I swear I didn't get no money from Tom Slaughter," I says. "Please just take my word for it."

"You can't be that dumb," he says, louder. "Turn out your pockets."

Which I was bound and determined not to do because I had something private in there, something strictly personal. I stood up and says, "I can't do it, Pa. I wouldn't do that for nobody, not even under a gun."

He didn't like the look of me standing up, and his face kind of scrunched up tight in the middle. "Maybe I'll just go get the shotgun and see if you know your own mind yet, boy."

"Jed," Ma says. "I need some dishwater."

"Just leave them dishes out in the rain, woman," Pa says.

Then he looked me up and down and seemed to relax a little and says, "So you aim to be treated like a man from now on, is that it?"

"Yes, sir," I says, feeling a long ways from home already.

"What you done to prove it so far?" he says, leveling out into his thin, mean voice he used to use with Kit.

"I ain't sure," I says, but I had the feeling I was going to have to prove it right there.

"Does Tom know you been playing tickle-wiggle with his daughter?" Pa says, grinning.

"Jed!" Ma says. "Don't you go saying that."

"Takes more'n a little trip up the milky way, Ike boy," Pa says. "I got started on that when I was twelve, but it didn't mean I was a man. Yet I'll tell you one thing: I was more a man at twelve than you are now."

"Miss Millie Slaughter is a decent young girl," I says, "and I got nothing but respect for her."

"You got nothing for her a-*tall*," Pa says. "Turn out your pockets, boy."

"If you want the wagon loaded, you better tell me what you want put in first," I says.

"Oh?" he says, pretending like he was real surprised. "You figure on doing a little work around here? Free of charge?"

"I don't want to quarrel with you, Pa," I says.

"And just what do you think this is you're doing here if it ain't quarreling?"

"I'm standing up for my rights," I says.

"Your *rights?*" he says, making his eyebrows go up and down twice like I had just brung up a comical new subject and he needed to roll it around in his head a minute to take some of the polish off. "And what in the wide world might them things be?"

I didn't know how to put the proper names to them, but I sure felt like I was about to have them stole from me if I didn't fight back. "I shouldn't have to turn out my pockets to you," I says. "And I—" I tried to think hard, but it ain't easy to do at the best of times, and trying to face Pa down wasn't the best time but the worst. "And I don't belong to you, not altogether." That didn't sound right yet. I moved a little to get out from under a drip from the roof and says, "You don't own me outright."

"No, I don't, boy," he says. "I agree with you. If I owned you outright, I'd of sold you long ago like a nigger and bought me a cow or a hog or whatever you'd fetch."

"Jed, no!" Ma says, starting her grieving, hand-wringing, shrinking, walleyed shuffle over by the wood box.

I don't know what come over me then. Seemed like I was in two or three places at once, though I was standing stock-still, and my tongue started running away with me. I'd never been much of a one for talking, specially around Pa, but now suddenly I could do it, and I says, "You'll find that newspaper goes on to say too many men come to the gold fields without no muscle to their backs and with their hands all soft from clerking in dry-goods stores, but I ain't like that now. I'm ready."

"Your fool mind's got a leak in it," Pa says.

"That's your own roof over your own head which I fixed as good as I could with no nails and no shingles," I says.

"You didn't have no trouble finding a pickax and shovel when you wanted to," he says.

"When I was digging them practice holes, some kids and jugheads from town would come out and watch and sit around and chunk a few rocks at me and tease me," I says. "But sooner or later they'd all wander off and find something else to waste their time on. Want to hear what I learnt digging holes?"

Pa looked a little confused, since he'd never heard that many words out of me in a row, but he stiffened hisself and come around to the edge of the table and says, "Just shut your mouth and turn out your pockets."

But I was heading downhill now, so I says, "I learnt

there ain't no gold in any kind of hole you'd care to dig in Cass County, and them that's got a Plan, them that's got a Vision of the Future, why, they always seem loco to the muddlers and the whittlers that don't want to do nothing or be nothing."

"If I'd talked like that to my pa, he'd of whup me till my ass rattled," he says.

"You better practice up on somebody else first," I says, getting ready to defend my rights, which I had begun to make out a little plainer now.

He seemed to relax some and shook his head in mock wonder and looked at Ma, who'd got herself all stirred up with nose blowing and blinking and lip biting and saying silent things at the floor and so on. "Ever hear the like of that?" Pa says. "That's what comes of going to school."

Which was a sore point with him he always brung up, no matter what or who he was mad at because me and Kit had both learnt to read and write better than him from Miss Wilkerson down the road.

Then in a mild, even voice he says, "All right, you tie up the pots, pans, and skillet in the tightest bunch you can and put them in the back part of the wagon that's out of the rain under the shed, if you're so anxious to do something for your country."

"Yes, sir," I says, ready to do anything sensible to cool the air down, and I headed for the bin next to the sink.

"But they ain't all clean yet," Ma says in a kind of wail.

"That don't matter," Pa says. "We're moving first thing in the morning, come Hell or high water or both."

And I made the mistake of passing too close to him and didn't catch sight of the piece of kindling till it was coming around on the backside of my head. It hit me a good solid thunk, and the light blazed up in my head like a bonfire hit with a bucket of coal oil. And when I come back to myself, stunned, I was laying on the wet floor, feeling calm and lazy like you might if you was to wake up in the middle of the night from a dream that hadn't gone too bad yet. Ma was beside me, clutching my head to her bony chest, and Pa was at the table under the candlelight, reading Kit's letter out loud, which I'd had in my back pocket.

He'd already got past the part about how Kit had teamed up with these three other men, one of them an old-time miner, and formed a company called the Colly-wobble and staked their claims on Slab Crick off the South Platte near Cherry Crick and had built them a hut to winter over, and how they was sure as sin going to strike it rich when the ground thawed.

In a voice that come blurry to me, Pa says, " 'I am sending this here map so's you can tell how to find me. Come on, Ike, the others says you can earn a share if you work hard. I told them you was good and strong and not no rumbuster. Am enclosing two flakes of placer gold worth seventy-five cents. Plenty more where that come from. Be here by April. Your brother, Kit.' "

Even with my head throbbing and thick-feeling, I could of recited the letter faster than Pa read it. Even laying sideways like that and with Ma getting her rough, skinny fingers in the way, I seen Pa turning over the flakes of gold with a miserable, doubtful, goddamn-the-luck look on his face. Then he dropped them careful into the folds of the letter and tucked it tight in his shirt pocket. He spread the map flat and leant on it, like I'd done a hundred times: it was almost two foot square on thin crinkly paper that made a noise like bacon frying when you handled it. He stared it over for near a minute, then folded it back up and shoved it in his pocket.

He seen me setting up and trying to get Ma to leave off swabbing me with a wet dishrag, and he says, "Well, I guess I got me two boys with big ideas and none of the brains to go with them." He shoved his hat on and took his yellow slicker off the peg by the door.

Ma was bawling without making no more noise than the

floor creaking underfoot (she'd learnt how to do that so's not to give no annoyance), but she managed to say, "Where you going?"

"Why, if it's any business of yours," he says with his chin in the air, "I'm going to have me seventy-five cents' worth of gold whiskey. If it's gold. Be the first time I ever got anything back from a boy of mine. After all I've laid out for *them*."

Well, he had laid *me* out all right, but I didn't aim to pay him back right then. I kept still and watched him stomp out into the gusty night, holding his hat on, and I wished him no evil on his mile-long walk to the Wagonwheel, where, I was sure, he'd make up some bragging tale or other about the gold flakes. Instead, I got my feet under me, tried to make sure my head wasn't busted, and when I had shook off most of the dizziness, I clumb up to my cubbyhole loft and begun making a waterproof bundle out of my extra shirt, extra drawers and socks, and my blanket.

At the bottom of the ladder, for the tenth time, Ma says, "He didn't mean it. Don't run off."

When I figured I could talk all right, I says, "I'm sorry, Ma. You picked him. I didn't. Or let him pick you. And if you want to go on making rubbage out of the rest of your life, there's nothing I can do. I ain't going to wreck mine nor salt it down neither. It ain't my fault if he busted your spirit." Which was the most I'd ever said or hope to say to her on the subject.

She cried some more up the ladder, making a little more commotion about it than usual, and she says, "He ain't a bad man, and he needs you."

"We don't own nothing he can't lift by his own self," I says. "And right now I need myself worse than him." I clumb down and kissed her between the eyes, which was about the only place there wasn't no tears.

"But I don't have no food to give you," she says.

"I got something better than food to go on," I says, putting on my own oilskin slicker, which had a long crack under one arm but would serve. I give her another peck on the forehead, right in the middle of the squint lines which made me feel deep-hurt and sorry for her, but I kept going into the windy drizzle, hanging on to my hat and starting to feel freer with each slog through the mud up to the road and not looking back—because didn't I have a World to Win and wasn't I Bound to Rise?

Chapter Two ★ ★ ★ ★ ★ ★ ★ ★ ★ ★ ★ ★ ★ ★ ★ ★ ★

☞ Later, I was bound to rise about six thousand foot, but now I done all my walking on the level. I felt miserable for a hundred yards, and bad for another hundred, and nothing for another, and pretty good after that, and by the time I'd slipped through town—I kept shy of the Wagonwheel because (1) I had got that map burnt deep in my mind's eye and didn't need it wrote on paper and (2) there's no use killing your own pa if it won't teach him nothing—I felt extra good and just hung out there at the split-rail gate for a spell, enjoying the rain.

But I come halfway to my senses pretty soon, specially when their hound dog Biltmore come out and commenced baying at me like I was the moon or a possum with six younguns on its tail. Tom come to the door with a lantern and a shotgun, but when he seen who it was, he just handed the lantern backwards to young Millie without even looking to see if she was there and let her come out by herself with her shawl over her head to hush up Biltmore and take me out to the shed like she'd done every night for nine days.

Pa had called her mighty pretty, but he never looked at nothing too close and maybe he just took somebody else's word for it. There ain't many women in Cass County, and most of them's little girls or mothers or old ladies, and of the ones in between, dang few of them's pretty, let alone *mighty*, and when there's so few around I guess you can't blame men for praising and flattering what there is. Truth to tell, Millie Slaughter was plain-looking—skinny and flat in front and long-legged and a pair of brown pigtails and snub-nosed—but she had great big dark-brown eyes and didn't talk much, and after a bit it got so all you could remember about her was her eyes and her shut lips pressed together kind of stubborn.

She led the way to the shed and shoved the door open and let Biltmore go bounding in ahead of us, whining and crooning with joy (which was about how I felt but couldn't show it), and then she hung up the lantern so's we could all three stand there and admire my wheelborrow.

Biltmore hoisted on it like he done every night, but that just helped season the wood some more, and it was going to need all the seasoning it could get for the Grand Journey. Summer and fall I had seen Pikes Peakers come through town in every contraption known to man and some unknown like the wind wagon which had been sposed to sail with its sloop rigging all the way through Nebraska Territory and uphill among the tributaries of the South Platte but which keeled over and broke up in Crocker's Canal five miles west of here and wound up patching chicken coops: I had seen full-fledged covered wagons with two whole families aboard, smaller wagons and carriages by the hundred, handcarts pulled by four men who couldn't afford to buy or feed mules or oxen, men on horseback and burroback, men afoot with nothing more to their name than a pickax with a carpetbag hanging on it. But the practicalest one-man rig I ever seen, needing neither hay nor horseshoes, ready for pushing or pulling, and big enough to hold what a man would need to travel five hundred miles and tools to work with after he got there, was a wheelborrow. And I had built the finest, sturdiest article in that line I ever laid eyes on.

It had an eighteen-inch iron-rimmed wheel which had been the flywheel on a steam pump that blew up over at Mossbarger's drainage ditch, and I happened to find it before he even come to. I'd had it for ten months, knowing it was going to be good for something, and there it was, all axle-greased and ready to roll again, only this time Ike Bender was going to be the head of steam behind it. I had made the handles and back legs out of clothes props with the grip ends rasped down smooth to fit my hands and not splinter. But the smartest part of all was the body, and I thought up the idea all by myself (which Pa would never of let me do if he'd been watching): it was the wood tub me and Tom Slaughter had used to dig his well, the kind you haul the dirt up with on a windlass. The rest of the wheelborrow was like a framework and the tub fit down into it and stayed put full or empty. But if I wanted to use it, all's I had to do was hoist her out, and then come the second smart part, if I do say so myself as shouldn't: I was carrying another piece of clothes prop, notched at one end, the same length as the handles, and forty foot of rope, so all I had to do to change my wheelborrow into a hole-digging, gold-digging truss was lift out the tub, turn the frame so's the wheel was up in the air, brace it into a tripod with the extra prop, tie the rope through holes I'd brace-and-bitted in the tub, shove through an iron crank I'd bent myself, and haul her up.

I had been proud of a few things before in my life, but always on the sly, having to be sneaky and secret. Now I had myself the sweet pleasure, for a little while, of being proud right out in the open. And there was Millie Slaughter and Biltmore to help me do it.

After a minute of watching me enjoy myself grinning and shuffling, she says, "I think you did a beautiful job."

For the life of me I couldn't act modest like a Christian's sposed to but went on grinning. "I'd like to try her out first, but I don't have time," I says.

"What do you mean, Mr. Bender?" she says, looking worried and big-eyed.

"I'm leaving right now," I says. "Tonight."

"I don't think Pa got all the things you asked for yet," she says.

"I don't care," I says. "He's done too much already." Besides giving me a place to work and loaning me saw, hammer, rasp, and square, Tom Slaughter was paying off my well-digging with a side of bacon and twenty-five pounds of flour and the old pickax and shovel I'd been using.

"He didn't get the blanket yet," she says.

"I don't need but one."

"He got the skillet and canteen," she says. "But he couldn't find any quicksilver. Nobody's got any."

Kit had told me to bring some quicksilver because they use it gold mining, but I couldn't stay around hunting for it. "It don't matter," I says. "Maybe I'll find some on the way."

"But it's raining," she says, her voice going up.

"It's always doing something outdoors," I says. "What's the use of being choosy the first night when I can't do nothing about it tomorrow night or a whole month of nights? I'm going to take what comes, and I expect the night to do likewise."

She says, "You have blood on your head."

She was always noticing things like that—broke fingernails and cuts and slivers and scrapes—so I let her fuss and cluck and run back to the house for liniment, while I got my oilskin bundle arranged right in the tub and wondered if Pa would come hunt me up when he got home from the saloon and admired my own carpentry and worried over whether I'd dug enough practice holes and scratched Biltmore, and then she was back and her father too.

"I don't think it's any too good an idea lighting off in the middle of the night," he says, while Millie made me stoop under the lantern and dabbed at the back of my head with a piece of flour sack. "How'd you hurt your head?"

Tom acted kind of shy about it, since he knew what my old man was like, but I could tell what he was getting at. "He won't blame you," I says. "I told him what I was going to do and he knows where I'm going and why."

Tom seemed to settle for that all right, but he says, "You don't have enough food to last you more'n two weeks, if that."

"I been eating trash and scraps all my life," I says. "I reckon I'll find enough."

"How much money you got for emergencies?" he says.

I was embarrassed to tell him, but then Millie give me a slap dab of liniment, and I forgot what kind of half-truth I was going to tell, while I yipped a little to cool it off.

"And your scalp don't feel too good when even a little bit of it comes off, does it?" Tom says. "How would you like to have the whole thing took off for you? I notice you don't have a gun."

"I don't aim to shoot nobody," I says.

"What if somebody aims to shoot you?" Millie says.

"I'm friendly," I says. "And I got nothing to rob—yet." I didn't like all this talk about hazards and what if this and that. It was sposed to sound practical but wasn't. "Mr. Slaughter, the main thing is *I'm going.* Everything else has to fall in line back of that. There's some things I can afford, and some I can't. I'm one man. There's some things one man can carry, and some he can't. If I run out of money, I'll just have to make do, and I won't forget about paying you back for all you done to grubstake me." He started to say no, but I had my oats up now and went right on. "I'll come back someday, and you'll get your fair share of what I got, even if it's only another stretch of digging. I planned this the best I could, and now it's time, and I ain't scairt."

He nodded at me and shrugged and shook my hand and shook his head and went off back to the house, so Millie could say goodbye. I think he knew pretty much what I knew: she was a little stuck on me, and I was a little stuck on her, and I suspicioned one of the reasons he give me so much help getting my wheelborrow and supplies rigged up and fitted out was he wanted to get me out on the road away from her before her and me done something foolish. And I can't say as I blame him: what did I have to offer except what I stood up in, some hopes, and a farm and a ma and pa all so run down they didn't amount to much but dead weight or worse? But even though she wasn't but fifteen and a half, I felt plumb funny about her. Weak and jumpy, like I was standing on a loose plank whenever I was around her.

Tom come back for a few seconds with the bacon and flour and saleratus (to make the dough rise), glancing kind of worried at her just standing there staring at me with them dark eyes, then left again, and I begun packing everything snug with the oilskin covering it and the pickax and shovel tied longways on the frame, one on each side.

"Are you really going through with this, Mr. Bender?" she says.

"Yes, I am."

"You haven't got enough clothes," she says. "All that walking. What if your boots wear out or your socks?"

"I borrowed enough things already," I says. "I don't need to borrow trouble too."

"I'll wager you don't even have needle and thread."

"I wouldn't know what to do with it if I did," I says.

"But I got me a compass needle. You just ease your mind off now, and maybe I'll write you a letter."

"Maybe?"

I could see I'd hurt her with that, so I says, "All right, I will. I surely will."

"Do you have pen and paper?" she says.

"Now don't go fussing over every little thing," I says. "This here's a wheelborrow, not a stagecoach. I'll *find* some."

"I know you don't want to go with one of those groups," she says.

And I sure didn't. There was messes of organized parties starting to form in every town around us, but I didn't want to spend no hundred dollars, which I didn't have but five dollars of, just to have company on the trip and a fat ex-major in a sombrero to point which way was west-by-north and stake out my corner of one of the hand-hauled carts as big as a buckboard.

"But couldn't you trail after one?" she says. "In case of trouble?"

"I'll do what seems best at the time," I says. "Now get your kettle off the boil and take good care of your pa and Biltmore." Her ma had died last spring, and maybe that was why she'd got such an early start wifing and mothering everything in reach.

"Are you capable of tender feelings, Mr. Bender?" she says, sounding just like Miss Wilkerson, who come from back East someplace.

"Reckon I could learn in a pinch," I says.

"That's hardly an encouraging answer. Would you say you had an excessively greedy nature?"

"I don't know," I says. "I ain't never been satisfied, if that's what you mean."

"I don't want you to think I'm shocked by sinful character traits," she says.

Millie had learnt to read off Miss Wilkerson same time

as me and Kit, but she kept right on reading even after me and him had slacked off, but she must of hunted up all kind of strange books because she didn't talk the same no more. Girls got the spare time for it, I guess.

She looked up at me hard and straight and says, "What do you really want to do? Just be rich?"

"Well, I wouldn't object none," I says.

"Aren't there better ways to go about doing that? Safer ways?" she says.

I give her a careful looking over and seen, underneath, she was hopeful and anxious and a little sad. It was all I could do to get myself to talk about it, but since there wasn't nobody else listening, I says, "I got a Destiny."

But that didn't stop her. "What kind?" she says.

"I don't know, but I can feel it coming and hear it calling," I says. "Can you keep a secret?"

"Yes," she says, and I believed her.

"I ain't the same as anybody else that ever lived in the whole world," I says. "Not better, but just not the same." And I had never told that to a living soul since I had found it out one night in the dark of my bed, with the leaky roof no more'n two inches from my nose. I was tired and cold and hungry and not sleepy enough to get over them facts, and instead of just falling off a cliff into the pitch black (like I often done at night) I seen what they call a Vision. I can't tell you what I done or said in it or what I felt because it would wreck it all, like telling a wish after splitting a wishbone.

"What's so different about you?" she says, kind of sassing me but looking like maybe she thought I really was.

"I'll just have to wait and find out for sure," I says.

"I hope you're not being boastful, Mr. Bender," she says.

Something made me take her slim little hand in mine, and I says, "I don't mean it that way. I just mean some good things have already been laid out ahead of me in my life, and I didn't do nothing to deserve it but be born different and have the luck to find out."

She kept still for a spell then, like she was mulling over what I said, and she seemed to like it all right, which made me feel good. She slipped her hand out of mine and took a half-pint bottle from under her shawl and held it up to the lantern to look through the red inch and a half in the bottom of it, then shook it and handed it to me, shy. "It's Dr. Barton's Iron Nerve Elixir," she says. "Pa doesn't allow liquor in the house, so it's all I could find. Would you do me a great honor?"

I was scairt she was going to ask me to drink it, but I didn't need no spring tonic. I felt like I'd already drunk up a gallon of it.

"It's presumptuous of me to ask, but I was afraid you wouldn't think of it by yourself," she says. "Would you christen your wheelborrow after me?"

"I thought you needed a preacher and holy water for a christening," I says.

"This is different. They generally use a woman to christen ships, and this is a kind of ship, isn't it?"

"I spose so."

"Well, all I have to do is break a bottle over it, and it's christened and launched both at the same time."

"Just don't bust nothing but the bottle," I says. "And don't get nothing sticky on the handles."

She had me line up with her by the front wheel, and in a solemn, clear, shaky voice, she says, "I christen this wheelborrow the *Millicent Slaughter*, and may it go in peace and safety and good fortune and come back the same way." And she hit the wheel a good lick and smashed the bottle and splashed Biltmore and scairt him out the door and begun weeping, all about at once.

I hadn't seen nor heard her do nothing like that before, nor no other grown female but Ma, and I didn't know what to do or act like. So I took the coward's way and patted her on the back and heisted the handles of the wheelborrow and headed for the door.

Sounding mournful, she says, "We could paint the name on, but I imagine it would just wash off."

"I'm much obliged to you and your pa for everything you done for me," I says.

"As I hope to go to Heaven, I wish you well, Mr. Bender," she says.

"As I hope to go to Pikes Peak or Bust, I thank you kindly, Millie," I says.

"Put down the handles just a moment," she says, catching up with me.

I done so, and we kissed each other on the lips, her doing most of the work at first, then going equal shares and not smacking loud at the end of it. It was our first one, and it was very peculiar, it being more bothersome than I'd reckoned on. I got myself and my wheelborrow out in the rain quick to simmer down and traded goodbyes with her all the way out to the road in the near-dark, and then I was along it and on my way at last. But the wheelborrow, as light as if it was empty, done more to balance me than me it, to start off with.

Chapter Three ★★★★★★★★★★★★★★★

☞ I didn't make it far that night—just three miles to an empty hay crib on the edge of Detweiler's ranch, where there was enough shelter to keep the rain busy trying to find me—but I wanted to put a little space between me and Pa, who was liable to start spitting sparks and saw teeth when somebody went against his grain. And I spent my first night using my back as a mattress and my belly as a blanket (I didn't want to unpack nothing when it was so tidy), feeling like a happy man because every time the worries commenced, such as Millie weeping and kissing me and how was I going to be worthy of her, or Ma bawling and shaking and maybe taking the thousandth drubbing of her bondage on my account, or Pa hunting after me with his shotgun, all's I had to do was touch that iron wheel I was laying beside, and I'd remember where I was and what I was up to: Here and Anything.

Come the first thin slice of dawn, and I was up and going again on that narrow road that hadn't been rutted much yet since the thaw and having nothing to eat but what they call a Mexican breakfast, which is you take your belt in a notch.

Now, the first thing you want to do if you're interested in pushing a wheelborrow fifteen miles a day (or thereabouts) for maybe six weeks is not to get mad at it. I made that mistake every now and then for the first few days, even going so far as to kick the *Millicent Slaughter* right in the tub when she pitched over on her side for the sixth or seventh time after she hit a hump I didn't happen to have my eye on. A wheelborrow don't want to be kicked no more'n a mule, and you get just about as much action in return, namely nothing. There's going to be plenty to vex you anyway without adding on a sore toe. I tried a little of Pa's kind of cussing, but I wasn't no good at it, and besides it made me feel like I'd brung him along with me.

No, if you want to get along with a wheelborrow, what you have got to do is look to its needs ahead of time, which isn't but a few: (1) it don't want to be pushed up over nothing—it has got to go around or else be pulled over, and (2) if you feel one of them handles pushing up against your hand or hauling downwards, you'd best start shoving and hauling the opposite ways or there's going to be a spillover. I got the hang of it pretty quick, though, and after a while, I switched from pushing to pulling and back even when there wasn't no rocks or humps or ruts or trash to go past, but just to shift off on my muscles and elbow sockets.

I won't go into blisters on hand nor foot. They come and go for a spell, then they harden up and you can forget about them. I took to wearing my extra socks on my hands the first few days, but I seen how foolish it was to wear holes in two pair at once, and then on, I just let Nature take over, which is the same as trying not to fetch up the Wrath of God.

The country was flat and barren and none of it plowed yet, some open range, and the dead bent-over grass was mud-colored, and you wouldn't of thought there was a hope of nothing new growing up out of that mess. But of course it was there already, down at the very base of them stalks, the pale-green shoots taking their first small breaths and a deep suck at the roots and trying to find a way to get past all the dead tangled-up old-timers bunched over them, leaning cockeyed and shutting out the light.

After that first night, the rain held off for the two days it took me to hit the Platte, and the wind blew from every which way, sometimes a help, sometimes a hinder, but you could smell more rain in it, just holding off till the right time, which nobody knew but it. I slept the second night out in the open because there wasn't no choice, not a tree or a shed in sight around sundown. After I'd made a little fire out of scraps from dead bushes, I cut me some bacon and fried it in the skillet, then borrowed a tin-cupful of water from a big shallow puddle in the field next to me and made up a flat chunk of pan bread and fried it in the grease nice and slow.

I'd scared off some long-legged gray birds smaller than chickens and skinnier, but they come to the puddle again when I'd got back to the fire, and I set there watching them go wading a couple inches deep and poking this way and that down in the mud with their long, thin, pointy beaks. I couldn't tell if they was finding anything, but they kept on doing it, wading and weaving and sometimes in a tight bunch and sometimes wide separate. And as I et my bacon and bread and watched, it seemed like I was getting a lesson. Them birds had picked a puddle that didn't look worth nothing, that wasn't no different than a thousand others probably all around us, that would be long gone and forgot by May if not sooner. But they was drawing their life out of it that evening, just like me, and happy to have it and know how to use it, finding things down in that muck nobody or nothing else knew how to find. And singing while they was at it too: short, high, far-off-sounding whistles like wind blowing across broke straw. And maybe not even finding much, or maybe finding nothing till tomorrow but still happy to be there, now, doing what they liked to do.

They flew off right at the last glimmer of dusk when the sky was going all ashy, not all of them together but a few at a time till there wasn't but one left. He took a few more swipes at the water and maybe caught him a last grub or whatever, then took off after the rest, maybe spending the night flying somewhere for all I knew. Before it was plumb dark, I walked over there and scooped up another cup of that water and drunk it down to them birds and myself and the Good Future, which I knew now had already started when I wasn't looking.

I had never traveled much, except for moving from Missouri to the farm, and I didn't remember a whole lot about it except getting sick over the side of the wagon. Besides, Pa was doing all that traveling, and me and Ma and Kit was just tagging along. It's different when it's you deciding where to camp and when to get up and which way to turn. Even the prairie seemed exciting because it was me pushing that wheelborrow on it, alone out there on my own two feet, not asking nobody's leave to spit or whistle. I begun to feel alive, which I hope to tell you is the best way.

Mid-afternoon of the third day, the wind dropped still and the sun come out blazing like June, and I tromped along through the quiet, beginning to feel strange. I felt like I was going uphill, which if you've lived on the prairie most of your life is a notion your knees can't understand. Seemed like every time I put my foot down, the ground was there to meet it a little too soon, and when I seen what looked like hills up ahead of me—low and domy-shaped and bare and sort of bluish—and when I seen the soil underfoot was getting sandier and looser, I reckoned I was coming to the Platte.

And right about then the wonders commenced. You're going to think I'm lying, but I don't need to. I don't mind a good lie, one with lots of decorations on it like a band-wagon that makes nice loud music and serves a little beer to help wash down the extra whoppers. (A mean, bare lie is different.) But I was never no good at lying. My ma was always saying, "Tell the truth and shame the Devil," which I been trying to do all my life, and the truth always seemed stronger and dreadfuller and funnier and sadder than any lie, so you can take my word if you feel so inclined and it won't cost you nothing but a little effort.

First off, them hills looked to be maybe two miles away, so I walked two miles (which happens to be 3,520 paces of mine unless I'm gimped up or tuckered out), but when I done it, they still looked two miles off. Well, that's no wonder, you might say, that's just bad eyesight. Then I walked another two miles, and they was *still* two miles off. And how's this for bad eyesight: halfway through that second two miles, I seen six men all dressed in black on one of them hills, just standing there like they was waiting for me. I got worried because I couldn't figure out what no priests or undertakers would be doing out here, so I sheered off a little to pass them by. But when I got closer, they went skittering along the ground and rose up in the air and flew off. I thought I'd been hexed or sun-addled, and even after they commenced cawing and I seen they was crows, the question in my mind was: how long had they been crows?

The hills left off playing their main trick then and stopped backing away and let me get halfway up one of them, and I was so excited to get to see whatever it was I'd see when I got to the top, I had a little wheelborrow trouble in the sand because these was *sand* hills. All sand. Just like I'd read about on the edge of the ocean or out on the desert. By the time I collected my wits and turned the *Millicent Slaughter* around and started pulling her up the last slope, I'd had my fill of loose sand and had lost my temper near as bad as Pa, but then I seen the giant.

It's all right to have sand hills with nothing growing on them, not even a blade of buffalo grass. I can put up with them. But over on the next one west of me, which looked to be a quarter mile off at most, there was some kind of dark-brown shaggy-looking monster—man or animal, I couldn't tell—and to make a short story tall, it was a good fifteen foot high.

I dropped them handles where I stood, and if it hadn't been sloggy sand, my wheelborrow would of rolled halfway back to the farm by itself. I didn't move none, since I didn't want to stir up nothing's appetite that was that thick and tall, and in a minute or two, the critter moved off over the slope away from me, shifting and jiggling its shape and shrinking down a bit and popping up higher than before and using six or eight legs to walk on and, at the last, just four legs like it was pretending to be an ox or maybe a buffalo.

The second it had went over the further edge, I grabbed them handles and made it the rest of the way up the hill in one long splay-footed gallop, and I was over the top and down a little ways before I stopped and took my first long look at the greatest wonder of them all so far: the valley of the Platte, the likes of which I haven't seen since and neither has nobody else.

I thought I'd seen a river before, and I had—the Missouri, when we'd got ferried across at low water to get to our farm. But this looked more like an ocean is sposed to look, except it was yellow, and here where I'd struck it, the valley looked five or six miles wide and the river took up dang near half of it. I could of been wrong, of course, since I wasn't used to measuring distances like that, there being nothing much to stand on and see from back where I come from. But it was mighty broad and flat and full of islands and side channels and meanders and backwaters, and there was just too much of it to take in. The sun was flashing on and off now as some clouds come puffing out of the northwest. There wasn't no wind on the ground, but it looked like they had plenty to spare up high. I stood there a long while, awestruck, forgetting I'd been a little scairt a while back. And I have found that to be the nature of wonders: if you try piling one on top of another, you start losing track of the first ones. A wonder takes up all your attention it can find and don't leave hardly any room for memories.

The air was shimmering and going light and dark as the sun blinked, and when I looked way off upstream, I could of swore for a few seconds I seen a lake higher than the river with skinny-looking upside-down houses beyond it, and I didn't know whether I was standing on my head or my feet.

What brung me back to sober daylight was the sight of about a dozen tepees and doby lodges of a Pawnee village below me and off to the right on my side of the river, so I short-cut off left away from them down towards the river road, not wanting to meet no Injuns if I didn't have to. They was mostly quiet and easygoing, but they'd only lost the land I was walking on a few years back, and some of them around home hadn't got used to the idea yet. I didn't feel like it was up to me to do powwowing or peace-piping or trading off, since all's I wanted to do was get on past, which I done.

But while I went downhill, letting my wheelborrow pull *me* for a change, I got to thinking: this other world had been laying out here all this time—not just laying but reeling and roving and gleaming and pitching—and I had been back home in the jail of my own head, not doing nothing to get away sooner. I felt shamed I'd been only three days' hike from all these marvels (and maybe more to come I couldn't even put a name to now), and had set and sulked and let Ma and Pa be the whole kitboodle of my life. After five years of looking at nothing but mud, corn, snow, or the end of my nose, I now felt flabbered and gasted and sort of joyful, like anything could happen, even something good. Where preachers (or whatever) could turn into crows, and critters taller than our house could roam around free and easy, and towns could float higgledy-withers, why couldn't I find me some gold and turn up happily ever after?

Chapter Four ★ ★ ★ ★ ★ ★ ★ ★ ★ ★ ★ ★ ★ ★ ★ ★

☞ The road was broad and looked to be well used, and whoever had laid it out had tried to keep it straight, even though the riverbank zigzagged something fierce, so sometimes you'd be right by the water—which was thick and fast and yellow-shiny—and sometimes you'd be off away from it a mile or two. The grass wasn't up yet, and nothing else was growing along the river, not even a bush. I seen some cottonwoods out on the islands, and here and there across a backwater slough I'd see some driftwood laying on a sand hummock, so it looked like I was going to have to get my feet wet if I wanted firewood at night. I put it off as long as I could so's not to have to take off my boots more'n once or lug the wood too far.

I come to a crick which wasn't but ten foot wide, but it was up and fast, and I was glad somebody'd bridged it, probably last summer or fall during the first big rush to Pikes Peak. It was made out of four-inch cottonwood trunks, not thick enough for logs nor skinny enough for poles, and it looked like somebody'd hauled off a few for kindling. But the dished-in rim of the front wheel just fit the curve on one trunk, and I pushed right across, keeping dry for a change instead of having to slog through like I done many a time with nameless little three-inch-deepers and three-foot-widers back on the prairie.

And I'd only been on the road a mile when I met my first wagon—coming back, not heading for gold. Its cover was all weather-ripped and half-patched, and the back wheels was sprung out sort of knock-kneed, and it was being hauled by a mule and an ox that didn't look like they admired each other's company none. The man holding the reins was a leather-cheeked, greasy-bearded old man with some kind of brown blanket tied around his head and shoulders, right over his cap and wool jacket.

He stared at me and my wheelborrow and let his team come to a halt, which they was inclined to do anyway, so I stopped too and set my handles down and says, "Howdy."

"Well, I hope you're the last one I'm going to see, but I doubt it," he says. "Is there any more like you coming?"

"I don't know," I says. I wanted to tell him about the marvels I seen, but he didn't look like he'd be interested.

"I mean, you reckon you could possibly be the last of a new batch of damn fools?"

I started picking up the handles again.

But he says, "No offense, young man, no offense. I call my*self* a damn fool willingly and openly, and an old fool is a sorrier sight than a young one. Where might you be headed?"

"Cherry Crick gold fields," I says, wary and standoffish now, like I recollected feeling toward Miss Wilkerson when she'd get me trapped in a dumb answer.

"I'm sorry to hear it," he says. "You aim to push that contraption all the way?"

"Push or pull, I reckon."

"Will you accept a piece of advice from an old man who

is sadder but wiser?" he says. "A man old enough to be your father, maybe even your grandfather?"

"Well, sir, I already had about as much advice as I can carry, but if you want to unload, go right ahead," I says.

He looked at me real solemn and shook his head a little —or maybe he was just shaking natural. "Turn around and go back where you come from, no matter how poor and miserable and godforsaken it may have seemed to you. I'll even give you a ride to Council Bluffs, if you want one and if these two bone-baggy critters can make it that far."

"No thanks," I says.

"That's what all the rest of them ahead of you told me," he says. "Son, you know what you're looking at? You're looking at a widower. I left my wife back there thirty-eight miles from Pikes Goddamn Peak under a heap of rocks because the ground was too froze to make a grave, and it was the same as if I kilt her myself."

"I'm sure sorry to hear that," I says. "But I haven't got nobody to kill but me."

"Don't go," he says. "You'll find more gold in the nearest dentist's office than ever you'll find in that jughead's paradise which you still got maybe four hundred fifty miles to get to. It's a hoax. You'll get skinned. If nobody else happens to do it in time, you'll skin yourself."

"I'm much obliged to you for your—cautions," I says. "But I mean to get ahead in this world."

"Yes, I reckon I'm a caution, all right," he says. "What's lying ahead of you, son, is not this world at all, but the bunghole of the next. Or the *previous*, not sure which." He flicked his reins at the ox and mule, but they didn't pay him no more mind than me. "If you make it as far as Fort Kearny, tell them Andrew Murchison made it at least as far as Elder Creek, no thanks to them."

"All right, sir, I will," I says.

"I hope you have a change of heart, young man," he

says, flicking harder and managing to stir the ox into taking a step or two.

"Well, I got a change of socks anyway," I says, and we passed each other by.

I didn't take no offense, but that's the way they like to do, lots of them old men: they want to take that smile off your face and get you squinting and squirming and feeling useless. Why should I believe him when I'd just seen I couldn't believe my own two eyes? I shoved on another couple miles with the road dipping down into near-bogs now and then but mostly staying straight. And the sky up ahead turned some brand-new colors and the sun glancing low off the sand and making it and the river golder than ever.

When I come to a place where a funny kind of ditch about a foot and a half wide cut all the way down from the top of the sand hills across the road and into the water (like somebody had took it into his head to make a crick and then couldn't find no water to go in it), I stopped and figured on camping. The ditch, near a foot deep some places and all chopped-looking, had knocked out a chunk of the riverbank so's the water was easy to reach, and I could fill my cup or canteen without no trouble. I was hungry and was going to need a fire for my bread and bacon, but the only wood I could see was over on a sand bar with fifty yards of water between me and it.

I took off my wool jacket and my gray slouchy hat, which I wear dished in fore and aft to cut down on the head winds and the brim turned up in front so's I don't look like Pa, and took off my boots and socks and jacket and tied my yellow slicker around my neck (I was going to need something to haul the wood in), and I was ready to have my first go at swimming the Platte. I hadn't swum nothing wider than a duck pond, but I had faith I'd be able to learn on the job, so before I could get worked up scairt about it, I went down that little ditch to the edge and jumped in feet first.

And dang near broke both legs with the surprise of it: the water only come halfway up my pants, and though the bottom was soft and runny-feeling and quicksandy, it held me just fine, and then I learnt another wonder: it never got more'n three foot deep all them fifty yards, though I could feel the current staggering at me in the middle. Later I come to find out there ain't many places in the whole river that's over a grown man's head, and why it don't just all steam off in the summer or sink in the sand, I don't know.

After I'd got me a slicker-load of sticks and driftwood, I waded back, started a fire, and begun rustling up supper. Naturally, the first thing I needed was a cup of water to make dough, but when I seen the color of it, I decided to let it settle down and made my bacon first. The sun was putting out its last level shreds now, and when I come to pour off the water, I seen the cup was a third full of fine sand. I tilted it into the light and give myself a terrible turn: it was full of bright little speckles like gold.

I squatted there on my hunkers just staring at it, not saying or doing nothing. It didn't seem possible the whole river could be full of gold dust and nobody'd noticed it. I tried to calm myself down and think reasonable, but the idea kept jumping up like something trying to climb out of my throat. Cherry Crick (and Slab Crick too) flowed into the Platte, and didn't they say Cherry Crick was full of gold? What was to keep some of it, maybe even most, from washing out and coming all the way down here and saving me 450 miles of shoe leather? Maybe people had been drinking gold for years, been wading and washing in it and never had the dumb luck to notice what was streaming by.

Suddenly I broke out of that squat and dug my big tin pie plate out of my wheelborrow and emptied that yellowy

sludge into it and got down to the water's edge and commenced trying to pan it out the way old Abner Nickles had
showed me how to do one day in town. But the light was
getting worse now, and far as I could see, pretty near all
the sludge wanted to slop right out of the pan with the
water and leave nothing behind. I was going to have to wait
till daylight, and maybe even then plain ordinary panning
wasn't going to work.

I made my bread in a kind of foggy trance, telling myself not to be a fool and yet going right on being one,
scheming up ways to get that gold out of the water by myself but not rightly knowing how. Maybe that was how
they used quicksilver, but I hadn't brought none and
wouldn't of known what to do with it anyhow. I et my
bread, and could taste the gold in it, faint and sharp and a
little crunchy, and how was I going to keep from going
loco in the night? And how could I stake a claim to a
whole river? A claim was only good for a hundred foot,
and I'd get an extra hundred as discoverer, but what was
to keep somebody from getting upstream of me and filter-
ing out all the gold before it ever got to my two hundred
foot? What if claims got staked all the way upstream to
Fort Kearny and past it to the North and South Forks and
along the South Fork to Cherry Crick? Then where would
I be? The Platte would probably be running clear by the
time it got to this place.

For a long while I fretted and stewed and simmered by
my small fire, turning rich and poor every other minute,
rubbing that pie plate with a smudge of sand in its bottom
like it was a magic lamp, and swelling up into a great man
and shrinking back down to a small, mean, sour-faced
doubter like Pa and generally having a rich-poor old time
of it.

I set there wrapped up in my blanket and wrapped up
in gaudy dreams, poking sticks into the fire nice and slow
and saving the big chunks so's they'd last while I got to

sleep (if I could ever sleep again), and I didn't hear nothing till a man's voice says, "Evening."

He was standing upstream of me about fifteen foot off,
which was about as far as the firelight went, and he looked
bulky in a short, thick, dark jacket and some kind of cap. I
nodded and howdied him back and kept setting.

He says, "Mind if I set a spell? Don't have any firewood,
and I saw yours burning."

"You're welcome," I says, but I didn't feel like he really
was. I had wanted to go on pipe-dreaming without a pipe.

He come closer, stepping over the ditch and circling to
the other side of the fire. "Name's Frank Pitt," he says.
"Leavenworth."

When he didn't offer to shake hands, I didn't neither.
"Ike Bender from near Plattsmouth," I says.

"You coming or going?" he says, hunkering down and
holding seven blunt fingers and one thumb, which was all
he happened to have on him, out to the fire. He had a half
inch of black-and-gray stubble on his face and a bent red
nose.

"Heading west," I says, and I tried to tuck my pie plate
far enough under the blanket so's it might seem like something I et out of.

"Pretty fancy rig you got there," he says, tipping his chin
at my wheelborrow. "You must be an ambitious young
man."

I don't know how to talk to people who say things like
that, so I usually say something just as dumb or keep still.
For no reason, I remembered what I'd heard a drunk yelling outside the Wagonwheel one afternoon last winter, so I
says, "I don't know where I'm going, but I'm on my way."

"Maybe I can be some help," he says. "I been out in the
gold fields all fall and winter. I been up and down every
crick and gully there is. Maybe I could trade you for some
good advice."

That made me feel real uneasy, so I says, "I'm going to

join up with my brother's company, and I ain't got nothing to trade."

"I could use a little food," he says, gruff-sounding, not begging.

He looked pretty fat in the face to me. "I don't hardly have nothing myself," I says. "And I got a long ways to go. How bad off are you?"

"Well, I et a little yesterday," he says. "But I'm not any too sure about tomorrow."

I knew I'd ought to feel bad and charitable, but I says, "All I got's a little flour and bacon to take me all the way. I'd sure be obliged if you could find somebody else to ask it off of."

He warmed his fingers some more, and I could see his eyes working over me and my belongings. "You've still got eighty miles to Fort Kearny. You must have more than just a little or it's going to be bellybutton-to-backbone."

"Well, it's all I got, mister," I says.

"Aw, come on," he says. "Don't be selfish. You can always buy some more at Fort Kearny."

"I got nothing to buy it with," I says. It felt like a lie because I had five dollars, but I didn't want to tell him.

"Well, just how far you aiming to go?" he says.

His voice had more of a rough edge along it now, and I didn't like the way he was looking at me, and if there'd been someplace to get up and go to then, I'd of got up and went. "Near Cherry Crick," I says.

"No money, only a little grub? What'll you do when you run out?"

"I reckon I'll go as far as I can," I says, and then I don't know what made me say the next thing, it just come out of my mouth: "Then maybe I'll turn into a crow and fly the rest of the way."

He set there squinting at me over the low fire and nodding a little, and he says, "You know, there aren't any fish in the Platte. Not a one."

"Didn't look like there was," I says, getting more and more worried but trying not to show it.

"Maybe you figured on doing a little hunting," he says. "I could give you a few pointers. Course, a lot depends on what kind of gun you got."

I opened my mouth to say I didn't have no gun, then shut it and changed to a different tune. "I don't enjoy killing nothing," I says. "Not my line."

"Maybe you'll take a liking to buffalo-chip soup," he says.

There wasn't no good answer to that, so I just studied him and the fire a bit more, and then I says, "I can spare you some fried dough and bacon if you don't mind the way I make it."

"I won't mind," he says, sounding offhand and not very hungry.

I stood up, keeping my blanket on and taking my cup the few steps down to the dark river. "And I *will* trade for a little advice," I says, scooping up a cupful and bringing it back and letting the sand and (I hoped) the gold dust settle in the bottom.

"I'd be glad to oblige," he says, not sounding glad about nothing, but gruff and level and well-fed.

While I mixed the dough, I says, "How do you go about panning gold dust if it's real fine and mixed in with real fine sand?"

"Well, you can pan some of it in the regular way if you're real careful and blow the dry black sand out later on, but you've got to use mercury to get enough to count."

I sliced off the smallest hunk of bacon I could without feeling stingy, and I says, "Is that the same as quicksilver?"

"Yes," he says.

And while I was at it, I let him get a good look at my nine-inch deer's-foot-handled spear-point hunting knife which I stuck back under my belt when I'd finished with it. "Spose I could get me some quicksilver someplace?" I says. "Maybe at Fort Kearny?"

He grunted, which I guess was his way of laughing. "Might as well buy gold while you're at it," he says. "Can't even buy calomel or corrosive sublimate between here and Pikes Peak. They've got mercury in them."

I put the skillet on with the bacon, and I seen his lip curl up more and quicker than the bacon when he seen the size of it, which wasn't much smaller than what I'd had myself. And that one third of a cup was setting there by the fire, maybe with enough gold in it to buy some quicksilver with, which I needed so's I could get the gold out in the first place.

"How you fixing to buy quicksilver and you with no money?" he says, smiling sort of unpleasant.

"I could work it off," I says. "I'm a welldigger by trade," which was the most likely one I could claim. I dropped the flattened-out piece of dough in with the bacon and let it sizzle.

He stood up a little too sudden, then relaxed and smiled when he seen I was watching him close. "This is a right nice act of charity," he says. "You must be a good Christian at heart."

"Haven't had much practice," I says.

"Well, why don't you practice up a little more?" he says. "Practice makes perfect. You could be a perfect Christian like the Good Book says and give your all to the poor."

"I'm poor my own self," I says.

"I reckon me and Sam are even *more* poor," he says. "So you could practice up on us, starting about right now."

I stayed crouched by the fire and knew I was going to have to get busy pretty soon and save my bacon and my Future. Meanwhile, I says, "Who's Sam?"

"Oh, he's a friend of mine about fifteen foot behind you there," he says. "Sam's shy and scairt of the dark, and that's why he carries the gun instead of me. Ain't that right, Sam?"

My hope he was bluffing lasted about two seconds because a voice not very far behind me says, "It sure is."

"Now you want to think very careful what you're doing," I says, as much to me as to them.

Raising his voice a little, the man calling hisself Frank says across the low fire and the skillet, "No gun, least not in sight. Hunting knife in his belt. That's all."

The voice behind me says, "Now stand up nice and be a good boy."

But I couldn't see no use in that, and if I let them take the little I had, I'd be Bound to Sink instead of Bound to Rise, so I leapt forward without ever coming out of my squat and went from the frying pan to the fire: I landed flat on the skillet and the fire both and rolled hard sideways, scattering the sticks and dousing what light there was. A gun went off in back of me, loud as doom, and Frank made a grab at me but was too busy yelling to do a good job of it.

Sparks had went flying every which way, but nothing caught fire, and what with the clouds, it was a real dark night and hard to see more'n a few yards, so I kept in a deep crouch, still clutching my blanket around me, and found the edge of the ditch and went scuttling up it, fast and quiet, getting a little distance while the commotion lasted.

Pretty soon they had enough sense to quit hollering what to do and keep still and listen, but by that time I was thirty yards up the slope, sprawled in the ditch, facing them with the blanket flat over me, and they could of walked right across me and never known I was there.

I heard them whispering angry and quick, and then Frank yells, "Hey, you, what's-your-name, don't do nothing foolish now."

Which I had no intention of doing, but the hard part was telling the difference between what was foolish and what was smart.

"Get that goddamn fire going so's I can see what I'm doing," Sam says.

There was more whispering back and forth, and then Frank says, "You couldn't hit the side of a barn if you was standing indoors of it."

Then they talked low some more, and I heard them rummaging at my oilskin. Laying down like I was, I could see their outlines crouched over my wheelborrow, and it give my heart an awful pain to know they was going through my things and taking what they pleased, which I'd had so much trouble getting together.

"Get me some light," Sam says, and Frank says something back, and Sam says, "Aw, don't be a Nervous Nellie, he's just a kid."

"With a knife," Frank says, and they lowered their voice.

I seen one of them go back to the fire and pick up a couple of sticks with red coals on the ends of them and commence blowing at them, and pretty soon a small flame popped up and he took it back to the wheelborrow and shielded it like a candle while the other one went on rummaging.

"He's got his money on him," Sam says loud enough for me to hear, and Frank hushed him, and they whispered some more, and then in a big full rough voice Frank says, "Tell you what we're going to do, boy. If you come back here right now, nice and friendly, and just hand over whatever cash you got, you can keep your food and your kit and this damn machine here. What say?"

I had my five dollars but aimed to keep it for a five-dollar emergency, and this seemed more like about a fifty-dollar one.

"We won't hurt you," Frank says, and the flame went

out but popped up again when he blew on it. "Think it over: just your money and we'll call it square."

And if that was his idea of square, I didn't want to find out what he'd call crooked, so I kept still.

"Otherwise we'll start a bonfire out of this heap of kindling here, have ourselves a feast of bacon, and send your sack of flour back to Plattsmouth by water."

Well, I knew then I was going to have to turn smoky whether I wanted to or not. I couldn't just lay there and let them burn my wheelborrow, and I couldn't just walk in with my hands up: Sam had shot at me once already and might like it better the second time. They'd probably think me better off kilt and my body hid up in the sand hills or buried out on one of them little islands than having me talking my head off to the first wagon I run into.

"Easy as pie," Frank says, holding the skinny torch close to my crumpled-up oilskin and looking all around in the dark for me.

They whispered and muttered some more and seemed to argue a little, and I begun crawling forward in the ditch, not really knowing what I was going to do or whether I could do it when I thought it up but just moving because I had to. Before the flame puffed out again for the third or fourth time, I seen what looked like a long pistol gleaming in Sam's right hand while he did some left-handed rummaging in my wheelborrow but halfhearted now like he didn't expect there was nothing in it worth the bother.

But it was worth any kind of bother to me, it furthermore being called the *Millicent Slaughter* whether there'd been time to write it on or not. So I kept kneeling my way forward, keeping low and holding the blanket out on both sides so's I wouldn't look like nothing much. When I was about ten yards off, I slowed down till I was just inching.

Frank got a stick blowed alight again, but he was holding it too close to his face so's he could blow on it and holler too, and I was sure I could see more by it than he could. Yelling, he says, "You got exactly one minute, boy, and up she goes." He was aiming it in the right direction, south, but too high and too far, and I could tell they thought I'd cut and run and wasn't up close like this.

Still standing by the wheelborrow at the edge of the shallow ditch, Sam was gazing off west someplace into the dark, maybe listening more'n looking. I dug my toes deep in the sand to get a good start and left my knife in my belt because I didn't want to hurt nobody bad, and I lunged forward at Sam—fast and knee-high—and he seen me just before I whaled into him, and he spun halfway around, bringing that long-nosed gun my way. It went off with a bang so loud I couldn't scarcely hear it, and at the same time I knocked him dipper-over-bucket backwards into the river.

I probably wouldn't of found the gun for a half-hour if it hadn't hit me on the shoulder on its way down: Sam had left it behind, along with his sweat-soaked old hat, being knocked loose of both of them articles by me running into him.

I got hold of the gun and switched it around quick at where I reckoned Frank would be, but he wasn't there. I stayed low, using the slightly paler sky to locate his outline but couldn't find it.

From over in the river Sam yells, "Get him, Frank."

But nothing happened, and Frank didn't say nothing, and again Sam yells, "Frank? What's the matter? Get him!"

Just to keep everybody thinking, I loosed off a shot at the sky. I hadn't never shot a regular pistol before, let alone a big old short-handled musketoon like this, and it was a good thing I had hold of it with both hands because it jumped like a jackrabbit.

First there was the sound of Sam splashing further and further from the bank, maybe headed out to the sand bar to think things over, and after that, nothing but my ears singing and ringing. I stayed crouched, worried Frank was playing my own trick on me, laying low and biding his time to jump me. Then I smelt wool burning. I made sure I wasn't laying on any hot coals my own self, then begun groping around one-handed toward where my fire had been, and I run into Frank's boots out flat and him in them.

I didn't want to strike no light with Sam still nearby—for all I knew he had another gun or at least a knife—so I hauled Frank off a couple yards by the boots and found the place smoldering on his jacket and rubbed it out. But there was no telling whether the fire or Sam's bullet had done the burning. My hand come away sticky with blood, and I could tell by the way he was all sprawled still, he'd been croaked.

And just so's there wouldn't be no doubt about it out in the river and so's he wouldn't be expecting no more help from shore, I took a deep breath and yells, "You kilt him, Sam!"

Chapter Five ★★★★★★★★★★★★★★★★★

☞ Now I had to calculate what to do, and I didn't have all night to do it neither. I could just leave Frank laying right there and break camp and get my wheelborrow going as many miles upstream as I could manage in the dark and just pretend like nothing happened, as long as I could get around Sam and keep ahead of him. I hadn't done nothing wrong. Frank had been shot, and I didn't even own a gun, except there I was with it in my hands. Well, I says to myself, I can just chunk it in the river and who's to know?

But if I did that, then I wouldn't have nothing to protect me from Sam sneaking back to get even. For all I knew, he could be circling back to the bank, upstream or down, to stalk me or lay for me. Right now, he was probably setting out there on the sand bar, thinking hard, and it was up to me to think harder. So I begun dreaming up all kind of other ideas I wouldn't of had no room for if it had been daylight and me my regular self, which I wasn't, being spooked and rattled and het up and chilled all together, never having had nothing to do with a corpus before except to see a few going by for funerals.

I thought of hauling the body up in the sand hills and burying it where nobody'd find it till Doomsday, if then. But that would mean leaving my wheelborrow behind, maybe long enough for Sam to come wading back and burn it. Or I thought I could just nudge Frank's mortal remains over the bank into the river, like he'd been going to do with my flour sack, and let him see if he could make it into the Missouri. Then there wouldn't be no blame to lay onto me right off, it being customary in Nebraska Territory for the Law to grab whoever's closest to trouble and hang on, just to have something to show. I didn't give much thought to hauling the corpus all the way to Fort Kearny, where there was probably a marshal or a general or somebody. That was four days off—or more, with all that extra load—and a corpus wouldn't be good company even in cool weather, not to mention the dark of the night.

It was a mean problem, and while I tried to figure it through, I got my kit tied back together best I could, including the skillet and the blanket, which had got a hole burnt in it somewhere along the line, because one thing was certain: I wasn't going to stay at the same campsite tonight and make it easier for Sam if he took it into his head to find out whether I could tell one end of his gun from the other. I was moving on, and the sooner the better so's he'd have less chance to bushwhack me up ahead, though there wasn't no bushes to whack out of.

And I come to the conclusion I couldn't do everything right in a problem like this here, so I had to pick what had the least wrongs in it: I just left the body laying there and everything like it was, come what may. What was the sense in being innocent if you wasn't going to act like it?

I hadn't shoved my wheelborrow more'n fifty yards, going cautious and quiet and peeling my eye for any sign of movement high or low, land or water, when I come to the next part of my problem. I'd half-wondered where Sam and Frank's packs had got to and whether they was afoot, and there ahead of me I could just barely make out the answer standing low-headed and humpbacked and not much bigger than some of the jackrabbits I'd heard tell about: it was a burro, and when I wheeled close enough to make sure I wasn't seeing things, it backed around to aim its kicking end at me. I give it a little soft talking to, and it settled down some so's I could get around front and let it smell me. It had been hobbled short, since there wasn't nothing for miles to tether it to, and it had a pack tree hitched on its back and a full canvas-covered load. It was as skinny as Biltmore, and I could feel its ribs sticking out.

And so I had to start thinking again. My mind was getting as much exercise as my arms and back, and it felt about as sore, but I managed to dredge up a couple of notions: if Sam stayed scairt off, this burro was going to starve, which it was halfway to doing right now, and hobbled like that, it couldn't even drink too good, the riverbank being a couple feet high in most places, so I was going to have to untie it. It crossed my thoughts to do what Sam and Frank had been about to do with me: run off with somebody else's food and kit. But then I got to thinking it might make Sam worse than he already was. He'd already kilt his own pardner, and I didn't want to starve him to boot. And I wasn't no thief anyway, spite of that revolver stuck in my belt, which I meant to get rid of soon as I'd got well off from Sam.

I untied that hobble, and the second the knot come loose, the burro trotted off into the night. Seemed like it was heading up for the sand hills, where it could maybe find some kind of food on the far side, scrub or dead grass. I worried after it for a bit, thinking Sam was going to have a hell of a time catching up with his belongings, but then I figured he could track it by daylight, and I'd a whole lot rather he'd be looking for a burro than looking for me.

We was all three going to be in for a busy while, but at least me and the burro had one advantage: we knew where we was headed and why and we hadn't kilt nobody and wasn't shivering wet out in the middle of the Platte on a moonless March night.

I covered a good ten miles before daybreak, having to move to keep warm but going slow because I couldn't see ruts, humps, or bogs. I pulled the wheelborrow instead of pushing in the dark: it was easier to pick myself up than it, so I went first to get the lay of the ground, crossing six or seven more of them long, narrow, shallow ditches like the one I'd camped by. I couldn't figure out what they was for but to stumble into, though I'd been grateful to lay down in that other one.

Long before sunup, I knew the burro was following me. I'd had to keep a check on all directions, expecting Sam to pop up out of the ground any minute like a prairie dog, and when the sky first begun to pale a little, I seen the burro about a hundred yards back, stopping when I stopped, going when I went, and keeping his distance. He still had the pack tree on, but whether he'd found some forage along the way, I couldn't tell. I didn't feel any too happy about him trailing after because what with my big feet and the wheelborrow and now his hooves, Sam wouldn't have but one direction to pick along a track anybody could see.

When I come to a few scraps of driftwood on the near shore which I wouldn't have to get wet collecting, I called a halt and made a small fire (it was light enough now so's I felt pretty safe), and cooked some breakfast. The burro kept back and had a drink of water, pretending not to watch me. And I was chawing the last of my fried dough and starting to settle back and think up ways to squeeze the gold out of the river and maybe even catnapping, when I snapped wide awake and realized I was seeing a man coming after me along the road.

First, I thought it was Frank come back from the dead because he was wearing the same kind of clothes, but this one didn't have no hat on and the hair was the wrong color, half gray and rusty-looking. I hadn't got too good a look at Sam before, but I reckoned I was going to get one now.

The burro didn't even let him get close but trotted off south toward the valley rim, putting on a little extra speed when Sam made a short run at him. I pulled out the gun and looked it over, not knowing much what I was looking at but seeing the two bullets left in it. I got up, held it in both hands, and stood my ground.

Sam quit burro chasing after a couple of zigzags, acting like a tired man who'd just as soon lay down as anything else, walking duck-footed and hunched forward. He come at me slower and slower and stopped about twenty yards off, breathing hard with his mouth open. He had a big fat face and a belly to match and didn't look like he'd been enjoying hisself lately except at suppertime. The burro had quit moving and took up a good spot about fifty yards off to watch the show.

"What the hell do you think you're doing?" he says.

"Pikes Peak or Bust," I says.

"You think you can get away with robbing me?" he says. "Kid like you?"

"I'm not robbing nobody of nothing," I says.

"Whose burro you think that is?" he says, scowling.

"Take him and welcome," I says. "He's none of mine."

Sam scowled some more, and I could tell he was sizing up the gun. "And how did he happen to get loose of his hobble?"

"Same way he's going to get caught now, I reckon: by the friendly hand of man," I says.

"You took Frank's money, and I'm going to get it back if I have to make you eat that there gun," he says. "You think I'd let you run off with what we spent months of slaving to scrape up?"

"I didn't take nobody's money," I says.

"Don't make me laugh, I got a set of sore ribs," he says, coming a few steps closer. "You better give me that gun before you hurt yourself."

"You're not going to shoot me like you shot him," I says, aiming at him but hoping I wouldn't have to pull the trigger. "Just stay put."

He says, "I didn't shoot Frank. You done it."

Well, that was a new one on me, but I could see he didn't believe it his own self. "I just shot up in the air," I says.

"That's *your* say-so. I'll say *you* shot him."

"What was I doing with your gun?" I says.

"Same thing you're doing now," he says, looking like he was straining to think. "No, wasn't my gun did it. You had one of your own, but I slung it in the river in a fight."

"I wish you health, long life, and happiness telling that story," I says.

He took a couple more steps but stopped when I squinted along the barrel at him. "Just give me Frank's money, and we'll call it quits," he says.

"Go on about your business," I says.

"All right, I'll settle for half, same as if we was pardners." He brushed his lanky hair back, nervous, and showed me how empty his hands was.

"I don't rob nobody, dead or alive," I says.

He give me a long, hurt look like I was telling him something downright painful. "His pocketbook was gone. I looked."

"It must of fell out, what with all that thrashing around," I says. "You must of missed it in the dark."

He give me another long stare, looking sick and trembly-chinned. "But he was just laying there. All you had to do was reach down and—"

"If you couldn't even find your own hat on the ground, you could of missed a pocketbook too," I says.

He run his fingers through his hair again. "My hat fell in the river."

"I beg to differ," I says.

Now he had that thinking-hard look on his face again and wasn't enjoying it none. "Maybe you're just dumb enough," he says, soft and puzzled.

"First man along that road after dawn can pick hisself up a nice pocketbook free of charge," I says. "How much was in it?"

He stood there, blank-eyed, seeing some no-account stranger picking up that smoky, half-baked pocketbook and counting out whatever it was. He says, "Enough," and took a couple more steps towards me.

But I straightened my aim and says, "Watch it, mister." He stopped. "If you had enough, what did you want mine for?" I says.

"You go on use that anchor and banjo you got tied to that wheelborrow, and you'll find out," he says. "Go dig up a little gold, and then see what's enough. See if maybe you don't want a little more and a little more."

"Reckon I'll find out," I says.

"I got to have some grub to get back there," he says.

"Run on your fat for a spell," I says. "You'll get no grub of mine."

"Then lend me the gun a minute so's I can shoot that burro and get my bedroll and some jerky," he says.

"No, sir."

"Then shoot him *for* me."

"I don't believe in shooting nothing, except you," I says. "If I have to."

"Then lend me that rope you got in your kit, and lasso the miserable little pigeon-toed stump-sucker," he says.

"That rope is meant for better things, and I'm not about to watch it go trailing off up into them sand hills and you chasing the bitter end," I says.

"Goddamn it," he says, adding it all up.

"Tell me," I says. "Just as a matter of common, ordinary interest: is Frank floating downstream now?" And I seen by the flush in his forehead and the quick glance he give me I'd guessed right. "How many miles do you reckon he'll make a day?"

He backed off a little now, which was a step in the right direction, and he says, "That pocketbook better be there." He sounded in earnest. "It had better be there waiting for me. Full. Or I'll track you down and have your tripes out for sausage."

I kept the gun steady, though it was getting to feel heavy, and says, "You sure he didn't move it to some different pocket? Or stick it in his boot for a change? You search him good before you rolled him in?"

His eyes flickered with doubt and worry, but he kept backing off. "If you value that stupid green-assed life of yours, you better be telling the truth," he says.

"I always tell the truth if I can locate it," I says, which was near true but boastful, and I watched him trying to stalk the burro again, which kept shying off, going just as slow or fast as Sam and acting fresher and stronger and maybe smarter. While they was playing that game, I renched off my skillet and broke camp fast, belting the gun and getting my wheelborrow moving west again.

By the time Sam had give up and noticed what I was doing, I was a hundred yards off and going brisk, and the burro was circling off south of us both, his pack tree waggling. Sam yelled something at me, to which I paid no mind, and the next time I glanced back at him, he had commenced the ten miles back to the other campsite to do some prospecting for pocketbooks, and I wished him neither well nor ill at it, feeling sure he was going to get about what he deserved—if not now, then later, starting off with one of them Mexican breakfasts I already told you about.

Chapter Six ★★★★★★★★★★★★★★★★★

☞ Most of that day I kept wheelborrowing, though I felt like I was sleeping standing up, and the burro commenced following me again, maybe since he couldn't think up nothing better to do. I tried to get close to him once or twice, but Sam had stirred up his juice on that score, and he wouldn't let me near. So I just kept hauling and shoving along the flats, next to the two-mile-wide, shallow, swift, dirty-looking river which had already been where I was going and seen what I wanted to see and maybe right now was rushing off east and south with more gold in it than all the landlords of creation had ever squeezed out of the mountains by theirselves.

I camped well before dark and made my fire with the sun still up and fell asleep before dark, trying to keep one eye open in case of more trouble. But you can't catch two nights' sleep with only one eye, so pretty soon I lost track of what I was doing and dozed off deep.

First time I jerked awake in the middle of the night, I seen a fire way downstream of me, no telling how far but like a campfire. Then I seen a couple more on the other side of the river, then three more up ahead on my side, and I reckoned I had more company than I'd figured on, heading for Fort Kearny. They felt like a comfort, even though I didn't know whose they might be, more comfort than Sam's revolver, which I stuck down the side of my wheelborrow (since I didn't want it inside my blanket with me where it might take a notion to go off). And I sank deeper than before and practiced panning gold in my sleep.

The burro wasn't nowhere to be seen in the morning, and I broke camp feeling sort of disappointed. But after I'd been hauling about an hour, I seen it off south of me, ambling down along the gradual slope from the sand hills, aiming to catch up with me at an angle. It slipped in about twenty yards in back and come along like it was part of a pack train.

It had had that tree on its back at least two nights now, and I was surprised it hadn't bucked and kicked it off, but there wasn't nothing I could do to keep it from getting galled, since it still wouldn't let me close enough to touch it, let alone unhitch it.

The day was cloudy and sharp-cool, and after I'd passed a couple of fair-sized campsites where the night fires had probably been, I kept finding wagon tracks in the boggier dips and reckoned some better-traveled side trail had joined up with the main road. I felt safer with company, but I begun to wonder how many people was headed for Denver City and how we was all going to fit and whether my brother's pardners had staked their claim good and proper and solid. It made me hurry up my wheelborrowing, since I didn't want to be left back on the runt's tit of Fortune.

Yet all day long I didn't catch up with nobody, and nobody caught up with me, so we must of all been in the same hurry, whether afoot or horseback or rolling on four wheels. I didn't see no marvels or upside-down cities, and I begun to get mad at all this *distance*. Every step I took I was going to have to take back someday, if I was planning on seeing Millie Slaughter again, so every step was like two steps—one now and one later—and that made it double hard except when I could shut off my mind's eye and keep my dauber up with sheer stubbornness (which run in our family the way red hair done in others).

The burro was following closer all the time now, and when I made another early camp, he took his water same as me and hung around a bit (still out of reach, though) and didn't take off to forage on the other side of the hills till it was near dark. He seemed to like my company but only in mild doses.

I didn't try to catch up with nobody, and the fires looked to be about the same distance off each way that night. The wind come up long before dawn, blowing dry but hard, and I laid there in the little shelter the wheelborrow could give me, listening to it whistle through the iron spokes of my front wheel. I didn't hear no mercy in it nor smell no perfume, and I flickered in and out of sleep all night like a coal-oil lamp with a cracked chimbley. I had begun to doubt, and I wasn't even near halfway to the gold fields.

In the morning the burro was still gone, but I had been joined by three visitors, heaped up and tangled with each other on the windy side of the wheelborrow: tumbleweeds the size of bushel baskets, all winter-bleached and knocked seedless by rolling butt-over-branches for many a mile. The wind was still going at it, and I was the only thing in their way for as far as I could see. Shivering and wondering how I was going to get a fire lit in all this ruction, I held one by the broke-off stem and felt it shivering even harder than me, like a horse or dog about to be turned loose to get at something it wanted bad. I let go, and that weed went sailing and tumbling east next to the river, doing what it was built to do and gradually knocking itself to pieces meanwhile. I done the same with the other two, giving them their freedom and watching them flop off, maybe to get caught by the next Pikes Peaker or maybe veer enough north to hit the water and try their hand at floating like Frank's corpus.

Or by tomorrow the wind might be blowing some other way, and they'd be scrambling with it just as hard and determined as now till something caught them and held them for good and all. The wind had them all going one way at the same time, and they acted like it was the best idea they ever heard of.

I had to buck that wind when I got going, and it made me keep my head down most of the time, so I didn't see the burro come back till he had fell into line again behind me, only ten yards off now, which was the closest he'd come. He was an undersized blue-roan jack with that stubborn-shy-patient look they all got, which they must of learnt from all the fool things men expect them to do.

"You finding something to eat?" I says. And then answered my own question, "Must be." He didn't seem tired or broke down, and I begun to wonder what was in them packs out of my reach. I could see the two bedrolls tied on towards the back, but Sam had mentioned jerky (which I would of admired to have instead of bacon for a change), and maybe there was other vittles too.

After five miles or so, I stopped, and he stopped, and while I set down between my handles with my back up against the tub to rest it, I says, "Mr. Blue Roan Jack, what you carrying on that pack tree?"

He switched one ear back to make sure nothing was sneaking up on him and left one aiming forward at my voice, which he hadn't heard much of. "Mr. Blue, I'd be glad to relieve you of some of that weight, in case you're wasting your time hauling trash, but you'd have to let me look."

He had his eyes half-slitted against the wind, which give him a shrewd, sleepy, horse-trading kind of look, and I says, "Your back's going to be raw if you don't leave me take that load off sometime."

I stood up slow and casual, holding my hands out so's he could see I didn't have no rope or hackamore waiting for him, and took a couple of small steps while talking soft, "Mr. Blue, we got to have equal shares in this company which you joined up with, free choice, and what's mine is yours and what's yours—" And that was about when he shied off his regulation twenty yards again and looked ready to make it fifty if I didn't get back to business and mind my duties, which consisted solely of leading the way.

So I give up and commenced wheelborrowing while he fell in behind again, putting them dainty hooves down, one right on a line behind the other, so's he could of walked a narrow plank over a canyon and not fell off.

Then I seen a lone tepee up ahead, which I had thought a half mile off was a wrecked wagon or a heap of wind-blown trash snagged on a tree (if there'd been a tree along there) but now made out as loosely sewed and half-ripped hides stretched over lashed-together ten-foot poles. I thought of circling up toward the sand hills to get around it, but I couldn't see no other tracks leaving the road, so the wagons ahead of me had just went on by with no trouble, and maybe I could too.

Somebody was setting out front of it near the flap and out of the wind, with a little fire going and heaps of stuff laying around. It was a messy-looking wickiup, and being all by itself like that, it looked even worse because there wasn't no competition nearby to let your eye stray off on.

Mr. Blue had pulled up to ten yards in back of me again, and when I got a good look at the man setting by the fire, I speeded up our train a little because he didn't look like nobody to spend the time of day with. He was wearing what had been a coonskin cap once upon a time but had shed most of its fur, including the tail, which hung down bare like a muskrat's, and his face looked to be about in the same condition: patches of pepper-and-salt beard sticking out this way and that. He had on a smoky-dark, greasy buckskin jacket and ripped jeans and dirty deerskin wrapped around each foot like some kind of bandages, and I could see tin cans and bottles sticking out from under a couple of moth-chewed buffalo robes on the ground.

I was aiming on getting by with no more'n a grunt and a nod, but he reared up when I come by and spread his long, skinny arms and let out a big, raw, gravelly voice past a full set of glistening brown teeth and says, "Welcome to the Hotchkiss Trading Post, goods for sale or barter, last opportunity till Dogtown, thirty-five statute miles, or Fort Kearny, forty statute miles, and you'll never find a man more willing to listen to reason."

"I got nothing to reason about," I says, slowing down in spite of wanting to hurry up because I didn't like to be rude.

"You never know when you might strike the bargain of your life," he says. "Opportunity don't always look like opportunity, no more'n gold always looks like gold."

He'd caught my interest with that, and I set my handles down. I seen a fat, coppery-brown, blank-faced squaw peeking around the edge of the flap, and I figured I must be looking at one of them squaw men Pa had always sneered over, which he done whenever somebody had done something he hadn't. "What *does* it look like?" I says, thinking of the river maybe full of it a hundred yards off.

"Why, it can look like me," he says. "Or it can look like that pretty little beast you got there. Or it can look like that home-built wheelborrow which I congratulate you for. Or—" His eyes, which wasn't nothing but a couple of deep black spots under his thick eyebrows, was roving all over me and mine, missing nothing they could help. "Or that Allen revolver I see sticking up out of the tub. There's some things worth their weight in gold, it all depends on where they're at and when. Opportunity and gold can both look like dirt to men of little vision."

Which sounded like something I might of thought up myself, and I begun looking at him a bit more kindly. "Well, I'm always on the lookout for a chance," I says.

"A man after my own heart," he says, showing me where that article was located by giving it a good scratch. "Avery Hotchkiss, proprietor."

"Ike Bender."

"Mr. Bender, I won't munch words," he says. "You're on your way to the gold fields, am I right?" He squinted at me like he had just guessed my age, place of birth, and grandma's maiden name.

"Yes, sir," I says.

"And I see you have a good-sized bundle of supplies to aid and abet your future endeavors along the way and once you get there," he says.

"I can't complain," I says.

"If that's true, you are the first spiritually serene man to pass along this road, in either direction, in a year and a half," he says. "And I want to congratulate you."

"Much obliged," I says, tipping my hat. "What color *is* gold?"

"Well, it might be brown and it might be gray and it might be green and it might be crystal clear," he says. "Depends on what you fancy."

I wasn't making much sense out of this, so I heisted my handles and started off. I'd heard Pa say all squaw men was loco, and maybe he was right for once.

"Just a minute, hold on there," Hotchkiss says. "How long have you been traveling?"

"About a week," I says, setting the handles down again because there was something urgent in his voice.

"No matter how careful your preparations may have been, no matter how careful you thought out your plans, you must be feeling the lack of something by now," he says. "Name it. You just name it."

"I'm getting a little tired of eating bacon and bread," I says.

"There, what did I tell you?" he says, glancing around as if a whole bunch was listening to him, though there was only Mr. Blue aiming one ear at him. "I've got canned raspberries." He went digging under the nearest buffalo robe and come up with a round can, bulgy top and bottom, and a flat can with part of a label still stuck on it, bulgy too. "And sardines!" he says. "Right fresh out of the ocean."

"What ocean?" I says.

"Sardines don't stay in any particular ocean," he says. "They move around, same as you and me."

"I don't have no money to spend at all," I says. "Don't even have any *not* to spend."

"Didn't you ever hear of trade and barter?" he says. "You don't need money with Avery Hotchkiss, long as you've got anything of value. And you obviously have some articles of value."

I looked back at Mr. Blue. "That burro don't rightly belong to me," I says. "He just taken it into his head to tag along."

Hotchkiss stuck the cans back, give his cap a twist, and stood looking at me, ducking his knees and grinning. "I'm glad to hear you say that, Mr. Bender," he says. "I perceive I am in the presence of an honest man, and I believe I'll offer you a little Taos lightning on the strength of it." He shoved another hunk of buffalo robe off a keg laying on its side with a wooden spigot stuck into it. "Would you do me the honor?"

"I don't believe so," I says. "I better get a move on."

He held up one hand. "Did you think I'd been chewing jimson weed when I spoke of crystal-clear gold? There it lies, kegged and cool, normally available to all comers at two-bits a mouthful, but offered to you free of charge because, Mr. Bender"—he held up his hand again when he seen me shaking my head and reaching for the handles—"because I saw that burro and pack go by here three days ago. Heading the other way. And I'd been entertaining doubts about your bona fides till you spoke up and said it wasn't yours."

"I don't know whether I'm bonafied or not," I says, "but I got to get moving, and I don't want nothing to drink, thanks."

"But we haven't completed our transaction yet," he says.

"I don't know what that sposed to be," I says, pretending I knew what he meant but only knowing it had something to do with railroads.

"I can't say for sure because I don't know yet what you want most," he says. "Soon as I know, we can get down to business."

"What I want most is to get to the gold fields," I says.

"And so the problem is how can we speed you on your way safe and sound and whistling a merry tune?" he says. "Would fifteen minutes with a nice plump warm squaw be of any interest to you?"

"I am safe and sound right now," I says. "And I learnt how to whistle years ago."

"How are you fixed for shoe leather?"

"Still plenty between me and the road," I says, but then I thought of the one thing I *did* need, though it didn't seem likely he'd have none. "You wouldn't be trading for any quicksilver, would you?"

"You mean you've got some?" he says, his eyes popping almost wide enough to see.

"No, but I could sure use some," I says. "If I knew how to use it."

"Sure I've got some," he says, hearty and offhand and

making me doubt it. "Got a pound and a half. Worth triple its weight in the gold it will surely find for the lucky man that's got it in his kit."

"Well, I don't have nothing to give for it anyway," I says.

"If that Allen revolver's in working order, son, you and me can work a deal right here and now," he says.

So there I was, stuck with a genuine temptation. You might say I'd won that gun in honorable combat, and if it was mine to sling in the river (which I had still been going to do) it was mine to barter off. But I didn't feel like that. It had kilt a man, maybe more'n one, and that made it seem like bad medicine, except maybe against Sam hisself. If I traded something for it, maybe it would turn out quicksilver with a hex on it—if Hotchkiss had any. Besides, I'd never seen no quicksilver before, and how would I know if his had gone stale or rotten or something?

"Do you mind if I inspect it?" he says.

"It isn't rightly mine neither," I says, feeling fidgety and bothered and not having nobody to get advice from but myself.

"Your honesty does you eternal credit," he says, coming over to my wheelborrow on a knock-kneed limp, trailing them deerskin swaddles on his feet, and he plucked the revolver out from the edge of my oilskin before I could make up my mind whether to let him.

He turned the chamber a couple of clicks and backed off, looking through it and hefting it and grinning some more to show all them teeth that looked like they'd been boiled in coffee a couple of months. "Two cartridges," he says. "Got any more?"

"Nope," I says. "Unless there's some in the burro's pack."

"Don't you know?" he says. "Haven't you looked?"

"Can't do much looking from ten yards off," I says, "which is about how far Mr. Blue likes folks to be."

"I tell you something else that happened to me three

days ago," he says. "I was held up and robbed by two men, name of Art and Willy, and they had that burro and they used this revolver, and they took all my hard-earned winter cash and tobacco."

"They was Sam and Frank when I met up with them," I says, starting to worry about where that gun was pointing.

Hotchkiss moved off from his goods to get partway upwind of me so's he wouldn't have to squint so much, and he says, "If they were the same men—and I don't doubt it —they were remarkably generous with you, handing over their gun and their burro and their worldly goods."

"Well, they didn't exactly hand them over," I says.

"I see," he says. "They didn't happen to hand over their money—*my* money—at the same time, did they?"

"No, sir, they didn't," I says, wishing I was in the guardhouse or whatever they use for safekeeping in Fort Kearny.

"As part of our transaction, would you be so kind as to unhitch that burro's pack and spread it out on the ground where I can see it?"

"Mr. Blue won't stand still to be unhitched," I says. "I already tried."

For a long minute Hotchkiss looked back and forth between me and Mr. Blue and back at his tepee and give hisself a scratch here and there with his extra hand, making up his mind, and then he says, "Suppose you try again."

I was agreeable, since I knew it wouldn't take no more'n three or four steps of mine to show what Mr. Blue could do in the way of shying off, and when he'd skipped sideways and trotted twenty yards with his stubby tail switching, I held still just in time to hear Hotchkiss say, "Hold it, don't spook him," then fall to cussing under his breath and gnawing a piece of his mustache. "I'd ride him down on my horse and bulldog him, same as I would have done with those two thieves, but they kilt my horse, Mr. Bender. With this gun."

"I'm real sorry to hear it," I says, wondering if I could

just pick up my handles and start off, but that gun was moving around in my direction, so I bided my time. "If it's any comfort to you, you can keep the gun."

He give me a curious, crooked, one-eyed look and says, "Your generosity does you credit, Mr. Bender, but I'll confess I had already aimed to do that." He let out a quick one-sided grin. "A man can go far by making a virtue of necessity."

"What I want to do is make time on the road," I says. "And if you want some more comfort, one of them two men is dead."

He looked surprised. "You're resourceful beyond your years. But I'm not vengeful. I just want my money." He wagged the gun barrel at me like he was shooing a chicken. "Suppose you back off about five steps."

I stood there a little bit, thinking about it, then finally done what he asked. He come up to my wheelborrow, which was between us now, and begun rummaging under my oilskin with one hand, his eyes moving from it to me and over to Mr. Blue, who'd come back a ways. His dirty hand was pawing over my bacon and into my flour sack, searching like I once seen a blind man do hunting for a penny that had dropped into a crackerbarrel. In another minute, he looked square at me and says, "I want your hat off, your jacket off, your shirt off, your boots off, and your pockets empty right there on the ground. Or you can save all that bother and just hand it over."

And there I was again. Seemed like everybody on earth wanted to see the inside of my pockets where I didn't have nothing at all now but five dollars and some string and a lucky stone out of the Slaughters' yard, not even Kit's letter no more. I says, "Mr. Hotchkiss, I don't have nothing of yours and hardly nothing of mine. I don't believe I'd care to do what you say."

"I'll shoot you, boy," he says, sounding like he'd never tried nothing like that before but might.

"No man's that big a fool," I says, hoping it was true.

"I got my pride too!" he says, almost yelling, then hushing hisself up and glancing at Mr. Blue, who was about fifteen yards off, ears pricked up and wary. Then quieter he says, "It's possible you may be telling the truth, boy, so I tell you what I'm going to do: I'm going to cripple that burro first and see what's in the pack, and then if we're both lucky and my money's there, you can just go haul yourself off west and forget about it. I won't tell anybody you kilt a man in cold blood and run off with his burro and belongings."

That was too much to swaller all at once, and I stood there trying to gulp it all down and reckon out my place in this crazy scheme, when I seen him aiming the gun at Mr. Blue with both hands and trying to stalk him a little closer. Hotchkiss kept glancing sideways at me and then having to line up his aim again, and Mr. Blue was turning restless, the way he usually done when somebody was shortening up on him.

And I was in the middle of taking my first jumping desperate step to land on Hotchkiss as the gun went off, making an even bigger slamming thump than I remembered, and I seen both Hotchkiss's arms go rearing up with the recoil and Mr. Blue rearing up even higher, with a dark splotch showing up on one side of his pack, and then Mr. Blue took off running and Hotchkiss took off running after him, aiming again, and I took off after Hotchkiss, stepping on one of his deerskin swaddles trailing along behind and sending him sprawling flat and skidding on his face while the gun went skidding on even further.

I run right over him without stopping and got the gun before he could and turned it on him, at the same time watching Mr. Blue head for the hills at full trot, which he done in a straight line without a limp or a wobble.

Not wanting to have no more to do with this Hotchkiss, I left him lay where he was, cussing and breathing short and glaring at me, and went back to my wheelborrow, sick of wasting all this time with poor folks trying to rob poor folks. All the salt and vinegar had went out of him when I looked back: he was braced up on one arm, looking like a tired old man. I belted the gun, tipped my hat to the squaw, who was peeking out of the flap to see what had went wrong this time, and started on my way again, neither sadder nor wiser nor happier nor dumber, but mystified.

Chapter Seven ★★★★★★★★★★★★★★

☞ I passed three covered wagons that day, two stopped for axle fixing and one getting ready to camp for the night, all three headed my way, but I kept my distance and didn't no more'n nod like you might do at somebody you seen every day around home. And when I made my own camp, I found me a place off the road and right down next to the river where another of them ditches come down from the sand hills into the water. This one was even more trompled-looking than most, and I reckoned it must be where the deer or antelopes come down to drink, though I hadn't seen none. I wanted to keep clear of people. I figured I could keep liking them and maybe even keep a charitable thought in my head if I wasn't running up against them all the time.

Mr. Blue showed up just before dark and had hisself a good long drink, sucking up that gold-looking water with his lips stuck out forward the way burros do, and he didn't seem bothered none by another lively day on the road. The bullet didn't look like it had bothered him none but had maybe hit a can of raspberries Frank and Sam had stole off Hotchkiss or a jar of preserves they'd been saving up for company.

While I made my grub, I says, "Mr. Blue, the trouble with you is somebody went and put pockets on you, and now everybody wants to see what's in them. Everybody wants to know what's in mine too, so I know just how you feel. Take my advice, and first chance you get, don't wear no more pockets. I'd be glad to help take that old rugged cross off your back if you'd let me, but you think I'm just like the rest, and you're right: I want to see what's in your pockets too. Now ain't that a dirty pity?"

He didn't say nothing but a snort or two over another drink and then set hisself about ten yards off, which seemed about what he liked for nighttime, and I scattered my fire before dark, since I didn't have enough wood to keep it banked all night and didn't want my camp showing so's people would find me when I wasn't looking and give me warnings or hold me up or cuss me out or try to trade me something or tell me to strip off or blame me for a dead man.

But I'll *be* blamed if one of them didn't find me, just when I'd got myself all rolled up good in my blanket and little hollows in the hard sand just right for my shoulder and hip. I heard Mr. Blue shift off and then somebody scuffing up, and I just had time to struggle my arms outside the blanket and get my hand on the gun when this clean-shaved, skinny, pale-looking man about thirty carrying a lantern and wearing a round felt hat pulled down to his ears and eyebrows come trooping along and says, "Oh, I'm sorry, I didn't know you were asleep."

He put the lantern on the ground between us and hunkered over it like it was a campfire and says, "You passed our wagon back about a mile, and my cousin and I saw you turn off, and then we saw your burro come out of the hills all by itself, and I just wondered."

"Wondered what?" I says, not feeling too friendly.

"Have you trained him to forage for himself? We're getting awful short of hay and grain for our oxen, and I hear tell there's none to be had at Fort Kearny, and I just wondered if you happened to know where there was some grazing."

"You'll have to ask the burro," I says, and we both took a look at him out there at the edge of the light. "He takes care of hisself. For all I know, the grass is six foot tall on the other side of them hills."

"I see. Well, I just thought I'd ask." He stared down into his lantern, looking solemn.

And I felt kind of sorry for him because I could see he was trying to figure out what to do when their oxen wouldn't go no more. I says, "If I was you, I'd start sawing my wagon down to handcart size."

He shook his head over that and smiled like it was a good joke. "I don't believe it'll come to that," he says. "The Lord will provide."

"The Lord will provide grass in about two months," I says.

"Have you been saved?" the man says.

"From what?" I says.

"From Sin and Temptation and Death," he says.

"I ain't even been earned yet, let alone saved," I says. "But I been luckier than some others I could name the last few days, and if it was the Lord's doing, you tell Him I'm much obliged."

"I see you are a young man full of pride," he says kind of sour-faced, standing up. "I would advise you to read this pamphlet." And he took a folder out of his hip pocket and handed it at me.

"You better feed that to them oxen you brung out here into the wilderness where any fool would know there wasn't enough to eat," I says.

He pulled the pamphlet back and says, "The Lord looks

after all creatures great and small if they believe in Him. If they *humble* themselves."

"I've also heard helping your own self spoke highly of," I says, getting mad, which I spose was another Sin.

"I will leave you in the dark where you belong," he says, picking up his lantern and walking off, huffy and stiff and spooking Mr. Blue out in a thirty-yard half-circle.

I watched his lantern bob and swing far off, and I laid down again, scowling and uneasy and provoked and cold, and I wondered, Could he be right, and I was in the dark, and off on some plain fool's errand? Five hundred miles was a long stretch to be a fool in, a long ways to go Following in Satan's Footsteps and all the rest of what they called it. Was I just off on a selfish hunt for gold? What did I want gold for anyway? I had told Millie Slaughter I was different than everybody else in the whole world, but was I? Maybe I was just one of this herd, which was starting to thicken up now, headed off into the unknown mountains because they couldn't think of nothing better to do. Or because their pa or ma or wife or the weather or their own selfs had made them so miserable, they was ready to walk or ride till they dropped, just to keep their head full of something new.

I laid there, thrashing around and vexing myself and heaving sighs and making more noise than the river and probably making Mr. Blue wish he'd stayed up in the hills where he didn't have to listen to nothing but coyotes and wolves. But then I come to my senses: I smelt the wind and heard the water and remembered where they was both coming from—out of the west, where everything was thick with strangeness and ripe with adventure and not all slab-sided and mucked over and figured out. And I felt the sand under my fingers, just plain sand, and it didn't matter whether it was gold or not, it was good enough for me because it was fresh territory and so was I. I begun to feel like I was my own campfire laying there, and I didn't need

no stars to look at nor ginger beer to drink nor Taos lightning neither.

All in a rush I felt like a happy man. Maybe I *had* been
saved, and if I'd had me a lantern, I might of hiked over to
that feller's wagon and told him so and his cousin too. Because this is what I felt like (and it don't look like much
when it's wrote down): I felt like *I'm Here, Right Here on
This Spot of Earth, and I Claim This Worthless Spot for as
Long as I Can Remember It.*

It felt like another wonder, come just in time, and I fell
asleep right on top of it.

I dreamt of thunder, and then I dreamt of the earth
shaking, and then I dreamt Mr. Blue was braying out a
long hee-haw, the first of his I'd heard, the wild cry of
what they call the prairie nightingale, and when I woke
up, he was still doing it, and the buffaloes was commencing to thunder by.

There they come, humpety-thump down the ditch, not
ten foot off from me, spread out in the dawn up in the
sand hills but narrowing down to single file, the lead bull
just lumbering past me when my eyes blinked open probably as red as his. I must not of looked like much to worry
about under my blanket because they went right by, looking huge and dark and shaggy, and went splashing straight
into the river and going right on out into it, on and on,
through shallows, swimming a sink hole, shelving up
across a little island, and I didn't know which way to look
nor what to do, so I just kept still, jolting up and down,
and felt thankful they kept to their ditch.

I don't know where they was going, but they sure in-
tended to get there. I couldn't stretch around to see how
Mr. Blue was feeling about all this, but he must of felt like
me: whatever them buffaloes wanted to do, they was welcome to do it, and all I asked was leave to keep out of
their road. Even the little ones was big, and they all run

sort of tip-tilty front to back like a hobbyhorse, their tails stuck out and some tongues too, and a lot of them letting manure fly as they went, so there was grass or brush growing *some*where.

Maybe two or three hundred went by while I kept dead still under my blanket, and then the last ones heaved into the chest-deep water and headed off north, and pretty soon there was no trace left but a wild stably kind of smell. They had decided to ford the Platte—or one had decided and the others had caught the fever—and they made no bones about it, not even mine, but just done it. And I was glad I hadn't taken up the habit of leaving my wheelborrow, making fire, or bedding down in them ditches.

I got an early start, thanks to them, and Mr. Blue joined me calm as you please. We passed five wagons and three handcarts in the first five miles, none of them up and going as soon as us, and by the time the sun was up full and had took the chill off, we come to a big trail junction and the road turned more and more rutted, and I could see dozens of wagons up ahead between me and Fort Kearny. I begun to feel crowded and not so happy. When I was by myself, I could make believe I'd used my head better than anybody else to get going in early spring, but here was all these other people that had used their head too.

Whenever I'd pass somebody, they'd scowl at me like I was racing them to the supper table, and whenever somebody passed me—it happened a few times: a couple of men afoot, a man with a pair of mules and a cart full of hay—I'd be trying to keep from frowning and thinking they had their stakes all sharpened up to jump my claim on Slab Crick. Only friendly thing I seen that whole day was when a stagecoach (which I heard somebody holler had come all the way up on the St. Joe Trail) bounced and jolted by me and Mr. Blue, and half a small arm come out the side window after it was by and waved a little lacy white wipes at us.

Soon after that, I passed up four men hauling a hand-cart, and they looked at me suspicious, like I didn't have no right to bust out of line and get someplace ahead of them, and they glanced Mr. Blue up and down with contempt, like he didn't know as much about hauling as them. I must of looked like a well-to-do, well-prepared prospector to the naked eye which couldn't see Mr. Blue running off whenever he felt like it, and them that didn't have critters to do their hauling for them didn't take too kindly to me.

In another mile I caught up with a young wheelbor-rower, not much older than me, shoving along with his head down and his arms looking like they'd been stretched down as far as they'd go and his feet goosing out sideways. He was stopping to rest about every hundred yards, which won't get you no place in a hurry, so I caught up with him pretty quick. His wheelborrow couldn't put a patch on mine, being an ordinary hod-carrying, slapped-up heavy-weight and not designed special like the *Millicent Slaughter*.

When he seen me, he tried to pull together and stay even, gritting his teeth and leaning his body forward like he was straining up a slope, and even though I wasn't going no faster than usual, he made me feel like we was racing.

When I begun to pull ahead, he says, "What's your hurry, you goddamn clodhumper, you?"

"I always go like this," I says, hearing him gasping and knowing he hadn't practiced up the way I done.

"Which one of you's the jackass?" he says, meaning Mr. Blue, and he tilted his wheelborrow sideways and tried to ram me, but I was too far past.

I didn't have no cause to fight and no time to spare for

it, so I just left him behind, wasting his breath and not en-joying hisself or his surroundings, probably not even seeing the way the sun come wavering off and on across the sand and getting hisself all worked up worrying about somebody else getting the best of him. I vowed then and there I wasn't going to do nothing like that, but do my work and take my turn and prepare for the worst and hope for the best and manage with what come along.

And the next thing that come along was Dogtown, which they call it after the prairie dogs that burrow and whistle all around there, and it wasn't but five or six doby shacks and a barn for the mail-wagon horses, what they call a swing station for the stagecoach, and people was camped out all higgledy-pig south of there, which must of give the prairie dogs a bad strain on their neighborly feel-ings. And from there on, it was only about five miles to Fort Kearny, and only a little over a hundred more to the South Fork of the Platte, and a little less than a hundred more to Julesburg, and then only about a hundred more to Slab Crick, short of Denver City, so all told I didn't have but three hundred miles and a couple of whoops to go.

The thought put some bounce in my boots, and I hove up toward the station hut to see if I could get some friendly advice for a change about where it was all right to bed down and where to get wood. I had begun to worry about Mr. Blue, him going all day on nothing but hope and water, but he went right around back toward the barn like he'd been there before (and maybe he had), and I let him take care of hisself, since he'd been doing a better job at it than I could of done for him.

But then my whole pile of thoughts, which I'd been heaping up all day in the bottom of my head, blew off sideways and left an empty hollow, because there by the shut door in the shade of that hut with dead grass growing out of its sod roof stood Millie Slaughter, in person, not my wheelborrow, wearing two wool shawls and a bonnet and looking straight at me with eyes big as horse chestnuts, and she had a small, thin smile on her face that looked like she'd been saving it up just for me.

"Good afternoon, Mr. Bender," she says. "I've been expecting you."

Which was more'n I could say of her.

Chapter Eight ★★★★★★★★★★★★★★

☞ I must of seemed dumbstruck to her, and I was, because she tried to help me inside by the elbow like I was blind or crippled up, but I couldn't leave my wheelborrow to get robbed, strayed, or stolen, so I says, "How in the living world did you get here?"

She looked surprised when I wouldn't let her tug me indoors. "I took a steamboat down to St. Joe and caught the stagecoach," she says, like it was plain as day what any fool would of done. "Would you mind accompanying me inside? I believe they have food to eat, but I didn't want to be unescorted."

I realized I was gaping at her, so I shut my mouth and took off my hat.

"I've been waiting out here three hours," she says. "I expected I'd have to wait two or three days for you in Fort Kearny. You must have been progressing very rapidly, but, Mr. Bender, you've been neglecting to comb your hair."

Which was true, since I didn't have no comb but my fingers. "Was that you waved your wipes out the window?"

"I waved my *handkerchief*," she says. "I couldn't get the driver to stop, and this place seemed more convenient anyway."

"Yes, but why'd you come all this way?" I says, still groping to get hold of the right handle on this problem because here she was, standing there and me facing her, and I was wide awake. "What's your pa going to say?"

"I expect he's already thought up a few things," she says. "I've been bouncing up and down on mail sacks for a number of days, and though I did manage to get some breakfast this morning, I lost it. So would you mind escorting me inside?"

There was something firm and scairt and resolute and desperate and awful young about her, and I could reckonize what was bound and determined, being that way myself, but I says, "I think they charge money in these places."

"I have some money, Mr. Bender, or I wouldn't be here," she says.

And I finally had to let her tug me through the door, leaving the other *Millicent Slaughter* to the mercies of all kind of passerbys and maybe dogs wanting to make the acquaintance of Biltmore.

She got us set down on three-legged stools at a big rough table, and we took turns breathing the greasy, smoky air while the stationmaster and a couple of hostlers and the cook set drinking coffee and gawking at us through the gloom (there was two coal-oil lamps and no windows) under the low, dirt-stained canvas ceiling, and she says, "Mr. Bender, I have run away from home. Temporarily."

Which was about what I had figured except the last part, so I says, "You mean you're going back?" That made me feel good because it seemed to scrape off some of the confusion. "When's the next stagecoach?"

"No, I mean my current status is temporary," she says, biting her lip and hesitating and not meeting my eye straight on. "I do wish they'd serve us some food."

"I've got bacon left out in my wheelborrow, but I'd have to build a fire someplace and—"

"Waiter!" she says, aiming at the other end of the room, and the four lunkheads seemed to like that one because they chuckled and said it over a couple times each, but finally one of the hostlers got up and stretched and strolled over with his coffee mug like he might want to borrow a little sugar, and she says, "We'd like something to eat, please. Do you have a menu?"

He frowned at her, then looked at me, and says, "We don't have none of that. All's we got is slumgullion, seventy-five cents."

"Well, I suppose that will have to do," she says. "We'll have two slumgullions."

"Just one," I says. "I'm not—"

"Two," she says, and the hostler strolled off scratching the seat of his buckskin-patched blue pants.

I got up to make sure my wheelborrow was all right, and when I come back she says, "I suppose I owe you an explanation."

"I'd be much obliged," I says, already imagining what Tom Slaughter was going to be doing and saying.

She took off her bonnet and set it on the table, and her shiny pigtails come down to lay on the front of her two shawls with two blue bows tied on the ends. "My mother left me a little money of my own," she says. "It's mine to use as I see fit at any time, and I'm mature for my years."

"How much did the boat and the stage cost?" I says, interested to find out how much I saved by hiking.

"I have some left, if that's what you mean," she says, nervous and a little snappy.

"I just wondered because I—"

"Mr. Bender, have you been thinking of me at all?" she

says, suddenly getting her eyes right on me and through me and her face going hopeful and hopeless, both.

I remembered many a night—and daytime too—when she'd been on my mind or around it or under it. "Well, yes," I says.

"And I've been thinking about you too," she says. "Mr. Bender, I have read too many stories in which young men go off to seek their fortunes, leaving their—their *ladies* behind to wait and—and pine for them. Those stories mostly have happy endings, but they take too long in coming."

"I can't help it if Slab Crick's five hundred miles from home," I says. "I didn't put it there."

"I'm not blaming you," she says. "Just—life. Those young men in the stories spend a great deal of their time helping damsels in distress."

"I haven't seen one single solitary—"

"—helping damsels in distress and sometimes being *won* by them," she says. "So I decided I couldn't wait, but would go along and if need be *I'd* be your damsel in distress. Don't you see: you wouldn't have to hunt for any."

"Well, I've had some distress already, but there wasn't any damsels," I says, but my mind was running around and running ahead of my tongue, up hill and down, both hunting and hiding.

The hostler come over and slapped down two tin plates full of something or other thinner than Platte River water, but she spooned right into hers without looking at it, not taking her big dark eyes off mine, and between swallers she says, "I don't fancy staying home spinning and being Pa's daughter and sewing and looking out the window for years. Would you?"

"Well, I—"

"I want to seek *my* fortune too," she says, earnest and full of a strange, drawn-out sundown longing, the kind I had felt alone out on the trail. "I have come to believe *you* are my fortune, Mr. Bender, and perhaps I can be yours."

I had never had no chance to practice up on this kind of talk, and there wasn't no time to learn, but when I tried to plunge right in, the way I done with the river, I come up shallow and practical. "It's more'n three hundred miles to Slab Crick," I says. "You're too—pretty," not wanting to call her young or weak or frail and not knowing how to tell her what was deeper down in my heart, which I had located right about where I catch my breath. "There's Injuns and bad weather and bad men and bad food and horrible hard work, and you don't deserve none of them. You're too—dear," which was near as I could come right then.

She seemed to grip on to that last word, and she dipped away at her slumgullion, still staring at me and not wiping her chin and starting to smile. "Dear?" she says, tasting it. "Am I really?"

I wanted to get up and check on my wheelborrow, but it didn't seem like the right time. "Yes," I says, not wanting to back off. "I have feelings too." And I recollected the first man I'd met on the river road. "Women can get theirselves kilt out here. Or get sick and die. I'd feel horrible if something went and happened to you."

"You would?" she says, looking mighty pleased at the idea, and her eyes went blurry and far off. "What would you say if I were dying?"

"How should I know?" I says.

"Would you hold me in your arms? And weep for me?"

"I wouldn't hold you in my arms if you had fell into some bottomless gorge or other," I says. "You'd best go on home to your pa and wait."

Her mouth went so stubborn she could hardly eat with it, but she got the spoon through a couple more times, then says, "And *you'd* best eat and keep your strength up."

"You can't walk three hundred miles," I says. "You don't know what it's like. Besides, it wouldn't be fittin', you being a girl."

"I have no intention of being a sister to you, Mr. Bender," she says with slumgullion on her chin.

"I hope not," I says.

"Whose goddamn burro's that out back?" one of the hostlers says.

"I was thinking of holy matrimony," she says.

"He tore the side out of a sack of oats and et about half of it," the hostler says. "If I catch that goddamn—" He heard my stool going over and seen me standing up, and he says, "Is that your burro, boy? If that son of a—"

"You watch your language around this lady," I says, "or you'll eat the rest of them oats yourself." I expected I'd have to fight him, since nobody ever done nothing I told them to.

But he turned all meek and smiley and ducked his head a couple times. "I'm sorry," he says. "I forgot myself. We don't get no women to speak of out here."

"I said a lady, not no woman." But Millie had started eating again, out of my plate this time, and she didn't seem interested in apologies nor wiping her chin off neither and looking ladylike.

The other three lunkheads was cackling and cawing at the hostler, but he backed off and shushed at them and went out the back door, and I stood there feeling strong till I remembered what she'd said. "Holy what?" I says.

"I didn't know you had taken to carrying firearms," she says with her mouth half full.

And sure enough, the butt of the revolver was sticking out between the front of my jacket, which must of been what tamed the hostler down. I took it out of my belt so's I wouldn't shoot myself if I bumped into something, and two more of the lunkheads cleared out, leaving the stationmaster whistling and thumbing through a newspaper.

"There's only two things wrong with you getting married," I says, keeping my voice down. "You're too young, and there's nobody for you to marry."

She polished off my plate and finally used her little lace-edged wipes on her chin, then dug into a round draw-neck black purse and counted out a dollar and a half. "That waiter doesn't deserve anything for his service," she says, as stern as ever Miss Wilkerson could of said it, but she changed over to a softer voice for me. "That's my trunk over there in the corner." She nodded at a leather-bound humpbacked knee-high trunk setting on the dirt floor.

"That's a good place for it," I says. "The stage driver won't have no trouble finding it when he picks you up to head back."

"Mr. Bender, I'd like to speak to you outside," she says.

Which was fine with me, since I never felt too good with something between me and my wheelborrow, so we went out and I was grateful to see it hadn't been messed with. It was getting on for dusk now, and the road looked empty both ways, and the river was more'n a mile off, shimmering in the flat light.

She says, "I made thorough inquiries of the driver before he had to move on. Do you want to know what I learned?"

I could tell I was in for some unwelcome information, but there wasn't nothing I could do but nod.

"The next stagecoach isn't for six days," she says.

"You should have thought of that before you—"

"But I wouldn't take it if it was to come in six minutes. Mr. Bender, don't you care for me?"

"I'm *trying* to care for you," I says. "You can't take care of yourself."

That made her mad, and her mouth tightened up. "Yes, I can."

"Just for instance, where do you expect to sleep to-night?" I says.

"I have a very practical suggestion on that score."

"I'd admire to hear it."

"I aim to sleep in your arms," she says.

Miss Wilkerson, when she was teaching the both of us,

claimed there wasn't but Seven Wonders of the World, but she must of quit counting too soon. While I was getting the taste of that one, I seen Mr. Blue come around the far side of the doby hut with his pack tree slung around upside down and hanging under him like some fool had tied him to the top of a little wood table whose legs was shorter than his. He tried to give it a kick but couldn't reach it right, and he didn't look too happy. "In my arms?" I says, trying to imagine it and keep track of everything else at the same time.

"I'm told the commanding officer at Fort Kearny is authorized to perform marriages and there's a preacher there too," she says.

"What in the world would your pa say?"

"If I were married, there's nothing he could say."

Mr. Blue come to a squirmy halt about ten yards off, still chewing on oats (there was some sticking out of the corner of his mouth) and looking mighty tired of that pack tree, specially upside down.

"I saw the burro from the stagecoach, but I couldn't believe it was yours," she says. "Isn't that perfect?"

"Nothing's perfect," I says. "Mr. Blue don't belong to me. He's just sort of stringing along."

"Why's his pack on like that?" she says, marching straight over and starting to unhitch it like she'd seen a package with the string tied wrong. Mr. Blue didn't shift a hoof, just give her a sniff up the side of the shawls while she was at it. When the pack tree and the bundles lashed to it fell down in a clump, I expected him to bound off like a colt turned loose into the spring grass, but he just stood quiet and content.

"Who owns all this gear?" she says.

"Hard to say." I didn't know which way that Sam was headed, so I couldn't exactly lay claim to whatever it was. "One of the owners is dead, and the other's off someplace."

"Well, *I* aim to use Mr. Blue if you don't," she says.

"You're going to wait for the next coach back if I have to camp here and see to it myself," I says, but I didn't sound any too sure of it. "You *can't* come along. Please."

She was down on her knees, unwrapping Sam and Frank's bedrolls and untying their kits and searching through everything faster than Sam had went through my wheelborrow. "You haven't heard me out yet, Mr. Bender," she says. "How are you going to provision yourself for the rest of the way?"

"Same to you," I says. "You think it's any easier feeding two mouths than one?"

"Somebody spilt blackberry syrup all over this blanket," she says, and then fell to tidying and rearranging and putting a can here and a knife there and looking over a pair of spurs like they might be can openers, and I didn't feel like telling her the troubles Mr. Blue had seen.

"If you happen to run across a pocketbook in there, I know who it belongs to," I says.

"That's what I'm trying to tell you, Mr. Bender," she says. "I have enough money to provision us and a little more besides. I'm offering to buy a partnership with you, which is what most dowries turn out to be anyway. Now would you please bring my trunk outside?"

I just stood there a minute, not knowing how to argue with her or which end of it to start on. Yelling wouldn't do no good, and I couldn't pull that revolver on her, and I couldn't leave her tied up for six days till the coach come, so what was I sposed to do?

She frowned at me, looking around the edge of her bonnet with them big excited eyes. "Don't just stand there," she says. "I have to get my belongings into a reasonable pack, don't I? We can't use any of this trash except the bedrolls, which are extremely unclean. And maybe this yellow slicker. I'll wash them out later."

It begun to look like Mr. Blue hadn't had nothing much in his pockets neither, but just hadn't wanted to turn them out for nobody. "I don't like to contradict a lady," I says.

"Then don't," she says. "Mr. Bender, do you want those men, those miners and your brother, to welcome you with open arms when we get to Slab Creek?"

"That's exactly what I want," I says. "But what'll they say when they see I brung a frail little girl along? They'll kick me out of the company and—"

"Mr. Bender, I have five pounds of quicksilver in my trunk," she says. "I bought it in St. Joe and paid dearly for it, and I invite you to try to find half that much anywhere in Nebraska or Kansas Territory."

I brung out her trunk for her, still hoping to change her mind, but anxious to see what quicksilver looked like so's I'd know it if I seen it again. And running through my mind quicker than any silver was a vision of all that gold might be in the Platte, and here was Millie with five pounds of the only way to find out, and by and large I was feeling pretty fuddled with trying to think in three or four different directions, upside, west, and crooked. I felt like Mr. Blue hauling somebody else's baggage on backwards and growling with hunger and smelling a jenny on the wind, all together.

She unstrapped her trunk and begun shifting a dress or two and holding some things all folded tight so's I couldn't see what they was and tossing away Sam and Frank's scraps and litter like I seen my ma at a rummage sale once over in Plattsmouth. A couple of kids had come over to watch, and I seen the hostler who'd backed off from me in the station come to the corner of the hut and stand there scowling, mostly at Mr. Blue.

"Millie, you have to understand," I says, making my last try at separating the confusion from the bald truth. "It may seem like a game to you now, but out on the road it's going to seem like pure Hell." I took a couple of swallers and moved closer so's the kids and the hostler couldn't hear. "I'll marry you someday, but back where I can put a roof over our head."

She stood up and faced me and moved real close till our fronts was almost touching and looked up at me, running her eyes all over my face and smiling slow and small. "I hope you're not going to think me immodest, Mr. Bender," she says. "But I'll have to take that risk because this is the turning point of my life. I hereby pledge and promise you all the wedded bliss you can handle in this world."

She went on staring at me, and I says, "What's that 'bliss' mean?"

"It's to your credit you don't know," she says.

"How's come *you* know?" I says.

"Women simply *do* know about things like that," she says. "And I have read a number of works of fiction."

I must of been blushing then because she touched my cheek the way you touch a stove lid to see if it's hot, and the kids commenced giggling and going "nyaah-nyaah" and wiggling around. Millie shooed them off without shooing off Mr. Blue (how she'd charmed him I'll never know, but wasn't the same charm working on me?) and then she got busy fixing her pack and getting me to heist it up on Mr. Blue, leaving off the pack tree.

She used Frank and Sam's rope to lash it on tight and neat. "This is the squaw hitch, in case you didn't know," she says, and I didn't.

"Please, now, we have to *think*," I says, but my mind was spilling over with quicksilver, gold, and Bliss—mostly Bliss—and once you get Bliss on your mind, it don't leave much room for sense.

"You!" she says at the hostler. "I need some tar or axle grease. This burro's been rubbed raw."

The hostler scowled some more, glancing at me, and says, "He et about two dollars' worth of my oats," he says.

"You should watch your stable more closely and not be

loafing around in other people's affairs," she says. "You fetch me a handful of axle grease, and you can have my trunk, which cost two dollars and seventy-five cents, and the rest of this gear, and we'll call it square."

The hostler disappeared, and she tied a short rope lead on Mr. Blue and says, "We'd best get on to Fort Kearny."

I still couldn't believe all this was happening, but here it was, coming at me item after item, one step at a time, and there didn't seem to be no way to keep the next thing from being next. I says, "It's five miles," half-hoping the mere sound of it might make her feet hurt.

"Walking will seem like a comfort after that stagecoach," she says. "And walking with you will seem like floating through the air, Mr. Bender."

What kind of answer can a sane and sober man make to something like that? Or a crazy and drunk man either? What I done was wipe my nose and get my hat on tight and try to keep from getting too full of myself.

When the hostler come back with a handful of grease, she took it from him like it was ladies' cold cream and slapped it on Mr. Blue and says, "There, that's better," and the hostler chased the kids off the heap of clothes and other gear and begun stuffing it all in the trunk.

"Mind me making one suggestion?" I says.

"Not if it's useful for our purpose," she says, holding a little heavy-looking crock with a clamp top on it and ready to stuff it in Mr. Blue's pack.

"If that's the quicksilver, don't trust Mr. Blue to have it on hand when you might happen to need it," I says. "He likes to wander off a day at a time."

She hesitated, then lifted up a corner of my oilskin and shoved the crock into my wheelborrow, and we started walking, side by side at first, but then me leading the way into what was left of the light, past women and kids from the wagons camped out hither and yonder, most of them hunting for sticks or buffalo chips or anything that'd burn, and us not saying much and me wondering if I couldn't hunt up somebody sensible at Fort Kearny to talk us out of this.

Chapter Nine ★★★★★★★★★★★★★★★★

☞ As it turned out, there wasn't no shortage of people willing to do that, starting with the first horse soldier we run into after about a mile and a half (which Millie done without complaint and even singing a little song about a bird in a tree though there was nary a bird come our way and no trees but a grove out on a big island in the river), and this soldier come riding up, stern and red in the face, and says, "Get the hell back where you belong, no foraging on Government Property, can't you *read?*"

"There wasn't nothing *to* read," I says.

"There's a sign on a stake back there, so you can just turn right around and go back and get somebody to spell it out for you," he says. "Git!"

Mr. Blue didn't like that kind of talk, but Millie had him firm by the rope, and I says, "If it was on a stake, it's probably been burnt for firewood by now."

"I'm giving you Official Notice, then," he says. "And the next form of notice is a boot up the rear end."

"I'm at a loss to account for this uncivilized behavior," Millie says.

The soldier give her a glance, then tipped his hat up so's he could hear better, and says, "Don't you understand plain English?"

"We both understand it a great deal better than you, I'll wager," she says. "And I won the only spelling bee ever conducted in Cass County, so mind your tongue. I wish to speak to your commanding officer."

Smiling with one front tooth broke off halfway, the soldier leaned over at me and says, "You better take that little girl back home to her ma before she starts sassing somebody that ain't full of the milk of human kindness like me. All you dang sodbusters ought to have more sense. There ain't any gold up ahead, no more'n there is underfoot."

"You ever looked underfoot?" I says.

He looked, and there wasn't nothing down there but hard-packed sand and a couple of horse apples. "No," he says. "I *work* for a living."

"And I wish you a rapid rise in your profession," Millie says. "But first you'll have to learn to be more respectful."

He smiled, even though it seemed like he didn't want to, and says to me, "Take Little Sissy Backtalk off home now or you'll get in trouble."

"I'm not his sister, I'm his bride-to-be," she says. "And I want to speak with your commanding officer about conducting a wedding ceremony. We have no time to spare: it's getting dark."

He chewed that one over, then says, "No foraging on Government Property, no livestock allowed."

"My wheelborrow don't eat nothing," I says.

"And this burro has just eaten his fill," she says. "And we're not sodbusters. And my father knows Major Kemper, and what does your name happen to be?"

The soldier didn't look too happy, and he reined his horse off to the side a ways. "All right, go on in," he says.

"But stick to the road. And if anybody asks, I'll say I warned you and you must of doubled back."

He rode off, and I says, "Your pa don't know any Major Kemper out here, does he?"

"No, but he might," she says. "And that's his real name. And the two together are enough truth for the purposes of diplomacy."

So we was one step nearer, and nobody'd stopped her yet, and my Future begun to look more and more like it was lining up with hers.

We come to Fort Kearny while there was still enough daylight left to see the few trees and the bare flagpole and the barracks buildings around three sides of an empty square and some doby huts and storehouses, but there wasn't no fort to it like I'd expected, no stockade or gunports or nothing, just the road turning rutted and sloggy till we had to sheer off and walk next to it to keep from getting bogged down.

After a long silence, I says, "You sure you still want to go through with this?"

"Mr. Bender, I've been waiting to hear your arguments against it," she says.

"I already told you," I says.

"And I believe I successfully rebutted everything you said." She held my arm till I had to set down the handles and look at her.

I didn't know how to talk pretty, and still don't, but I felt like kissing her then, and I done so. I was improving in that department, or maybe she was doing all the improving (it's hard to tell with kissing), but when we had finished for a while, I had something to say which I hadn't even thought up but had come unbidden, and I never felt more surprised at anything to come out of my mouth. "I love you," I says.

"I love you too, Mr. Bender," she says. "Our lives may

be difficult and hard, but they'll be beautiful and wonderful too, and at least *bearable*, which is more than I can say for a life without you."

I had never heard any music like that before, and I would of stood there a long while, holding her hands and enjoying it, but something new seemed to take charge of me, and I says, "We'd best find that Major or there won't be no wedding night left."

"There's always a wedding morning too," she says. "And a wedding afternoon and evening." But she sounded giddy and cheery and young and dizzy, and I knew exactly how she felt, being of the same persuasion myself.

We finally tracked down Major Kemper after being told No three times each by a Sergeant and a Lieutenant, and he come out on his piazza (which is what they call the long covered porch in front of his two-story wood house), with a napkin jammed into his collar and his jaw still giving his supper a work-over under his broad mustache, which was brown over on the cigar side and gray on the other. He listened about halfway through what the Lieutenant said—which was what the both of us had told and told and told so many times, it seemed like it had already happened—and he says, "Go get Reverend Applegate."

And while the Lieutenant went and done it, the Major looked me and Millie and my wheelborrow and Mr. Blue over and says, "Well, you two have a nerve, I guess."

"We have all the nerve we require for the purpose, Major Kemper," she says.

He went on chewing a bit, then pulled his napkin out, mopped his mouth, and hollered over his shoulder, "Clara! Come on out here a minute." He looked Millie up and down and says, "How old are you, girl?"

"Don't you know it isn't polite to ask a lady's age?" she says. "If you and your men have won any medals yet, they are undoubtedly not for gallantry."

The Major sucked his stomach in and glared at me like I was to blame for it all and says, "Don't you know better than to take a raw girl afoot all the way from here to Denver City or wherever you're bound? Are you crazy?"

"It wasn't my idea," I says.

A chunky woman in a long gray dress come to the door and says, "What are you shouting for? Don't shout."

The Major says, "I merely wanted you to come see—"

"Shouting my name outdoors at night across the parade ground," she says. "As if it were some kind of *order*. As if you were giving me *orders*."

"I'm sorry, dear," the Major says. "I merely wanted you to lend your weight to the argument here." He looked from me to Millie. "There's bound to be an argument."

"What's my weight got to do with it?" his wife says.

The Major used his napkin on his forehead and says slow and soft and reasonable, "These two very young and very foolish emigrants, who are on their own, want me to marry them. Right now. Tonight."

His wife come out on the piazza and squinted back and forth at us to see what she was sposed to be thinking about. "Them?" she says. "Ridiculous."

"We're no more emigrants than you are," Millie says. "And certainly no more ridiculous. We are full-share members of the Hearthstone Mining Company and are quite prepared to pay our way. What's your usual fee for a wedding ceremony?"

Which was the first I'd heard of any Hearthstone Mining Company but it sounded grand.

"I perform very, very few weddings," the Major says. "And then only for my men and only if *necessary*."

His wife leaned close to inspect Millie and says, "How old are you, girl? Fourteen? Fifteen?" She said the years like they was the worst possible ones.

"I happen to be Sweet Sixteen," Millie says, holding her chin up high. "And I had better warn you that my bridegroom-to-be is quite prepared to defend me from any slurs."

"I surely am," I says, and I was, if I'd been sure what they looked like. The Lieutenant fetched up a squat little man in a black suit, and when he got in a slice of light from the doorway, I seen his red face and watery eyes.

There was nothing wrong with the Major's eyesight neither. He says, "For God's sake, Applegate, are you drunk *this* early?"

"It's not early," Applegate says with the Lieutenant holding on to his arm.

"How do you expect to exert any moral authority when you're three sheets to the wind?" the Major says. "And on my brandy, I might add."

"Our brandy," his wife says, still looking at Millie, disapproving and giving little shakes to her head.

"Are you a man of the cloth?" Millie says.

Blinking so's he could get her lined up straight, Applegate says, "Yes."

"How much do you charge to conduct a wedding ceremony?"

All this talk about fees and charging made me uncomfortable, since I didn't want Millie to part with no money she didn't need to, and if you go around talking like that, you won't get something for nothing as long as you live.

"That's out of the question," the Major's wife says. "I couldn't permit that."

"Two dollars," Applegate says. "But I've been known to take one."

"You've been known to take one too many," the Major says. "Now just hold on a minute. Let me explain the circumstances."

"There's the matter of posting of the banns," the Major's wife says. "That's three weeks right there. Now I have a suggestion to make."

Applegate says, "Why, I haven't posted any banns for—"

and he begun fumbling at his vest pockets like he'd had some of them banns around someplace but lost track.

"I said I have a suggestion to make," the Major's wife says.

Millie says, "I will pay two dollars for the wedding and an extra dollar to shorten up the banns from three weeks to three minutes."

"Sold," Applegate says.

"Or maybe I could dig somebody a well," I says. "In exchange."

"Mr. Bender, we don't have *time*," Millie says.

"Wouldn't be no more'n ten or twelve foot this near the river," I says.

"Is anyone interested in hearing my suggestion?" the Major's wife says loud enough to scare up a little echo from the barracks across the square.

"Yes, dear," the Major says.

"First of all, where are your mother and father, girl?"

"My mother is deceased, and my father has given me his blessing," Millie says, which I doubted.

"Just answer my question, please," the Major's wife says. "I asked for his whereabouts."

"He runs a farm back near Plattsmouth," Millie says, sounding a bit younger.

"And why did you have to come all the way to Fort Kearny to get married?" The Major's wife didn't wait for no explanation. "Is it possible you've run away from home? We had a daughter that ran away from home."

"Now, Clara," the Major says.

"Wouldn't it be wiser to wait till we can write back to your father and be sure he's given his consent? You seem to be of a suitable age and deportment for domestic service. You could earn your keep as a maid, perhaps, in the meanwhile. If your father consents, well and good—if by that time you and this young man are still of so foolish a disposition—or if we don't hear from your father and you have matured a little, the Major and I might give *our* consent."

The Major says, "I doubt very much—"

"*In loco parentis*," his wife says.

"Loco is right," I says, stepping down off the piazza and getting hold of my wheelborrow handles. "Come on, Millie."

"If Applegate's willing to be responsible, I don't see how I can interfere," the Major says.

"Applegate is never responsible for anything except outrages," his wife says.

"I'll make that four dollars," Millie says, "but there's got to be a certificate."

"Sold again," Applegate says.

Glaring at the Major, his wife says, "Are you going to permit this kind of disgraceful behavior?"

"The church runs its own business, I'm afraid," the Major says.

In a clear voice Millie says, "Mrs. Kemper, you may have difficulty recognizing a determination superior to your own, but if you watch and listen closely, you may be able to detect the difference between a housemaid and a Handmaiden of Love."

"Love!" the Major's wife says, giving a little snort and heading for the door. "Very well, I wash my hands of it."

Millie got Applegate's arm away from the Lieutenant and tried to get him started off in the right direction.

The Major come down off the piazza and half-whispers, "Well, good luck. As long as you're set on this, I hope you'll be happy."

"Thank you, sir," I says. "We aim to be."

Still half-whispering, he says, "Do you—uh, have a place to stay tonight?"

"Stay?" I says, and I realized I hadn't got that far in my thoughts of Wedded Bliss yet.

"Perhaps we can arrange some sort of shelter for you at least," he says. "But I don't know about privacy."

"William!" his wife says from the doorway. "I won't stand for it."

"Yes, dear," he says, fumbling quick in his pocket and handing me fifty cents without moving his arm much.

"If you think I'm going to have newlyweds rattling around on my piazza all night, you've got another think coming," she says.

He slipped a cigar case out of the inside of his tunic and offered me one, and I took it just to be polite, and he half-whispers, "You've got a determined young lady there, but don't mistake determination for being right. They're not always the same thing."

"William!" his wife says. "Don't you dare help them, you hear?"

"Yes, dear," he says. Then to me, "This is a damned hard road you've picked, son, and don't forget it. This end of the Territory is tougher and crueler than the other end, which is no bargain either. Nearly every man over thirty's been married twice, and nearly every woman's a widow, some twice over. Don't go into it blind."

"William Kemper!" she says.

"I'll keep my eyes wide open, Major," I says, and I went wheelborrowing off after Millie, who was leading Mr. Blue and Reverend Applegate along under a dark, leafless row of cottonwood trees, but I didn't know whether to trust my eyes any more'n my brains.

"Man that is born of woman has but a short while to live," Reverend Applegate says with his rear end shoved up against the altar, where there was a red plush cloth hanging down and held in place by a stack of collection plates.

"Those aren't the right words," Millie says.

And truth to tell, they didn't sound any too good to me neither. We had come indoors for the ceremony, even though it meant leaving my wheelborrow and Mr. Blue out in the thieving night for a spell: you don't get married any too often, and you might's well have everything nice while you're at it.

"Ashes to ashes, dust to dust," Reverend Applegate says, spreading his fingers like he was sprinkling it.

"That's for the burial service," Millie says.

Reverend Applegate hadn't found his book, but he'd located the certificates, and Millie already had one made out fair and square, and the ink and quill laying beside it ready to finish off. We was standing side by side, and I patted her hand to gentle her down and says, "It's probably still legal."

"I'm not paying any four dollars to get buried or baptized," she says.

Reverend Applegate pulled hisself together a bit and says, "Do you take this woman to be your lawful wedded wife?"

"Don't ask me, ask him," Millie says.

"I do," I says, amazed to find it was so easy.

"And do you take him to be your lawful wedded husband?"

"I do," she says, her voice high and fluttery.

"To have and to hold, from this day forward, I forget how it goes," he says. "I don't know what happened to that damned book."

"Mr. Bender has to put the ring on my finger, and you have to pronounce us man and wife," she says.

"I don't have no ring," I says.

"Oh, yes you do," she says. "I've got it right here in my reticule." And she fished a gold band out of her draw-neck purse and handed it over, and I slipped it on her like she showed me. "Go on," she says to Reverend Applegate, giving him a prod in the vest.

"All flesh is grass," he says, yawning and his eyes watering.

"Pronounce us man and wife," she says.

"I do, I do," he says, getting annoyed. "I can pronounce anything."

"Now sign it." She dipped the quill and got it in between his fingers.

"Where's my four dollars?" he says.

She showed him the money but held it out of reach, and he scrawled his name on the certificate, letting it sag down below the dotted line but staying on the paper anyway.

Then I had to kiss the bride because Millie said it was the custom, in spite of Reverend Applegate and his housekeeper and the housekeeper's crippled-up sister watching (they had been drug in from next door to sign on for witnesses), and even though it had commenced drizzling outdoors, Millie and me refused Reverend Applegate's kind offer to let us bed down on the pews for the night, me because I didn't like the look of them planks and Millie saying she had to get used to her husband's Way of Life (which was the first time I'd heard I had one), so we walked out of there Mr. and Mrs. Ike Bender, all official, got back on the road west, and done two or three happy miles in the pale gloom of night.

When we had put plenty of room between us and Fort Kearny and stray horse soldiers, we pulled off the road a ways and camped, unhitching Mr. Blue but hobbling him because around so many campers he might get shot or dog-bit, and I give him the cigar to eat so's he'd have something to celebrate on. Then Millie showed me her best idea, which I should of thought up myself: she'd brung along a sheet of canvas, and we flung it over and pegged it down on each side of the wheelborrow with our blankets spread under, and then we slid ourselves in below the tub and handles till our feet was almost touching the wheel. It was like a pup tent, only better and drier and safer—

feeling, and then she told me what was in her heart, which I can't tell because that might spoil it, and I managed to tell her what was in my heart, which I couldn't tell even if I wanted to because I can't remember how in the wide world I ever got it said.

And you can guess what happened next, and you'll *have* to because I'm not going to tell except to say the greatest wonder I'd found or was yet to find, on that road to many a wonder, didn't come while I was shoving the wheelborrow ahead of me or hauling it along behind me but was underneath of it.

Chapter Ten ★★★★★★★★★★★★★★★★★

☞ When we woke up, we was still married, and we was married all morning into Doby Town (pop. 300, not counting the people who might be drifting up and down among the huts and shacks trying to figure out how to stretch their little bit of money into loads of supplies or, if they was coming back from the gold fields busted and disgusted, how to change their supplies into something easier to carry), and we was walking around smiling and happy among all them worried, scairt, sour-looking, doubtful people, and there wasn't no kind of advice or lies or discouragement you couldn't hear.

You didn't even have to ask for it but would have it shoved onto you every place you turned: some said the dumbest knothead in the world could earn five or six dollars a day if he knew enough to slop a pan back and forth, but all the good claims was taken; some said there was no gold at all, and the whole rush was hoaxed up by merchants in Kansas City and Fort Leavenworth and St. Joe and Nebraska City so's they could sell cheap supplies for big prices; some said everybody was sick and dying in Auraria and Denver City from having et their mules in the winter; some was trying to sell guidebooks, and some stood next to them saying what a raw swindle and cheat the books was and we'd do better to read the family Bible and use the maps of the Holy Land because they was just about as accurate on the subject of Cherry Crick; some wanted to sell us a plot of land, sight unseen, where a big city was going to be, spang up against the best paydirt and how could we go wrong?—and a baker's dozen wanted to sell us shares in claims that was bound to pay off a hundred-fold, just as soon as the thaw set in and the water come flowing in the cricks again, and every one of them had a little chunk of gold-streaked quartz and some rusty-looking pebbles or a goose quill of what they said was gold dust, which they would take me aside and show me secret and careful and spying around this way and that to be sure we wasn't being overheard.

I had smelt some strange places back around home and heard some tale spinning and been filched out of a few pennies and marbles and a jackknife from time to time, but nothing to put a patch on this Doby Town. Yet through it all, while Millie was inspecting the beans and flour and jerky and coffee in the general store and I was trying to keep Mr. Blue from lighting out for open country so's he could hear hisself think, we was still being married and close and the good feeling kept running up and down the inside of my backbone, and I didn't mind all this scurrying and meanness and scrabbling and desperation. Hadn't the sun come up? And wasn't it the middle of a free day, handed out to us free of charge and full of promises and spilling over the best kind of daylight ever invented? It seemed *right* that every other word you'd hear was *Gold.* Gold this and Gold that and Gold over yonder and No Gold No Place. I listened to the swearing and read the covers on guidebooks and looked at little chunks of rock and took a nibble at the buttery thick language on Deeds and Certificates and Bills of Sale and Shares in the Blackleg Mining Corporation and the Holy Smoke Lode and considered my nomination as the Assistant Town Treasurer of Goldville, which was only twenty-eight miles from Pikes Peak if anybody could find it among the pine trees, and I felt glad to be a living witness to all this fine confusion and meanwhile kept my jacket buttoned and my hat on tight and one eye on my wheelborrow and one eye on Mr. Blue, sharing in the laughter and talk coming out of the Sure Fire Saloon without having to join in or join up.

What begun to puzzle me most was I felt surrounded by liars and fools, yet I didn't think I was neither. And I wondered could I be a liar and a fool without knowing it? How could it only be me and Millie, out of all these people, who was honest and smart? Didn't make sense, but that's how I felt. And then I figured maybe being in love was the foolish part I couldn't reckonize but other folks could, and that was how they'd take me for a fool like everybody else. I looked at Millie arguing with the storekeep in that sweet, steady, quiet way she had, and I realized she had to be a fool too, no matter how smart she acted, because wasn't she joining her life up with a fool like me? After that, I didn't feel so plumb much like an outsider.

The next man that showed me a little pinch of caramel-colored dust in his palm and told me it was gold and tried to sell me shares in his company, I says, "Did you use quicksilver to separate that?"

He says, "Yeah, sure," tipping his sweaty sombrero back and putting one foot up on a patch of boardwalk and looking at me square and earnest.

"How do you use quicksilver to get gold dust?" I says, that being what I hadn't found out from nobody yet.

"You buy into this claim and you'll find out quick enough," he says. "Hasn't been a pan out of her that didn't show color."

"You just put some quicksilver in the pan, and then what?"

"I'm letting you in on the ground floor of a lifetime, boy," he says.

"Tell me about the quicksilver," I says.

Already looking around for another customer, the man says, "Makes an amalgam with the dust, and you got to squeeze it through a filter and heat it up in a retort to vaporate it off."

I didn't understand much of that. "What's a retort?" I says. "What kind of filter?"

But he pulled his hat down and strolled off, scouting for a live one.

Millie didn't tell me how much she finally spent, but to judge by the look of her mouth, it was more'n she wanted to, and we had three more bundles to add to the load, two for Mr. Blue and one for my wheelborrow, which was going to look humpbacked till we had et it down a ways.

We stopped alongside a grander hut which was the home station for the weekly mail coach, and I thought it might be my last chance to keep Millie from a lot of suffering, and I says, "Won't be but five days till a stagecoach comes back through here. We could camp nearby, and you could catch it back home."

"I don't propose to catch anything," she says.

"You're married now, and you'd have something to think about while you was waiting," I says.

She snapped a quick look at me and says, "I don't want merely to think about life. I want to do it."

"I mean planning things and getting our Future lined up," I says. "Safe and sound."

"Right now my home's underneath that wheelborrow, wherever it might happen to be," she says.

"Or you could take the coach the other way and wait for me in Julesburg," I says. "You wouldn't have but a hundred miles to go after that, and you could practice hiking while you was waiting."

"I've already ridden part way," she says. "You don't seem to understand, Mr. Bender: I'm wedded to you now. I want to see the same things you see and learn what you learn and be your helpmeet. I'm strong. I always did more chores than Pa wanted me to."

"One of the parts Applegate left off was 'in sickness and in health,' " I says. "If you get sick or hurt, what would I do?"

She come up real close to me then, something I found out she always done whenever she wanted her way and meant to get it spite of flood or brimstone. She says, "He also left off 'till death do us part.' And that means only death can do it, not some mail wagon. If you want to get rid of me, Mr. Bender, you're going to have to make my deathbed somewhere along the line, but don't expect me to lie down in it willingly."

"I won't do no such a thing," I says.

"Very well. Then I suggest we commence our journey," she says. "Three hundred miles is no different from three hundred yards if you think about it properly."

And we done so, though I must not of known how to think about it right because even the first day seemed like a long ways to me. I was mostly worried about her feet: the round-toed, thick-soled brown boots she was wearing seemed all right, but I knew they was a whole lot bigger than what was inside them, and I was scairt she'd blister herself bad. And I kept trying to figure out some way to shift all, or most all, our pack into my wheelborrow so she could ride up on Mr. Blue if he'd let her.

Nothing's more tiresome than worry, and the first few miles seemed like twenty to me, since I was taking all her steps for her and trying to fill up her boots with my feet, but she was so cheery and excited and pointing at things, pretty soon I begun to trust her to do her own walking and me mine. Doby Town disappeared behind us, and even though we could see some wagons up ahead and a few in back, it was like we was mostly alone. She would touch me on the arm now and then (since I couldn't touch her without letting loose of a handle) and say, "You're still there," which I found funny and a comfort because I wasn't any too sure *where* I was. I felt like I was one of them strange marvels I'd seen further back on the road, like I was a crow man or a monster or a top-turvy village my own self, shifting and changing.

I told her about seeing them things and about how the hills had stayed far off, and she says, "They're called mirages," which didn't make them no less a wonder. We kept our eyes skinned for more on that endless flat stretch that rose up to low rolly hills on the left and down to sandy water and long skinny islands on the right, but it was too chill a day with the wind gusting sideways and the light grayed out, and she figured mirages done best in the calm heat and brightness.

Over and over in my mind I kept fumbling with "filter" and "retort" and "vaporate" and "malcom," wondering how I was going to rig up anything that complicated, but I didn't dare waste the quicksilver fooling with it, so I finally just clamped my mind shut like a lid on a crock and didn't think about the Platte maybe being gold-choked.

From time to time we'd come across pieces of furniture that had been thrown out of wagons to cut down the weight for tired, underfed mules and oxen, most of it hacked up for kindling, but some not—specially the bigger pieces that had fell out or been pushed into the shallow river when somebody'd tried to ford it in the wrong place and got bogged down or quicksanded: highboys and buffets and sideboards, some already bleached like driftwood, and Millie would cluck and exclaim and turn sorry and hold her hands flat on her cheeks like a housewife watching an heirloom get scratched or spilt on.

We camped near one of them: a chest of drawers sticking up about two foot out of the water and ten foot from the bank, and I roped it and hauled it ashore with Mr. Blue's help and stood it up next to my wheelborrow to shut out the breeze and to save having to get myself wet for firewood out on an island. At first Millie didn't want me to bust up one of the drawers, but she seen the sense of it after a bit, and I got a fire going, and we set there eating beans and bacon and sipping skillet coffee (which is fine if you don't mind a little grease in your grounds) and looking at that chest with one drawer missing already.

And she says, "Somebody meant to have that in her bedroom out in Oregon or California or someplace, and now look at it."

I put another chunk on the fire. I think it was cherry, and it burnt sweet and slow. "Well, you can have it in your bedroom tonight," I says.

"I wonder what she thought when she had to leave it behind and saw it sitting there in the river, lost forever," Millie says, clutching her knees in close under her shawls and letting her eyes go even bigger in the firelight.

"She probably cussed a streak and blamed whoever was nearest," I says.

"Mr. Bender, you should cultivate a more romantic nature," she says. "You mustn't feel that a tender sensibility might be a drawback to your future success. Many wealthy, well-educated men are not ashamed to weep over just such an object as this chest of drawers. Even in front of others."

I tried to think it over and see it her way, but I finally had to say, "They shouldn't of hauled something that heavy this far. Don't make sense."

"Perhaps it had sentimental value," she says. "Part of a family heritage."

Though I hadn't inherited nothing but trouble so far from my family, I had to admit she could be right. "Well, I'll feel sorry if you want me to," I says. "We didn't have no chest of drawers at home. I don't have but two pair of drawers anyway, so I don't reckon to need no chest for them."

"It could just as well have been her hope chest," Millie says. "Perhaps she lost that too." Her eyes was shiny.

"I've got plenty of hope," I says. "But I keep it in my own chest."

"You have mine full of hope too," she says, touching her own small bosom so I could see her do it.

I got over on my knees and kissed her, which I had been doing so much of since the night before, my lips felt wore down to the quick, but I never wanted to stop. "Mind if I freshen up the fire one more time?" I says, meaning I had to break up the bottom drawer to do it, and I didn't want to hurt her feelings.

"You might as well go ahead," she says, touching one side where the water had wore off varnish and stain and left it all yellow. "It's of no more use to anyone except for thoughts."

I had to rattle and yank the drawer and finally persuade it a little with my pickax, but part of the front come loose then, and it was all full of women's clothes, soaked the color of the Platte so's you couldn't hardly tell what they was sposed to be exactly.

Millie pounced on them and fished one out and got it untangled, and it had lace around the bottom edge and some embroidery around the top and was short, but I didn't get too good a look at it because she crumpled it up and held it behind her and says, "Mr. Bender, these are a lady's unmentionables." Her mouth dropped open, and her whole face was spelling the wonder of it. "Perhaps some poor woman's trousseau."

I started to pick one out of the drawer myself to have a look, but she stopped me.

"Gentlemen are not supposed to deal with garments like these," she says.

"I have looked at many a clothesline," I says.

"You never saw silk and sateen and linen and cambric and zanella cloth like this," she says, standing so's I couldn't see good and holding out piece after piece to the firelight. "Not in Cass County anyway. And not on clotheslines." She rummaged some more, and I done my best to see, which wasn't too good. "I suppose they're all ruined and shrunk," she says.

"Well, most women are bigger than you, so maybe they've shrank down to your territory," I says. Being married lets you start talking out bold like that.

"I really don't think we should discuss unmentionables any more," she says, but I seen her holding up one of them to her own front and looking down to see if it fit.

"If they're not sposed to show or be talked of or seen or known, why's there so many different kinds of them?" I says.

"It would be too difficult to explain," she says. "The next creek we come to, I'll see if they'll rinse out any. I wish I had more soap." And she took another one out of the busted drawer, still showing pale blue through a layer of river silt.

"I know what that one is," I says. "That's a corset." Gawking under the swinging doors of the Wagonwheel, I had seen one of the dancing girls peel down to that two years ago, and Alfie Cutler had told me what it was. My ma didn't own one, or need one neither.

"I won't inquire how you happen to know," she says.

"I'd be obliged if you'd tie that rope from the chest of drawers to the wheelborrow and back again."

"Won't neither one wander off in the night," I says.

"I intend to dry these garments, Mr. Bender, even if it means your getting a look at them. You'll just have to exercise restraint."

"I've exercised everything else today," I says. "Might's well give that a workout too." And I rigged up the clothesline for her, and while she was draping them unmentionables over it, crooning and clicking her tongue and muttering at them and being hen-fussy, I turned Mr. Blue loose without his pack so's he could start his night foraging again. I had to take the chance he'd keep coming back for more of us, since all we had was a little emergency sack of oats for him.

When she'd finished, we got ready to bed down under the wheelborrow, pegging the canvas like before, and I didn't let her see me looking at the chemises and drawers and what-all waving in the breeze and glimmering ghostly in the last of the dim firelight. They seemed as much a mystery as what was sposed to go inside them, but not near as heart-squeezing. As I laid there with her, she still had lots of clothes on, mostly mentionable, it being our policy not to get froze in the night, but our bodies had begun to know each other, and clothes have a way of getting out of the road and fading off for a while and there's many a helping hand to lead them.

After a time, she says, "Mr. Bender, I hope our intimacy hasn't made any new problems for you."

The idea had never occurred to me. "I think you're wonderful, Millie," I says.

"It's very difficult being a woman," she says. "But very exciting too. I have the feeling it would be exciting even to be miserable and unhappy."

"I hope you never find out," I says.

In a quiet voice, soft as the breeze going through the

lace on our clothesline, she says, "I have opened my chaste treasure to you, Mr. Bender. I hope you've found it worthwhile."

"I am a wealthy man," I says, and meant it. And then I says something out of nowhere, which I didn't understand because I had never even said it in a church. "You're my salvation," I says.

She come even closer after that, and then we fell asleep.

Chapter Eleven ★ ★ ★ ★ ★ ★ ★ ★ ★ ★ ★ ★ ★ ★

☞ "I didn't know we had to go through a forest," she says. "Perhaps it will be a pleasant change of scenery. Instructive too. We must learn to take instruction from Nature."

Up ahead, I seen what she was talking about, but it didn't look like no forest I'd ever saw back in Missouri. It was too dark and too low and like the wind was blowing over it, but there wasn't no wind.

We'd been walking for days now, and she hadn't turned footsore or complaining and hadn't wanted to stop and gossip every time we passed a wagon coming or going that had a woman in it and hadn't made no trouble I couldn't of made myself and had been a boon and a companion and a joy, and we was getting more and more married. Mr. Blue had taken to the new routine just fine and held most as still for me as he done for her and seemed like ours, though I always felt guilty in the back of my mind about not having paid nothing for him.

The sun was out full but not hot, and it seemed like the

air ought to be clear but it wasn't, not when you looked up ahead at them trees. Instead, the air looked kind of shaky, and sometimes the trees was small as bushes, and other times they swole up higher than any elms or cottonwoods I'd seen along the valley. Nothing looked right or felt right, and I says, "We better stop."

"You said you wanted to make ten more miles today," she says.

The woods kept moving even when we didn't, so it wasn't just my eyes jogging: they stretched up over the sand hills where I'd never seen more'n a weed grow before, if that, and now slow puffs of something—smoke or dust or mist—commenced coming from in amongst them. They seemed to stretch as far ahead as I could see in the wavy air, and some was even growing in the river, which I *knew* couldn't be.

We had passed a couple of wagons heading for Fort Kearny a while back, but things looked empty up ahead except for them trees, which of course wasn't trees at all. "I don't think they'll trample us even if they stampede," I says. "Long as they can see us far enough ahead. Just stay still and hang on to Mr. Blue."

"What are you talking about?" she says.

"Buffalo," I says.

"But they can't be buffalo," she says. "There are too many of them."

The noise started then, rumbly and far off with little crackles in it like branches getting broke, and trying to watch the herd was like trying to look at something through clear fast water: you're pretty sure what you're looking at, but it keeps shifting shape on you. After a minute, there wasn't no doubt about it: they was galloping, some toward us, some up the slope to the valley rim, louder and louder, deeper and heavier, till the roadbed begun to make my feet buzz. I herded us off right to the low riverbank fifty yards away and got us set, with me and the wheelborrow in front, figuring the lead bulls would keep out of the water if they could and maybe give us time and room to jump in if we had to.

The herd—the biggest one I ever did see, though I lived to lay eyes on many another—had split into three separate streams, maybe more, since I could hardly see the other end of them, at least two going up the slope to the hills and the prairie beyond but one coming straight down the road toward us. And now we could see what had fussed them up so: a half a dozen parties of men, afoot, on horse-back, some on mules, was firing rifles and handguns into the clumps, all heading in different directions and running into each other and for all I knew shooting each other as often as any buffalo, though by now there was so much thundering commotion from hooves, the gunfire was all silenced over.

"Are they harming those poor beasts?" Millie says, looking astonished from me to them.

"Hang on," I says, meaning to Mr. Blue, but she used one hand to clutch the back of my belt like she was more scairt I'd run off, which I might of done if there'd been a safe way to haul her and someplace to run to.

But there wasn't, with them shaggy heads bouncing up and down toward us, some of them taller than me and too big to believe in, their brown beards scraping the ground and tufty tails sticking straight out. I got my revolver out of the wheelborrow, which might of been some use if it had been a cannon, and held it up in the air with that one bullet in it, ready to make a little noise if I couldn't do nothing else. "Can you swim?" I yells.

"I have never attempted to swim," she yells back.

"It's only three foot deep," I yells, hoping this was one of the regular shallow places and not some sink hole.

"Don't you dare shoot any of those creatures," she yells.

But before I could explain, the lead bull must of decided we didn't look like nothing fit to trample and sheered off, wheeling to our left and going upslope the way the rest of the herd had, and we stood there, our knees rattling with the ground thunder the huge buffs made.

A tall, skinny man on horseback came busting out of the side of the cluster near us, whooping and yelling and aiming his rifle into the side of a big cow, most touching it, and when he fired, she went skidding forward on her knees and stayed down, flopping and floundering while the others run past, and the man went galloping with them, aiming another shot into a bull and keeping the same pace as them.

I think the cow had been lung-shot because she laid there, struggling and coughing bright red blood and not getting her legs under her, gouging at the sand and looking like she might be bellering too, but we couldn't hear it.

Millie started like she was going to run over and help, though there wasn't nothing worth doing, but I held her back, and we stood there about ten minutes while the buffalo cleared off south over the hills except for the dead ones and them dying like the cow near us, who lasted about half that time before she stiffened up and quit.

Down the whole long stretch ahead of us I seen the carcasses sprawled out or half-dragging theirselves after the herd already gone and the men dodging amongst them, letting off more gunfire and now some wagons coming too, some pulled by hand, and pretty soon it was meat-cutting time, and for two miles ahead it was a slaughterhouse with men yipping and cheering and finishing off the wounded and not being too careful which way their guns was pointing. The hard sand looked all churned up, and there was buffalo manure dropped everywhere.

The skinny man come trotting back, yelling something at another man, who'd dismounted a hundred yards off and was already hacking away at a carcass, and they was either pardners being happy or enemies laying claim to each other's buffs, I didn't know or care, but when the skinny man took out a bowie knife and commenced taking that cow apart, I got our little party under way and tried to get us past before anything too bad could happen.

But Millie stopped close and says, "Don't you fear to suffer the same fate?"

I don't think he heard her right, being down on his knees and occupied up to both elbows, which he had rolled his sleeves back from, and he turned his head and grinned and says, "Want some, girlie? Which part do you fancy?"

She says, "Don't you fear the savages may capture you out on the prairie and gut you and flay you and scalp you just the way you're doing to that poor beast?"

He understood that all right, and he glanced from her to me and back, then started cutting again and says, "Help yourself before the Injuns and coyotes beat you to it, and don't go laying curses on your elders if you don't want to get spanked."

"I'm not cursing you," she says.

"Come on, Millie," I says. "Leave him alone. He's just doing what thousands done before and thousands more to come."

"Aren't you interested in cultivating your more refined feelings?" she says to him. "Don't you want to rise above your brute nature?"

Still working, he says, "At the moment I'm rising above it by not starving to death, little girl. It's been a long winter."

"Come on, please," I says.

"At the moment, are you any better than the worst savage?" she says to him.

"At the moment I'm a whole *lot* better because I'm in

here first with the knife," he says, grinning over his shoulder again and giving me a wink. "You taking this Sunday-school teacher someplace out west?"

"I draw my lessons and conclusions from what I see seven days a week, not just Sundays," she says.

"Well, I wish you'd reach a conclusion right about now," he says, getting back to work.

I got her moving then, and we went along that bloody stretch, keeping quiet for a while and steering as far off from the strewn carcasses as possible, which wasn't too far because there was dozens and dozens with men and a few women now from wagons hacking away and carting off red chunks and strips and some more skinning off buffalo hides for robes. Mr. Blue wasn't enjoying the smell none and kept shying away and helping us zigzag through.

Finally she says in a small, tense voice, "How much faith do you have in men, Mr. Bender?"

"I try to have as little as I can get by with," I says.

"Don't you believe we must strive for our rightful and dutiful position, which we're told is only a little lower than the angels?" she says.

"Well, I believe in striving all right," I says. "But I don't expect to crowd no angels while I'm at it."

"But you *do* aspire to a higher life, don't you?"

"That's what I'm doing with you," I says. "I think."

There was only a few more carcasses between us and the open road again, and they had been gone over already and didn't look like nothing earthly, and up ahead there wasn't no forest now, just the shimmering flat river with now and then a half-hint of a mirage like something trying to melt. We passed many a wagon that had come back for the kill, and by the time we'd left the churned-up, dung-covered stretch behind, I couldn't see nobody in front of us, and the ground turned smooth and innocent-looking. "You have to remember your family didn't come by the name of Slaughter by learning off of angels," I says.

"Mr. Bender, I have changed my name," she says.

"Well, my family must of been bending something to get ours," I says. "And maybe it went and broke."

About dusk the next day we come to a six-foot crick with nice clear water where it looked like many had camped before, and I carried Millie over (always get your feet wet at sundown so's at sunup you can walk dry-shod) and got us all set for supper, including a fire made out of a busted platform rocker somebody had heaved off a wagon. But instead of cooking, Millie made me do it while she renched out them unmentionables and had washday on Sam and Frank's blankets with a cake of yellow soap, doing her hair while she was at it too.

She went a bit upstream so's I couldn't see too good (but how was I going to learn what women like to wear underneath if I don't keep my eyes open?), and I think she slipped off some things she was wearing under her dress and added them to the pile, maybe sposing I couldn't tell the difference and wouldn't ask nosy questions, which I am inclined to do. And I knew it was hard for her because we didn't have no walls to separate us, no doors we could shut and be private, no roof to keep the sun and moon minding their own business, just darkness once a day. It takes some getting used to.

While I unhitched Mr. Blue, I pretended like I wasn't watching her, but I was. Everything she done was neat and straight and no waste motion to it, and when she had a pile of them wet underwears next to her and unbraided her brown hair and knelt forward and dipped her whole head in the crick and her hair went streaming along the sandy bottom like part of the water, I felt like everything she done was a kind of prayer. I felt foolish and mush-headed about it, and I caught Mr. Blue looking at me with one bulgy brown eye like he couldn't calculate why it was taking me so long to turn him loose.

(No, that's not right. You can't never tell what a burro's thinking by looking him in the eye: he's usually got his other eye aimed off somewheres else, and *that's* the one he's thinking with. I've come to believe burros mostly don't like what's going on around them. They know how things *should* be but never get it served up to them that way, and never will, and yet that don't stop them from knowing exactly what they want. They never get what they want and they *still* hold out for it. I admire stubbornness on that scale, and I reckonize some of it in myself.)

I says to Mr. Blue, "She's a wonder."

He blinked once, and I could tell his mind was off on something else. He would nibble her hand any time of day and let her scratch his ears, but would have little of me or mine. I slid his pack off onto the sand and begun to rig up a clothesline for her, using the sawed-off clothes prop from my wheelborrow, and watched Mr. Blue set off in a fast walk for the hills.

And just when I had got the bacon fried and the pan bread on the way and the blankets wrung out and stretched and everything was peaceful and she had strung up the unmentionables (some of them was showing colors now, pale green and blue and pink), and she seemed even shyer about them than before, I heard the horses.

There was three of them, an Injun and two squaws, riding scrawny paints not much bigger than Mr. Blue, and they come from behind us and splashed through the crick and reined up and looked us all over without talking, and I done the same. The squaws had on long, floppy deerskin dresses with just a little beadwork and all stained, and they was small and dark and round-faced and looked like sisters, but the Injun was a sight to behold and then try to forget. He was near as big as his pony and looked even bigger now because he was wearing a fresh-skinned buffalo hide without the head, bloody-side-in like he was saying *I'm the buffalo now*, and he had blue paint on the left half of his face and red paint on the right, meeting between the big dark eyes and coming right down the middle of his squashed-looking flat nose, and he had his long hair braided and tied with little feathers and rawhide, and he was only wearing a small flap on his front, and where a white man would of had a saddle, he was setting on raw meat. That pony was a walking butcher shop with slabs of dripping dark flank steak and what-all heaped over the butt and draped over the mane and under the Injun's legs where he was setting right smack on it.

His eyes squinted over Millie and the clothesline and the wheelborrow and the skillet and me, and he says something short and deep in Injun (I don't know whether he was Arapaho or Cheyenne or Kiowa, but he wasn't like no Pawnee I ever seen), and the two squaws swung off their ponies and come to look closer at the unmentionables, reaching out to touch.

"No!" Millie says, getting her wet hair bunched back behind her shoulders and stepping between them and the clothesline.

The Injun says something else, and one of the squaws says, "Tobacco, sugar, coffee," and held out her hands like she was going to catch it falling out of the sky.

The other squaw says, "Two bits," poking her forefinger in her palm. "Two bits. Meat."

The first squaw tried to reach past Millie to touch the corset, but Millie pushed her arm aside and says, "What would you advise me to do, Mr. Bender?"

"As little as possible," I says, standing by the fire and thinking of the gun in my wheelborrow and the knife in my belt and not wanting anybody to get hurt over a bunch of underwears.

The second squaw says, "Meat! Meat!" She made a gobbling motion with fingers to mouth and pointed at all that raw flesh the Injun was setting on. He swole out his chest a little, all streaked with fresh blood, and looked proud of hisself. I couldn't see no gun, but there was a knife handle sticking out of the buffalo roast in front of him like a saddlehorn.

The first squaw says, "Whiskey," and she went poking her nose into the wheelborrow, where the crock full of quicksilver was showing near the top, and when she reached for it, I knew I had to get busy.

"All right," I says, nice and loud, and everybody stopped what they was doing or about to do and looked at me, and I says, "All right," and got out my coin purse from my back pocket with the button on it and fished out two bits and got the purse buttoned back in before the squaws could get after it. I held up the coin at the Injun. "Meat," I says.

He lit up with a big smile and says something deep and grunty, and the first squaw made a come-on move with her hand and says, "More, more."

Millie's hand come out from under her shawls with a two-bit piece in her fingers she'd plucked out of someplace and held it up, and the second squaw grabbed hers and mine both.

The Injun slung one leg over and clumb down from his pony and lifted off two hunks of meat the size of pot roasts (I was glad to see he didn't pick the slab he'd been setting on directly), and come over to us, holding one out in each hand and grinning and nodding. I don't know where Millie was directing her eyesight, but this Injun's unmentionables was on the small side and kind of askew, and I took the chunk of meat from him quick. Still grinning, he clapped both arms around me (I felt the meat swat me in the back) and touched our foreheads together. He smelt like life and death and everything in between, sweet and rancid and good and gamy and horrible and manly, and with my head right up against his, for a few seconds I couldn't tell who was which.

He turned me loose and headed for Millie, his bare flat feet hitting the ground heavy and proud, and when he handed her the other roast, she says quick and gentle, "What would you advise me to do now, Mr. Bender?"

"As much of nothing as will go with your womanhood," I says.

He give her a hug just like mine and touched foreheads, and she stood there, keeping the meat betwixt them and closing her eyes, and then he backed off and turned, dragging the dusty end of his raw buffalo hide on the ground, and took a running jump onto his pony again without knocking none of the rest of the meat off, and the squaws remounted, chattering at each other and each biting one of the two bits. Then the Injun stuck one of his blood-covered hands out straight, palm down, and said something that sounded like a blessing (or at least it didn't sound like one of my old man's cussings), and they rode off.

Millie just stood there, holding that meat and looking kind of sick, and I didn't know what to do with mine neither. I had blood on my shirt, and I could feel it turning crusty on my forehead. Then finally Millie dropped hers on the ground and run to the crick to wash her hands and face.

I picked up her chunk and held it with mine till she come back, and she looked from me to the meat and seemed to get a grip on herself and says, "I suppose we ought to be practical and keep our strength up, but I surely wish there were more vegetables in this world, Mr. Bender."

"What did you used to do at slaughtering time?" I says, remembering her pa kept hogs.

"Run and hide," she says, sounding meek.

"Well, there's lots of room to run out here," I says, "but not much place to hide." I hefted that meat, which I didn't relish any too much myself. "Would you like me to bury this?"

She smiled a little nervous at me. "Couldn't you just take it off a ways and let the coyotes find it?"

I done so, then washed my own hands and face, and come back to hear her weeping soft and quiet by the fire, which she was poking at with a piece of the genuine hand-carved oak headrest of the platform rocker. She quit when she seen me, and I set down and held my arm around her and rocked a little with her, just like we was setting by the fire at home and not burning an heirloom of somebody else's.

Chapter Twelve ★★★★★★★★★★★★★★

☞ Walking is a sure way of getting someplace in most kinds of country because there don't seem to be much to taking a step or two and, while you're at it, taking a couple more and, once you get going, taking a couple dozen more. And pretty soon you don't notice how many you're taking (unless you're pacing off miles like I done sometimes), and you don't have nothing to wear out or break down except you and what you stand up in. And walking's an interesting way to get someplace because you don't miss much of what's going on like you do when you're memorizing the rear end of an ox or a mule and wondering which fly is bothering it the most. And with walking you never lose track of how far one place is from another, the way you can in a wagon or a boat if you doze off and start learning the inside of your eyelids by heart.

But one thing you have to say about walking is it takes time. Yet it didn't seem like ordinary time with Millie along, but some new kind, with more room in it sideways, fuller, thicker, and more noticeable. It wasn't just her talking, though she done plenty of that, and me too, mostly answering. It was the way I *looked* at everything because I knew she was looking at it too, feeling it out and feeling it through, and I become more alert about everything under the sun because of her. There wasn't a minute of the walking day, with me wheelborrowing and her leading Mr. Blue, when something didn't catch my eye or ear or seem to wake up some new part of my head, and I come to think of it as one of the best parts of love. (I wasn't afraid to think the word no more nor say it neither.)

Day after day and night after night, instead of catching myself napping or going dull-hearted, I'd catch myself breathing and waking up for the sheer wonder of something most folks wouldn't of noticed, including me back before Dogtown—the shape the current makes turning aside at the head of an island; the plain, miserable pleasure a hostler can get out of being mean to strangers at a mail station; the way rain turns all colors falling through sunshine; how fearful it is to listen to somebody else's heart beat and know yours is doing likewise and they'll both stop someday; the way a burro goes about appreciating oats, turning his lips in tight and bulgy like an old man gumming his mush; the feel of your own hams touching the ground when you haven't set on them but once or twice all day; how proud you feel when you make a fire in a place where it didn't look like there was nothing left to burn for miles around; how many different sounds a coyote can make when he settles down to it and has a little neighborly help; the way the moon can turn so bright some nights, you can't look at it no longer than if it was the sun; the way a girl's face can be fifty faces a day, all different, and all enough to make you ache for her; and on and on like that, forever if you've got a mind to.

We seen and heard more folks coming back from the gold fields without having stayed there but overnight, glum and burning mad and some even raving about all the gold being in the storekeeps' teeth, about wanting to lynch the liars back on the Missouri River that had set them on the road to ruination, and we seen old wrecks like Hotchkiss setting theirselves up as trading posts, waiting for the huge flow of new springtime fools, which we was among the first of, and it's certain sure it would of been enough to discourage us if we hadn't been so happy to start off with.

And since we'd already come more'n halfway, it didn't make no difference which direction we kept walking but might's well keep on going and see for ourselves. People would lean out of wagons and yell at us and call us idjits and fall to cussing, and some had crossed off the "Pikes Peak or" on the sides of their wagons and left "Bust" by itself, maybe adding a "By God!" But them people didn't even like where they stood or set *right now.* And we did. They didn't see or feel what we seen or felt *right here,* so how could we trust them about someplace we hadn't laid our eyes on or set foot?

Many a time Millie says to me, "Isn't this beautiful, Mr. Bender?" walking along a barren stretch of road. And it was. She was right. And half an hour later some lunkhead would be jawing and blaspheming at us about the godforsook valley we was in and the sonofabunching Platte and all like that. (I had long since give up defending Millie's ears from foul language, since it would of took too much time to fight a thousand men.)

People see what they believe, I spose, or see what they're set to believe. And me and Millie done a lot of looking at each other in the meantime, when we wasn't bumping into other wonders.

One day she says, "Do you think I'm too tenderhearted, Mr. Bender?"

"No," I says, but it was one of the subjects I'd worried about because I didn't want her getting heartbroke or heartsick over some of the miseries we'd seen and was bound to go on seeing.

"I believe it's one of my many faults," she says. "At least I'm not tender-*footed* any more, but how can I get over the other without turning *hard*hearted?"

"I don't know," I says. "Maybe you better not try."

"I have always believed it was a good idea for all of us to cultivate *feelings,* but now I'm not so sure," she says. "I want to be the most useful kind of wife to you and not a drawback."

For the life of me I couldn't figure out why she wanted to be any kind of wife of mine, but I didn't say so because there's no fit answer to a remark like that when you're already stuck. "You're no drawback," I says. "And it was true what you told me about that Wedded Bliss."

"I'm very glad to hear it," she says, smiling and blushing and giving Mr. Blue an extra twitch on his rope.

Which made me blush too but the same time I wished it was sundown already and us setting by the wheelborrow tent waiting for it to get dark enough to slip inside. Then, like I done most every day, I says, "Are you sure it's not going to be too far for you? You can still catch a mail wagon or stagecoach part ways."

And as usual she says, "Mr. Bender, I'm getting stronger every day, not weaker."

And truth to tell, she seemed to be. She wasn't losing weight and getting scrawny and hollow-eyed like many another I seen on the road. I didn't have no idea what *I* looked like, but she didn't seem worried about me.

If I'd had a mind to it and the muscle and the wagon space and a couple yoke of oxen, I could of set myself up as a blacksmith in the gold fields: by the time we begun the long curve southwest on the South Fork, where there was a couple good fording places for wagons aiming at Fort Laramie and on to Oregon, we'd passed six or seven good-sized anvils laying on the ground and tongs and pinchers and a box full of horseshoes and a stack of rusty sheet iron and plowshares and scythes and bar iron and grindstones and a bellows, all thrown overboard along the way to lighten the loads or maybe just out of disgust with that line of work. The stuff just laid there, and nobody had room to pick it up. Or maybe lots of people done what I done: they'd see something heavy they liked and pick it up and cart it along for a spell, even a day or two, then chuck it away again as too blame heavy. Probably some of them tools had been picked up and flung down again dozens of times and might make it to Denver City by relay in a year or two. The only things I hung on to and tied them alongside my wheelborrow was a two-handled whipsaw that had a beautiful set of teeth and hardly rusty at all and an ax.

"What do you intend to use the saw for?" Millie says.

"I expect I'll saw something with it," I says. "It don't look much good for digging gold."

She give me a peckish frown and says, "I was merely wondering why you'd want to weigh yourself down any more than you already are."

I kept it anyway and two big pocketfuls of two-inch nails out of a heap that must of been from a keg but somebody had burnt the keg for firewood. And one night we camped by a cookstove somebody had tossed out, and we got it set upright and built a fire in it and baked some pretty near real bread and biscuits and then set beside it a long time, even after dark, enjoying the comfort like we was in our own kitchen except for the wind and the coyotes. When we left it behind the next day, Millie kept looking back at it, but even if I'd tossed out the whipsaw, ax, pickax, spade, and quicksilver and give up all thought of striking it rich, I don't think I could of brung it along without spraining my back or breaking down the *Millicent Slaughter*.

We seen our first pine trees mixed in with the cotton-wood out on the river islands, and I knew we was getting

onto higher ground. Every step had been a fraction of a
fraction of an inch uphill, and the country was beginning
to change. And then late one afternoon on a deserted
stretch where nobody was catching up with us and there
wasn't nobody up ahead—just some traces of smoke from
campfires on the other side of the river, which was still
near a mile wide, even though it'd been halved back at the
fork—a party of eleven Injuns on horseback come over the
low valley rim and rode straight down at us, coming pretty
fast like they meant business, and I got my gun into my
belt and stood in front of Millie and Mr. Blue and commenced worrying as hard as I could without showing it.

"Are the savages hostile around here?" she says.

"I hope not," I says, keeping my voice calm, like she
had asked was the chokecherries ripe yet.

I don't know too much about Injuns, not having got
friendly with none back home who'd tell me what *they*
knew (such as how to live on the prairie without dirt farming, which dang few white men can do), but I thought I
could reckonize a war party when I seen one, and that's
what this was. When they come up close and reined in,
using their thin little woven horsehair or rawhide hacka-
mores that didn't look like they'd control a newborn calf,
let alone a wild-eyed skittery paint without no bit in his
mouth nor stirrups nor saddle, I seen they wasn't much
older than me and some younger. But they had painted for
war and carried bows and arrows and coup sticks and a
couple old rifles and looked fierce and joyful and full of
vinegar.

The leader—I didn't have no trouble picking him out—
was an uncomfortable sight and not just because he was
taller and stronger-looking and had a bad wound down the
side of his neck and was going bare-chested under his
blanket even in the chilly weather: what bothered me most
was the way he set still and stared while the others let
their ponies do shifty, tight-footed little dances and

laughed and chattered at each other. His pony didn't lift a hoof, and he looked like he'd growed up there on its back, and he was wearing his hair all swooped around on one side and down in a single braid, and behind the one ear showing he'd stuck a small blue bird with its beak pointing forward, dead, I guess, but maybe not. And to make it worse, he was staring at me like he'd just found the man who'd give him that half-healed wound.

"I don't believe we're going to be able to cover this matter with a twenty-five-cent piece, Mr. Bender," Millie says.

"Don't do nothing," I says. "Not yet."

A smaller and younger-looking Injun with two big feathers sticking up out of the back of his head jumped down off his pony and come toward us hunched forward and smiling. Some of the others was cackling at him and saying words, and he looked back a couple times at Blue Bird (which is how I thought of the other one right off) to see if he was doing something wrong and getting no sign one way or the other far as I could see. He had a bowie knife and a feather-tipped coup stick and a loose buckskin shirt with a narrow kind of bib down the front of it made out of skinny bird or critter legbones and streaks of white paint all aiming out from his nose and mouth, and hanging around his neck on a strip of rawhide like a necklace, he had a pair of gold-rimmed specs with one lens busted out.

He stopped within arm's reach of me and straightened up and begun acting puffed up and solemn and pursing his lips, which must of been what I looked like because all the others except Blue Bird laughed and howled to egg him on.

I didn't do nothing, since being mocked at is no worse than a little bad weather and a considerable improvement on going hungry.

Then this Specs started clowning around bowlegged, imitating me pushing the wheelborrow with arms pulled down stiff and straining, and while he was staggering off in a circle and getting some more cackles, I moved three or four steps forward to give me some elbow room away from Millie in case there was going to be fisticuffs or worse, which I prayed not, eleven opponents being no fit number for a sane man with a wife to protect.

He seemed a bit surprised when he seen I wasn't in the same place no more, and he come back acting crazy and teasy but a little annoyed too. Some of the others was giving him advice now, it seemed like, and he didn't want none of it. He dubbed me quick on the shoulder with his coup stick and sobered up a few seconds to see how I'd take it. I reckoned that to be a kind of insult, a way to score off of me, but I didn't mind. I didn't have no stick of my own, but I tipped my hat to him and give him a little bow and a smile just like he was a nice old lady who'd said Good Morning.

He frowned over that and got some more advice from the other nine and nothing but that same long stare from Blue Bird.

"How much money would you suggest I give them, Mr. Bender?" Millie says.

"None," I says. "Just wait."

I was scairt bad, mostly for Millie and Mr. Blue and the Future and Wedded Bliss, but some for me myself in my personal skin too. "Does anybody talk English?" I says.

But there was no sign from any of them, no change. I'd heard tell a lot about the way Injuns fight, and I felt pretty sure if they'd been feeling really smoky, they'd of done their killing and scalping at the first swoop. This was more like bullyragging back home where a lot of kids will pick on one or two that's different and torment them a while, then go off and think up something better to do. The only one that didn't fit was this Blue Bird, who looked man enough to face down eleven white men if the situation had been turned inside out. Seemed like I only had two choices: I could try to be as big a clown as Specs or I could try to be as steady and dignified as Blue Bird, and the trouble was I didn't think I could handle either one of them parts very good.

So then I had an inspiration, and I spread my arms out solemn and used the best voice Miss Wilkerson had learnt me how to get down in my chest, and I says:

"O sweet and strange it seems to me, that ere this day is done,
The voice that now is speaking, may be beyond the sun—
Forever and forever,—all in a blessed home—
And there to wait a little while, till you and Effie come—
To lie within the light of God, as I lie upon your breast—
And the wicked cease from trouble, and the weary are at rest."

That seemed to shake them up a little. Specs backed up and forgot to make faces, and the others talked it over a bit like they'd just heard the first part of a Peace Treaty.

"How can you possibly expect savages to appreciate Lord Tennyson?" Millie says.

But I wasn't trying to get them to appreciate nothing but our right to keep on walking (in case we had any right), and I says, "In about a minute, they may take everything we own, Millie, including our scalps, so I might's well try giving them something that don't cost nothing first."

They'd begun to stir at the sound of my normal voice, and I seen Specs maneuvering to get his audience back: he begun to stalk me, circling a bit like I was a strange dumb animal, gliding his moccasins along the ground and feeling out each inch of foothold, so I spread my arms again and says,

"I grieve for life's bright promise, just shown and then withdrawn;
But still the sun shines round me, the evening bird sings on,

And I again am soothed, and, beside the ancient gate,
In this soft evening sunlight, I calmly stand and wait."

Which wasn't any too appropriate or even true but was all
I could remember offhand from Miss Wilkerson's elocution
lessons, where even when I done my best I embarrassed
myself something awful.

Specs had pulled back a ways and was scowling like he
was scaired I might be making medicine, and I *was*, the only
kind I knew how, because I didn't want nothing of mine or
Millie's to wind up decorating their necks like whoever
had brung them gold-rimmed eyeglasses this far west and
was now having a hard time reading fine print—wherever
he was—or maybe even breathing.

Spreading his arms out like I'd done and puffing up his
chest, Specs tried mocking my voice, but he wasn't any too
good at it. And after just a few words, which I think was
neither Injun nor English but made up, Blue Bird stopped
him cold and silenced him with one little grunt. Then we
all just stood there for a spell, the other nine leaving off
their joshing and joking and me not remembering no more
poems, and Millie commenced singing.

From behind me come her thin, clear, high voice, and
she sang:

"Though our way is dark and dreary,
And we toil from day to day,
While the heart is sad and weary,
At our home there shines a ray.
Kindly words and smiling faces,
Gentle voices as of yore,
Loving kisses and embraces
Ever wait us at the door."

Which I hadn't heard before and sure didn't sound like no
home of mine, but the Injuns was listening hard and quiet,

and even Specs held still like he might learn something.
  She sang:

"Here we turn when all forsake us,
  Here we never look in vain
For the soothing tones that wake us
  Back to joy and peace again."

  Then she loudened it up a good bit and poured on the
chorus:

"Kindly words and smiling faces,
  Gentle voices as of yore,
Loving kisses and embraces
  Ever wait us at the door."

  Well, there wasn't a smiling face in the bunch, and I'd
sooner been kissed by Mr. Blue than one of them, but
when she quit, nobody was scowling neither, not even
Specs, who had backed off near the others.
  Then Blue Bird come to life and slipped off his horse
and held his rust-colored blanket close around him and
took his slow, sweet time coming straight at me. So I took
my hat off, partly out of respect and partly to hold it over
my waist so's I could get hold of the revolver handle, but
even then knowing I didn't have no use for one bullet.
He'd seen the gun already, and it must not of worried him,
and I was in a total fluster inside my head, wondering
what to do, but I didn't let none of it get to my face. There
still wasn't nothing on *his* face but that dead, deep stare
and a white circle painted on his forehead.
  I let my hat slip down to my side so's he could see the
gun again if he felt like it, but his eyes didn't turn that
way, just kept boring into mine. He'd been hit bad on the
neck, where the jagged cut was all crusty with blood and
something that looked like dry leaves crumbled up, and

now he let his blanket fall open, and I seen he didn't have a gun but a knife the size of mine and a stone ax with a stick handle wrapped in thongs and an old deerskin pouch the size of a goose egg tied around his neck. And hanging down from his waist was two long clumps of black hair with bloody patches at one end, and they hadn't grown on no trees.

He was near enough to touch now, and I was hoping he'd decide to bump foreheads like the buffalo Injun and we could call it a day, but instead, without no change of expression, he took his ax out of where it was stuck under the drawstring of his deerskin leggings and lifted it up high in the air aimed right at the top of my skull. He was an inch or two taller than me and had an arm on him as thick as most legs, and it looked like my hour had come.

In the smidgen of an instant I had thought up all the things I could do: knife him and offer to fight the rest one at a time, start bargaining off our goods, shoot him and pretend the gun was full of bullets, recite another poem even if I had to make it up as I went along, beg for mercy, and so on—the only thing that never occurred to me was to shoot Millie, which I had heard of being done by others to spare their spouses a Fate Worse Than Death, it being my opinion that nobody can decide what's worse than death for somebody else. Meanwhile, I done absolutely nothing but stand there, and when I thought it over later, I figured out I didn't *believe* Blue Bird was going to do nothing bad. There was just something too manly about him, and I think that's what he was looking for in me.

He put on a good show of raising that ax over my head and starting to bring it down hard right on top of my skull-bone, which would of taught me a lesson not to trust no dignified-looking Injuns, and raised the start of a shriek out of Millie, who, I believe, was about to tackle him. But he stopped it a few inches short, while still staring deep and fixed into my eyes and me staring back and not flinching (though I say so, as shouldn't) because I *knew* everything was going to be all right. How could I have a grand Future if it wasn't?

He stood holding that ax over me, then just barely touched the crown of my head with it, and let a little smile come at the edges of his broad, thin lips. He stuck the ax under his drawstring again (all the other Injuns was keeping dead still, and Millie had shut off her squeal before it hit full pitch) and nodded at me. Then he spoke in a deep, slow voice and touched hisself between the eyes and on the crown of his own head and touched along his scar. The other Injuns made a noise like an agreement, and he took the bird from behind his ear and kissed its beak, and I was scairt for a minute he was going to give it to me (what would I of done with something like that?), but he stuck it behind his own ear again like a storekeep with a pencil.

Well, I didn't know quite what to do to show my appreciation and sympathy and whatever else he wanted, so I just picked the nearest thing and took out my revolver and handed it over. It wasn't mine anyway, and I didn't like guns, and it saved me chucking it into the river like I'd planned.

Millie says, "Mr. Bender," like she was beginning to protest, but I shushed her, which I wouldn't ordinarily do, believing in free speech.

The Injun looked the gun all over, smiling broad now, and the other Injuns made them approving sounds again, and I seen Specs climb back on his horse like he knew this little game was over.

Blue Bird took the pouch from around his neck and put it around mine, backed off and says something ceremonial-sounding to me and waited, I guess expecting me to do likewise, so I says,

"God is great, God is good.
Let us thank Him for our food.

> *By His goodness we are fed.*
> *Give us, Lord, our daily bread."*

Which was the only other poem I could think of offhand besides "Mary Had a Little Lamb" and "Little Jack Horner" and like that. But he seemed to like it fine, and if it was good enough for him, it was good enough for me, and when he swooped back up onto his pony (they make mounting up without stirrups look easy, but try it sometime wearing a blanket) and galloped off, me and Millie stood there waving till they was gone out of sight, and we didn't have to explain to each other why we was going to camp right there on the spot and not move another step in what was left of daylight: our knees just wouldn't of behaved.

Chapter Thirteen ★★★★★★★★★★★★

☞ We laid in more supplies at the sutler's in Julesburg, which wasn't but nine or ten doby huts and more people arguing and looking for somebody to lynch and always forgetting to blame their own selfs when they reasoned it out at the top of their voice. We heard the same kind of complaints as back at Doby Town and along the way, but it was too late to turn back now, though some actually done it. It was the middle of April and still cold and seeming to get even colder as we went along, and Millie bought a green wool scarf and a wool cap for her and a pair of wool gloves for me with only one finger missing off of a family that was headed back to Missouri and needed money for food. Some people was having auctions right out of their wagons, but we didn't stay for none of them. There'd be three or four people trying to sell for every one buying, and it was too sorrowful to watch their face when something precious they couldn't eat—like an old watch or a patchwork quilt—got sold off for next to nothing.

There was even some talk of busting into the storehouse and making off with the flour and corn meal and bacon and gingersnaps and hardtack and sardines they couldn't buy, including the tanglefoot and popskull at twenty-five cents a saucerful they was longing to drown their sorrows in but couldn't. So me and Millie stored up what we could carry, quiet and quick before it got stole or burnt, and got as far away from that anger as we could.

"I want you to keep a close count on the money you spend out," I says. "Soon's I dig us up some gold, I'll pay you back." We was going along slow at first, breaking in boots that wasn't exactly new but had been broke by other feet back in Julesburg, still keeping close to the river. The country was turning slopier and hillier, darker and older-looking, and the ground was harder but not froze. There was more and more groves of pine and cottonwood in spite of some being chopped down and even some bushes which Mr. Blue chawed on whenever he got a chance, though they only had hard buds instead of leaves.

"I'm spending *our* money, Mr. Bender," she says. "Another part of the ceremony Reverend Applegate left out was 'With all my worldly goods I thee endow.'"

"I didn't expect nothing like that," I says.

"Well, you should have," she says. "What *did* you expect?"

I thought it over and didn't know and says, "What would I of done without you buying me food?"

"I'm glad you thought of that," she says, not smug or sharp but just plain.

"I'd of had to dig a right smart of wells and privies," I says. "You spose I'd of turned back?"

"I doubt it, Mr. Bender," she says.

"Maybe I'm just as big a fool as them poor, suffering, cussing, busted boys back there and was just dumb lucky to have you," I says. "Maybe you should of stayed home and let me come back skinnier and wiser."

"You don't need to be much skinnier or wiser than right now," she says.

Which sounded like such a grand compliment, I didn't know how to handle it but gulp and shrug. I says, "You come to my rescue like I was a damsel in distress, and I didn't even know it."

"You came to mine too," she says.

We walked on a bit, and I says, "Do you realize where we're at?"

"Yes, I think so."

"We've got about a hundred miles to go," I says. "How's come you wanted to marry me *this* much?" I don't know how I dared to ask a question like that, and I almost took it back for fear I wouldn't like the answer.

But she says, "I admired your modesty and pride, Mr. Bender."

I thought that over, then says, "Much obliged, but don't them two mean the opposite?"

"To some people, perhaps. But you combine the two very admirably."

"I'd never of known it," I says.

"Why, that's admirable too," she says.

"It is?" Maybe one of the best things about falling in love and getting fell in love with back is you hear about so many good qualities nobody else thinks you've got.

"And you are dauntless in the face of adversity," she says.

"I am?" I shoved my wheelborrow along a ways. "What does *adversity* mean?"

"A time of peril and despair," she says.

I thought I knew what *dauntless* meant, so I put the two together and says, "When was that?"

"Perhaps you're too brave to notice," she says.

"Or too dumb."

"You are *not* dumb!" she says.

"Pa says I was dumb."

"I believe he was too dumb to notice the truth," she says.

We strolled along another hundred yards under the gray, wrinkled sky, and I says, "Well, I don't talk good like you."

"You talk quite well enough, Mr. Bender," she says. "If you have some rough edges, I'm sure you'll either smooth them or sharpen them in time."

"A man my age shouldn't be taking so long to smooth out," I says. "He don't have as much time as a rock on the bottom of a crick."

She laughed then, and it was sure a beautiful sound, and she says, "There. You just proved my point."

"I did?" I says. "How?"

"By making a pretty speech," she says.

I couldn't remember saying nothing pretty, let alone a speech, but I pretended like I understood, which you have got to do *often* if you want to feel good and married.

We pushed on a ways further, and all of a sudden she commenced singing, which she liked to do and which I would of had a try at too if I'd been able to carry a tune in a wheelborrow.

She sang:

"Over the mountains
And over the waves,
Under the fountains
And under the graves,
Under floods that are deepest
Which Neptune obey,
Over rocks that are steepest,
Love will find out the way."

Which I hope to tell you is a true thought (as far as it goes) and made me hum along and shortened the miles like the strongest kind of Injun medicine.

The second day out, we come to a clump of letters and newspapers strewn out of a ripped mailbag by the side of the road, all rain-soaked and jumbled and the ink so smeary on the letters you couldn't tell what was wrote and the newspapers not prying apart without ripping.

We turned over a few. "You reckon somebody robbed the mail wagon?" I says.

"They did this twice in the stagecoach I was riding," Millie says. "They threw sacks overboard in the middle of the night, in the middle of nowhere, just to lighten the load and make a little room. They called it 'Delivering mail to the Injuns.'" She held up a pretty pale-blue envelope, the color of some of them unmentionables, and says, "How do we know whose heart is breaking up in the gold fields because this love letter didn't arrive?"

She likes to think up things like that, and then look moony and teary at me with her head a little sideways, showing her tender feelings. I have tried to practice up being tender, but it's hard to learn, so I says, "Maybe it was just plain old bad news, telling how everybody had fell sick at home, and you better dig up a gold mine in a hurry."

I was just fooling, which you're not sposed to do with tender feelings, but she took me serious and says, "Well, we'll never know," and she stirred through and found a couple more envelopes that looked like they'd come from women but all soaked and crumpled and glanced around at the rest of the mail laying all hither and skelter. "We're going to a land where the mails don't reach, and that means the Law probably doesn't reach it much either, and we'll be on our own, and our lives may hinge upon desperate chances."

"They might at that," I says.

"Would you say our path was fraught with danger?" She stared this way and that.

"Well, I spose that's the general idea," I says. Then because she was round-eyed and enjoying it, I helped her along some more and says, "We may come up against fearful odds."

"Exactly," she says, looking pleased. "I wish you hadn't given away your revolver."

All I'd got in Blue Bird's pouch was some little gray rocks which Millie liked to look at and sort of play with like jacks, so I let her carry it in her reticule to save me having to take it off my neck all the time. "Far as I know, that gun never hit nothing it was aimed at," I says. "And I think I'll take my fearful odds with as few bullets as possible flying around."

While we was standing there amongst the mail and wondering if maybe I shouldn't make a fire out of it, wet or not, along upriver I seen a raft coming with three men on it, the first one in a long while, the Platte not encouraging that sort of foolery with its fast, shallow current and sand bars.

They was about fifty yards out, and we watched them dodging along, going bumpety and wavery whenever they scraped bottom, and we both waved, but they didn't wave back. They had a heap of goods covered with a blanket in the middle of the raft, which was skinny, tied-together logs, and they was getting their feet wet in some mighty cold water and not looking too happy and maybe wishing they'd built theirselves a wheelborrow or handcart instead.

One cupped his hands at us and hollers, "Turn back, you dash dash dash! You'll freeze your dashing dashes off if you dumb dashes don't starve first!"

I wasn't sure Millie had heard all them dashes before. They happened to be unusual ones, even in a country that was pretty free with dashes in about every sentence. But I just waved some more and so did she.

We watched them go rickety-drifting past us and downstream and nose one corner into a sand bar, and while they tried to pole off it, the raft spun around sideways and dunked under, slow and calm as you please, and the water come up to their thighs for a few seconds and twisted the raft right out from under them. It happened so casual and clean, it seemed like they done it a-purpose, and when the raft come bobbing up clear again, they was standing up to their waist in the river, bidding goodbye with many a dash to them logs that would make a week of campfires for somebody somewhere along the line.

I hiked up my wheelborrow handles and started off toward Slab Crick, but Millie hung back and says, "Shouldn't we go to their rescue?"

But they was already wading for shore, using their poles to test the bottom, and I says, "They're only a day from Julesburg, and they can dry off walking, and I don't like their tone of voice, and I don't need no more discouragement than I can think up myself, and we don't have no way to shelter them."

She come along then and says, "Yes, Mr. Bender."

Which made me feel like I'd just been elected Governor of this country called Me and Her and Mr. Blue (pop. 3 and Bound to Rise).

Chapter Fourteen ★★★★★★★★★★★★

☞ I couldn't tell how many was following after us to the gold fields (I knew there was some, of course) because I couldn't see backwards or ahead far enough to take a count. But there was sure a heap coming back the other way, and we didn't miss none of them unless they took to traveling at night, which some done if they was mad or hungry or cold enough. And everybody we run in to seemed mad or hungry or cold or all three, specially when they seen us smiling and walking along cheerful.

During one of the gaps when there wasn't nobody coming for a half mile, Millie says, "Mr. Bender, I believe we give offense to people. Maybe we should try not to smile all the time."

I tried to keep solemn for the next wagon that come along. The driver, a blue-nosed, stubble-faced, hollow-eyed man trying to get a yoke of skinny oxen moving faster, just stared at us and shook his head (like many another done) and give his scrawny, long-jawed wife a look as much as to say

Ain't you glad we're smarter than them? And what with both of us looking so gloomy a-purpose, I believed they'd have passed us without a discouraging word.

But I had stretched my face too straight and couldn't keep it that way and busted out laughing and give the whole show away. Millie only lasted a few more seconds, then got mad, then had to laugh too.

The man and his wife both peered around at us, and the wife says real loud, "You better laugh now, you won't find nothing up ahead to laugh at."

And her husband says, "Leave them alone, Ma. Ignorance is bliss."

They went creaking off, slow and wobbly, and if them oxen ever made it to Julesburg, I'd be surprised. But what he'd said bothered me, and after we'd gone along a ways, I says, "Do you think we're ignorant like he says?"

"There are all kinds of ignorance in this world, Mr. Bender," she says. "But bliss is not one of them."

I figured she meant Wedded Bliss, and I had to agree. But it seemed like the man was talking about some other kind of bliss. We went along another few miles, ducking out of the cold breeze and trying to keep it from sneaking into our clothes, and we passed some more loudmouths full of gloom and damn-you's and you'll-be-sorry's. One rough-looking stocky man riding muleback (after I'd declined his offer to trade me stock in a mining company for a side of bacon) says, "I don't need to tell you to go to Hell, boy. You're already here and don't know it."

We shoved on through the afternoon and had to ford a small crick, which got my feet soaked good and proper, so we decided to camp there and dry out, and I says, "Maybe they're right. Maybe I'm leading us straight to our Doom."

"I never expected to hear you talk downhearted," she says, wringing out my socks and stringing them up near our fire made out of a genuine mahogany armchair we had found busted near the crick.

"I'm not downhearted," I says. "And I'm not afraid of my Doom, whatever it is. I don't spose a little Doom ever hurt nobody."

"I have always believed I was destined to be happy, Mr. Bender," she says. "And I thought you were of the same opinion."

"I am," I says. "Bound and determined."

"Well, if you're bound to be happy, might as well be happy along the way to it, and keep your feet tucked under that blanket," she says.

While I watched my socks commencing to steam, I says, "Mind if I ask you a personal question?"

"That's a husband's privilege, Mr. Bender."

"Why don't you ever call me Ike?" I says. "Don't you like that name?"

She hesitated, not looking at me, then says, "I don't want to hurt your feelings."

"I don't have no feelings to speak of," I says.

"That's not true!" she says, getting all het up. "You have a very highly developed sensibility and a great delicacy in all manly emotions, and you're not just blindly intrepid but thoughtful, and you mustn't ever downgrade yourself to me or I'll be forced to argue with you."

Well, that was too much to keep track of, and I felt confused and gushy about it. "You sure you're talking about *me?*"

"Yes, I'm sure, Mr. Bender," she says. "And I'll call you Ike if you really want me to, but the other seems more dignified."

"You can try me on Isaac, but it didn't take back home," I says. "Now what kind of dignified Doom do you reckon we're in for out here?"

"Beans and bacon," she says. "And let's hurry up and eat it before some wretched soul begs it right out of our mouths. I have a strong strain of mercy in me, Mr. Bender, and you mustn't let me give any more of our food away."

She had already doled out enough to worry me in the last three or four days, but I hadn't said nothing, it being hers to give or keep.

"We have to keep body and soul together," she says.

I turned my socks over to get them done on the other side and says, "Yes, I don't spose they'd be much use separate."

But the next two days we seen many a body that the souls looked to be trying to get loose of. By then, we had stepped onto the edge of the map my brother Kit had sent me and Pa had took, and was heading more south than west along the thinned-down river, and the Rocky Mountains sprung up out of nowhere soon as the morning mist cleared off, ten or fifteen miles away, and Pikes Peak was way down south of us someplace, maybe in sight, maybe not. I didn't ask nobody to point it out because I didn't want to hear more cussing than come natural, which was a good deal.

I begun feeling sorry I'd give my gun to Blue Bird, since the mere look of it sticking out of my belt would of saved us a lot of wasted time telling people we couldn't hand them over no food. We could of stripped ourselves of supplies twenty times over along that last stretch and come to the gold fields empty-packed, empty-bellied, and empty-headed like most of the people that was trying to get out of there. But we agreed to hold firm, including Mr. Blue's oats, which he was able to space out by chomping on cottonwood saplings and some dead weeds and left-overs from us (he fancied beans). Yet there was so many folks on the road now, either moving out or camped and trying to decide to, I didn't need no gun to keep us safe: there was always somebody watching and no privacy to get robbed in.

The river had narrowed down to about 150 foot by the time we come to D'Aubrey's Post a few miles short of

Cherry Crick (where Auraria and Denver City had been laid out), and we ferried across to the mouth of Slab Crick (it cost a whole dollar and a half, which come out of my pocketbook) without even seeing them big sinful settlements because I was following the map in my head now and getting excited and didn't want to spend time taking in the sights. And when we got off on the west side of the South Platte and commenced heading upstream (Slab Crick wasn't but six foot wide and shallow) past the staked-claim notices and a few strung-out tepees and a couple of log huts with sod roofs, I got such a spring in my step, I felt like I could of run the rest of the way.

"Can you feel that gold underfoot?" I says. It had been snowing lately, and the slush was sort of mean, but we were on a broad, rolly, mostly bare kind of country, none of it steep till you got to the foothills of the mountains where Slab Crick was coming from and us going.

"I don't believe so," Millie says. "I'm afraid my feet are numb."

"It's only a few hours more," I says, feeling kind of crazy, having tromped, scuffed, slogged, slewed, clumb, and stumbled more'n five hundred miles, not counting zig-zags and now wondering whether I could make it a few more without turning greensick with joy. I was snuffing the air like a horse with his head in the apple barrel, and if my wheelborrow had all of a sudden sprouted wings, I wouldn't of been surprised but would of sprouted my own to match.

"Why do you want gold so badly?" she says, striding along behind.

"I don't know, but it sure seems like a pleasure thinking about it," I says. And it did. And when we come to the first miner down on his hunkers panning gold, I felt like stopping and admiring that grand sight and even digging out my pie pan and joining in the fun, except I didn't know if it'd be polite to squat down and wash somebody else's paydirt for him. Judging by the way he scowled when we howdied him, I kept going up the crick.

"There don't seem to be many people washing gold along here," Millie says.

"All the more for us," I says.

"Are you sure this is the right stream?" she says.

"Kit drew it all clear and plain." After a couple miles a little side crick joined in from the other bank, just like it done on the map. After that, Slab Crick was only about half as big, though the gravelly bottom stayed about the same, which meant it had more water *some*times.

"I have a stitch in my side, Mr. Bender," Millie says.

And I slowed down a little then and tried to enjoy the last of our journey like a good meal, instead of bolting it all down at once, but even when my legs behaved their-selves, my mind's eye kept racing around inside my head, and I didn't need no mirages or natural wonders to spark up my admiration for the Future: about every ten steps I seen a place where I reckoned I'd ought to dig a hole, and I seen myself doing it and seen it panning out and me and Millie yipping and dancing around it and tossing gold up in the air by the handful and letting it rain down (which it done nice and slow, even the coins and nuggets I dreamt up), and for sheer blind happiness that short trip up Slab Crick would be hard to beat (bar Wedded Bliss) because I shed nary a drop of sweat in all that dream digging nor had no disappointments nor felt a half ounce of doubt nor put myself to the trouble of doing no chores but pickaxing and shoveling straight to pure gold.

"Why are so few people prospecting?" she says.

"I reckon they don't know what Kit knows," I says. "And maybe it hasn't thawed enough water yet." But I didn't let anything peck away at my bumper crop of good cheer.

She glanced around like she might not be having quite the same daydreams as me, but says, "It looks like rich country, and I love being here with you, Mr. Bender."

Which was too good to pass up, so I set down my handles a minute and give her a long kiss without begging Mr. Blue's pardon or asking leave of another old-timer sloshing water around in his pie pan fifty yards upstream of us. But kissing Millie always brung up other daydreams of a different order, and when we commenced traveling again, I had got the gold digging all mixed up with sleeping next to her under the wheelborrow, and my mind dreamt up some mighty unlikely events in the combined history of Love and Mining, which I wouldn't care to tell.

But she had called me back to the world with one sentence: it *was* rich country, and I loved being there with her too, and them were the two most important matters, and all the rest would have to line up behind and wait their turn.

We followed Slab Crick all the way to the foothills, which rose up sudden out of flat country and shut out the sight of the mountains beyond, and the last miles was the hardest we done in the whole trip: up slope and down ravine and through cottonwood, serviceberry, and chokecherry thickets, and it was all I could do to haul my wheelborrow through some of them squeaky places where the crick come down steep. But it leveled out again once in a while, giving us a chance to breathe a few times, and then after a long uphill stretch and up over a hump, we come to the hut, the only one we'd seen in the last three miles.

So we got a plain look at the headquarters and main office of the Collywobble Mining Company, which had dead grass on its flat roof and smoke coming out of a little chimbley on one side and a couple windows made out of scraped deerskin and a low stoop-down door. And there it was, all laid out in front of us: the hard, crusty ground shelving down to the crickbed and clear water running down the middle of it and a forty-foot, sharp-edge clift along the opposite side and the hut set back fifty foot on our side and a little stand of mixed pine and aspen. And our claim was right there, looking like the Promised Land, shimmering even in the gray late-afternoon light and so full of gold it probably didn't matter none where you scratched gravel for it. I felt like untying the pickax and shovel and starting right to work. Somebody had built fires here and there along the bank, and I seen where some dirt and gravel had been scrabbled off under the scattered charcoal, so I reckoned the ground was still froze and that's why they was all still in the hut and not out washing for dust.

I trundled us right up to the front door and knocked and stood there holding Millie with one arm, feeling shaky and proud and tuckered out and ready to bust with excitement. It seemed like I could smell the gold all around us and hear it singing.

The door opened a crack, and an old man stuck his nose out, frowning, and says, "Who's that?" and the same time a younger man wearing a sleeveless jacket made out of what looked to be black-bear fur come around the outside edge of the hut aiming a rifle at us.

But that didn't slow me down none. "Well, we made it," I says.

"Made what?" the old man says.

"You kids get the hell off of this claim," the man in the bearskin says.

"I'm Ike Bender and this here's my wife Millie," I says. "Where's Kit?"

"Jesus God, another," the man in the bearskin says.

"What do you want?" the old man says, blinking out at us with his head tilted and his long thin gray hair hanging down almost to the end of his beard.

"Aim that someplace else," I says to the man in the bear-skin. "There's a lady present."

He let his rifle sag and says real loud, "Badger! Come here!"

"Kit told me to come and join up with the company, and I done so," I says. "I kept my part of the bargain."

"Well, you're some bargain all right," the man in the bearskin says. "What's that thing?" and he prodded the *Millicent Slaughter* in the side with his rifle barrel.

"That's my wheelborrow, in case you never seen one," I says. "Where's Kit?"

"You pushed that thing all the way across the Territory?" the man in the bearskin says like it was the best joke he'd heard since the tent show.

"Well, sometimes I hauled it instead of pushing," I says.

"Kit's upcountry prospecting like a goddamn fool, excuse me, ma'am," the old man says. "Ain't used to talking around a woman."

"That's perfectly all right," Millie says. "I have heard enough foul language in the past weeks to burn my ears forever if I'd let it, but I prefer to let it pass me by."

A fat man in a red fur hat with a red pointy nose and dewlaps come around the edge of the hut, wearing a patched homespun shirt and a whole deerskin over him like a long shawl.

The old man stepped halfway out of the door and says, "That's Badger and John Staggs there, and I'm Zack Orfrey."

"Pleased to meet you," I says, giving my hat a little heist.

"Kit didn't say you was coming," the old man says. "He just told us he was thinking of asking his kid brother to come on out." He acted sheepish and kind of apologetic.

Staggs scratched hisself through the bearskin and says, "And I told him No Siree loud and often."

The one called Badger come forward and give our packs and Mr. Blue a squinty look and says, "Looks like that burro's old lady might of got herself tallywhacked by a gopher."

Staggs got a big guffaw out of that, but the two of them looked like they'd been crossed with three or four kind of critters: pretty near everything they had on from head to toe had been skinned off something else's back. Yet I didn't want to start gnashing back at them and spoiling the company, which it begun to look like I didn't belong to.

Zack, the old man, says, "Well, you better come in and set a spell while we get this figured out."

"Wait a minute," Staggs says. "I don't recollect inviting nobody to come into this house I helped build with my own two hands."

"Me neither," Badger says.

In a quiet, reasonable voice Zack says, "Now just think it over, boys. What if *your* brother was to hump it all the way across the Territory looking for *you?* Wouldn't you give him a—"

"I'd shoot his ass off," Staggs says.

"I don't have no brother," Badger says.

"Wouldn't you give him a place to set down and a bite to eat, seeing he'd brung along a sweet little wife young enough to be your daughter?" Zack says.

"Hell, no," Staggs says, but smiling a little now.

"That's better," Zack says, shoving the door all the way open and getting out of the way so's we could file by, Millie first. "Come in and welcome."

It didn't smell any too rosy in there, that being the way men get when there's no women around to wash up and rench out and scold, but they had added something extra by using one whole wall for meat hangers. I didn't reckonize much of it because it was upside down and skinned, but I seen Millie drinking it all in by the dim light and wished we was outside again.

"We been wintering in here, so you'll have to make allowances," Zack says, getting both his suspenders up and his long-tailed blues tucked in. "Would you like a stool, Miz Bender?"

There wasn't but a rough table, a bench, two stools, a tubful of water, an iron pot and skillet by the fireplace, and three heaps of pine boughs with blankets over them on the dirt floor along one wall. I could of touched the ceiling made out of skinny logs laid crossways.

She set down with her back to the meat and says, "Thank you, sir."

Staggs had come in and was leaning by the door with one leg hooked around his rifle butt, but Badger was still outside.

"Well, now, the Collywobble Mining Company ain't exactly closed up and finished off," Zack says, "but if that fool brother of yours shows up next week or whenever the thaw gets going good, and we get organized proper with our long tom, there won't be much room for another pardner."

"No room at all," Staggs says.

"See, we got it all staked here," Zack says. "I got my working claim and an extra for discovery, and Staggs has got one and Badger one and Kit one—the furthest upstream—that's five hundred foot of crick. Now if you want to stake yourself one up past Kit's, you're welcome, but I'll tell you it don't look any too good to me, and I seen myself staring back out of many a pan in my day, boy."

"Well, Kit says if I was willing to work hard and pitch in, you'd take me on," I says.

"He didn't have no right to say that," Staggs says.

"See, we don't know how good it's going to be," Zack says. "Might be nothing much here, might be pockets full of glory down on that bedrock. But it wouldn't do to give away a big chunk of it, not knowing, just to be nice to a young man like you."

Staggs give out a chuckle. "You ought to be selling stock down in Denver City, Zack."

I had two things going on in my head at the same time,

and they didn't mix too good: I was trying to shape our Future (including that very night) to fit what I understood about this talk, and I was trying to keep from being too uneasy about my wheelborrow out there with that Badger maybe nosing around it.

"How much would a share in this company cost?" Millie says.

Zack shook his head. "Well, you just can't figure a thing like that without—"

"How much you got?" Staggs says, standing up straight.

"Now wait a minute," I says. "Maybe Kit'll go shares with me on *his* claim. Or maybe there's another crick around here someplace." I was strolling to the door, which I seen was open a crack.

"That's up to him," Zack says. "But your brother's got a bad case of the gold colic, boy, and I wouldn't count on him giving nothing away till I had it wrote down and filed at the land office."

Staggs was sort of blocking my way without quite showing he was doing it, and he give me a big fish-eating grin and says, "If you wait around a month, Bender, maybe we could use a hired hand or two. You and the burro a dollar a day each to haul tailings and your wife there fifty cents to cook."

"How can you stand to live in an abattoir?" Millie says.

"A what?" Zack says.

"Excuse me a second," I says to Staggs, trying to get past him, but he give me a little budge with his elbow like he was joshing me.

"That's good wages for a boy," he says. "And that burro won't spend nothing on whiskey."

"I am referring to the carcasses and corpses and entrails and skins hanging on your wall," Millie says.

"Well, Miz Bender, we're out here in country where the corn don't grow," Zack says. "I tried eating rocks but it didn't work."

"I want to go outside a minute," I says to Staggs.

"Calls of nature out back," he says.

"Couldn't you at least hang the corpses outdoors somewhere?" Millie says.

"The bears and Injuns would love that," Zack says. "But it wouldn't do us much good at suppertime."

I finally had to shove Staggs out of the way, being as polite as I could without giving ground, and I ducked out the door, knocking my hat sideways, and I seen part of my kit untied from the wheelborrow, and when I run to the side of the house, there was Badger fifty foot up the slope carrying my whipsaw over his big fat shoulder and the crockful of quicksilver in his other hand.

Chapter Fifteen ★ ★ ★ ★ ★ ★ ★ ★ ★ ★ ★ ★ ★ ★

☞ I grabbed the ax off of my wheelborrow, not wanting to go empty-handed, and lit off after him, and I says, "Mr. Badger?"—not yelling so's to keep everybody else from getting worked up, it being my belief that the fewer folks involved in a fight, the shorter it's likely to be.

He stopped, looking surprised and shifty-eyed and mad, holding the little crock behind his deerskin leggings in case I hadn't seen it, and then he put on as good a face as he could, since he didn't have but two choices—run or talk —and running's hard work.

"I believe you've got something of mine there," I says, stopped two steps off. There was a little pine grove a few yards up ahead, and I was glad we hadn't gotten in amongst them and lost our elbow room.

He grinned on one side of his face and says, "Just going to saw me a couple planks, boy, long as you wasn't using it."

I seen a stack of rough-cut, six-foot-long sluice boxes— the kind I'd seen tore out of *The Miner's Own Book* and nailed up at the general store back home—and a couple of sawhorses, but Badger hadn't been heading for them but off slantways into the woods, and I says, "You didn't ask my leave."

"People don't have time to go through all that neighborly talk way out here," he says. "And no sheriff to learn them how." He looked at my ax. "You fixing to chop some wood?"

I felt ashamed about that ax. He was a whole lot fatter than me but no taller, and after all that walking and hauling, I was as strong as I was ever going to be, with hardly nowhere on me you could pinch if you was a mind to. But the whipsaw was a mean-looking chunk of steel with teeth as big as a bobcat's and five foot long from handle to handle, and I didn't fancy being mistook for no pine tree. So I just hefted the ax to show him I knew which end was which and says, "Yes, sir, I was. And I reckon I'll need that whipsaw to go with it. And my quicksilver too, if you don't mind."

He looked down at that heavy little crock as if he'd forgot all about it. "I just borried a taste of this jam to sweeten up the sawing. Ain't had a taste of jam in eight months."

"Badger!" I heard old Zack's voice yelling from back by the hut, but I didn't let my eyes stray off.

"Here, you can have it back," Badger says, holding the crock out a short ways. "If you want to be a stingy little button-pocket puckermouth all your life."

I could see I was going to have to get too close to him, and though that meant he couldn't swing the saw good, I didn't fancy rassling with nobody that fat. I says, "I'd be much obliged if you'd just bring both them things back to my wheelborrow and put them the way they was."

"Well, who was your slave last year, boy?" he says, flexing the saw by one handle and making it sing.

"Goddamn it, leave me alone," Zack yells back behind me, but I didn't turn to look.

"You're mean just like your brother," Badger says, grinning. "I reckon I'll make you fight me for this trash here, just to teach you how we do things on Slab Crick."

"Mr. Bender?" Millie says, loud and high.

"Which leg do you reckon you can best do without?" I says, hefting the ax and trying to act like I meant it.

He tossed the crock off to one side, and I heard it thud and roll but kept my eyes off it, hoping it hadn't broke. Badger took a half a step backwards and had both hands on one of the saw handles. "Which of them heads of yours would you like to have lopped off?"

From near behind, Staggs's voice says, "You raise that ax on my pardner, boy, and I'll shoot you right in the spine."

Half out of breath, Millie says, "Is there anything I can do, Mr. Bender?"

"Yes, stay clear," I says.

"Now what in the hell is going on?" Zack says. "What you doing with that boy's saw?"

"Zack, you dumb bastard, why don't you go take a walk and practice up lying?" Staggs says. "No sense to quarreling among ourselves."

"Mr. Badger walked off with my whipsaw and my quicksilver, and I want them back right now," I says.

"Go on, give him his saw, you damn tub of lard," Zack says.

"Quicksilver?" Staggs says. "Where at?"

Out of the corner of my eye, I seen Millie scampering and stooping and picking up the crock, and I kept my ax ready for all the bad things that could happen any second now, hoping I wouldn't have to chop nobody.

"You can't just rob a man out in plain sight and expect him to lay down like a lump," Zack says. "Not unless you're aiming to kill him."

"Might just do that," Staggs says behind me. Then he shifted off further to one side and says, "Little girl, let me look at that crock a minute."

"This happens to be our property, Mr. Staggs," Millie says. "And it's not open for inspection."

"Now you just do what I say," Staggs says.

"Well, I've had me some meatheaded pardners in my day," Zack says. "But if this don't take the rag off the bush, excuse me, *ma'am*."

Sweat was coming down Badger's jowls now (I don't know what was coming down mine, being too busy trying to make up my mind which way to jump, swing, or at least look), and he says, "Staggs?" with his eyes flicking over my shoulder at what was going on.

"Just a second," Staggs says. "Now, little girl, I'm not asking a whole lot. Just a peek inside there."

"Under the circumstances, that is an unreasonable request," Millie says. "And I don't mean to oblige you."

"Staggs?" Badger says, starting to look mighty worried about my ax.

"Give him his goddamn saw before we have to use it to get your leg the rest of the way off," Zack says. "Of all the pecker-necked phildoodlers I ever had the displeasure of—"

"All right, all right, I only borried it a minute anyway," Badger says, holding out one handle at me.

I took it in one hand, and for a second he held on to the other handle, and I thought we was going to play tug-of-war but he let go with a shove and turned and walked off past me toward the hut.

Which give me time and room to see about Staggs, who was holding one palm out to Millie and wheedling at her while she backed up, keeping the crock behind her. I set the whipsaw down so's I'd have both hands free for the ax and says, "Leave my wife alone."

Staggs come to a halt and turned on me, smiling and aiming his rifle down around my feet, but before he could say anything, Zack says, "Let's have some sense here now."

Staggs says, "All I asked for was a—"

"I know, I know," Zack says, looking at me and shaking his head like an apology. "We been winterbound, and it makes a man tetchy. You get to quarreling over nothing, and first thing you know, somebody's got theirself shot or cut. Seen it happen many a time."

"Listen," Staggs says. "How much quicksilver you got?"

He sounded halfway reasonable, so I says, "Five pounds."

Zack give a little whistle and smacked his lips like a kiss, and Staggs says, "If your brother has went and froze his ass off up in the mountains someplace—which ain't any too unlikely, believe me—why, it'll be all right with us if you inherit his claim, long as you throw in the quicksilver and the burro. We all work the long tom and share and share alike. What say?"

I picked up the whipsaw, got it over my left shoulder, and nodded Millie ahead of me down the slope toward Mr. Blue. "We'll think it over," I says.

"Nothing to think over," Staggs says.

"Kit wasn't fool enough to get froze," Zack says, but didn't sound too sure about it.

They come along behind me, and I says, "How long's he been overdue?"

"A week," Zack says.

"And in another week or so, the crick'll be up and the dirt loose enough with a little coaxing and we'll be ready to roll, and if he ain't here to help, why, we'll give his share to you," Staggs says. "Won't we, Zack?"

"I don't know what'd be legal," Zack says. "We'd have to go down to town and—"

"If we can't make up our own mind about our own god-damn company, what the hell's the use having one?" Staggs says.

I begun tying the saw on to my wheelborrow, while Millie tucked the crock under the oilskin and tied it down again. "We'd best wait till Kit comes back," I says. "I wouldn't want to take nothing off him without his say-so."

"He won't be saying much with a mouthful of snow," Staggs says.

"What makes you so sure he's froze?" I says.

"Just talk," Zack says. "You set around talking all day, and pretty soon you forget the difference between what you dreamt up and what you know."

"If Kit was all right, he'd be here," Staggs says.

Zack put his thumbs under his suspenders and stomped his feet a little to warm them up. "Unless he found something better."

I got behind my wheelborrow handles, but Staggs got around in front of the wheel and says, "Now don't go off half-cocked, boy."

"You can bed down in the hut tonight," Zack says. "Not too comfortable, but—"

"No, thank you," Millie says, beating me to it.

"It gets *cold* up here," Zack says. "Not like down on the flat. What's the sense in—"

"I'd be much obliged if you'd show me where Kit's claim leaves off," I says. "Is it staked?"

"Boy oh boy, these Benders all got shit for brains," Staggs says.

"Watch your foul mouth," Zack says.

"Oh, kiss my ass," Staggs says, turning to go to the hut.

"Mark off a square, you're *all* ass," Zack says. "Excuse me, ma'am."

"After we have established the Hearthstone Mining Company on a sound legal footing," Millie says, "we may consider the possibilities of a merger."

From over by the hut door Staggs let out a cackle. "Well, she don't talk like a Bender, but she sure thinks like one."

"Be sensible now," Zack says. "You hadn't ought to fool with the weather up here."

"We don't mean to fool with nothing or nobody," I says. "Where's those boundaries?"

The hut door slammed shut, and Zack walked us down toward the crick and along it and says, "If you're going to be stubborn about this, you got about an hour and a half to sundown, maybe less, and you'd do yourselfs a service to at least knock up a lean-to. Know how?"

"Well, I seen a few along the way," I says.

"I can show you," Zack says. "If it ain't against your principles."

We went up the crick along fairly level ground, while Zack pointed out the claim stakes every hundred foot, and when we come to the far side of Kit's claim, the little gully had narrowed down and steepened. Up ahead I seen where the bank turned near as steep as the low clift on the other side.

"Is there some way I can lay claim to this?" I says. "If I was to wade another hundred foot upstream, I'd have to drive a stake in sideways. Does sideways count?"

Zack says, "If you can't get up there to drive it, nobody's going up to see if it's been drove."

But the first ten foot next to Kit's was pretty level, and up from shore a ways Zack picked out two pine trees standing side by side about eight foot apart, and says, "Cut yourself a pole and lash it between them two, high enough so's you can sit up underneath. Or stand, if you're feeling like that much work. Then lash some more poles back from the first pole to the ground and lay your pine boughs across, commencing down low and building up so's most of the rain or snow or whatever else is going to fall out of this damned sky will mostly drip off. If we get anything heavy, you'll have to run a ditch along each side toward the crick. Now, you want to have the open end facing this way because the winds here either go upstream or down, and you don't want no smoke in your face nor snow in your lap, and you don't want no drifts building up in back of you and crunching you down in the middle of your sweet dreams, so get to work."

"When does it leave off snowing around here?" I says, getting out my ax and some nails and heading up for the pine grove.

"Son, this is still April, and it's liable to do most anything you can think of," Zack says. "Even in May. And if you got any more surprises in that kit of yours besides quicksilver and real nails, you'd best not let Staggs and Badger find out. They don't just hunt birds and beasts, them two, and as a matter of cold fact, we're pretty scarce for white women in these parts too, and I wouldn't leave this young lady alone much if I was you."

"I'm perfectly capable of taking care of myself," Millie says. "I don't permit forwardness or familiarities from strangers."

Zack shook his head. "Most men in the gold fields don't ask for no permission in matters like that. They just barge on ahead."

"I have already become acquainted with most forms of human wickedness, Mr. Orfrey," she says. "It would take a great deal to surprise me."

"I wasn't worried about you being surprised," he says. "But hurt."

"I'm grateful for your concern," she says, "and I suppose forewarned is forearmed."

Zack helped me trim some saplings, and when I commenced nailing one up about seven foot high between the pine trees, using the butt of the ax for a hammer, he says, "My God, you building a lean-to or a house?"

"When you've lived under a wheelborrow for six weeks, you want a little head room," I says.

He helped me knock together a sturdy framework to slant back from the crosspole, while Millie used my knife to cut some boughs, and he says, "I still wish you'd bunk down with us back at the hut. Sometimes it's safer being close to trouble than a little ways off by yourself."

"No, thanks," I says.

"Do you have a gun?"

"I had one but I give it away," I says. "I don't like to shoot nothing."

"I wish you a world of comfort with that notion," he says. "But it don't seem very likely. You aim to hunt with your bare hands?"

"I don't aim to hunt at all," I says.

"We'll go down to town once a week for provisions," Millie says.

He shrugged over that but didn't say nothing, and pretty soon we was all three cutting boughs for the slant roof, and he showed how to turn them upside down and a foot thick for a bed inside. "It'll seem grand and soft the first night," he says. "And tolerable the second, and hard and lumpy the third, and then you have to make yourself a new one."

"What do you think we should do about Mr. Blue?" I says, when we stood back to admire our brand-new house, which looked more like something that had fell down by accident than done a-purpose.

"Turn him loose and hope he don't get shot for a deer," Zack says. "He knows more about getting along up here than you do. Why, if you knew what he knows, you'd have damn little to worry about."

"And I wouldn't be up here gold digging neither," I says.

"You're dead right, son. A burro's got too many brains for that."

I had got him off a ways while Millie fussed with the bed, and keeping my voice low, I says, "Mr. Orfrey, you know the Platte River, don't you?"

"Know it a whole lot better than I want to," he says.

"You know how it's all full of that yellow grit?"

He spit and says, "I ground up enough of it hunting for the water in between."

I felt embarrassed bringing it up, but I says, "I don't spose there's no gold in that, is there?"

He give me a long blank look.

"I didn't think so," I says.

He chuckled then and says, "You'll think you see it lots of places where it ain't. And then maybe someday, by God, there it is for sure."

Millie come over to us then, and I says to Zack, "I reckon you know a lot about gold digging."

"Son, I know so much about it, I don't even *know* what I know."

"Then how's come you're not rich?"

He smiled through his gray beard, showing a row of gray teeth. "I *been* rich. Twice. But I didn't like it much neither time, so I spent it all." He held the flat of one old knobbly-knuckled and scarred hand up. "Don't ask me why I'm trying for three. It's the *looking* I like. I even like the finding. But what happens after you find it is too much for my guts. All gold is fool's gold if a fool's got ahold of it, and I'm a fool."

"I reckon I am too," I says.

"You most certainly are not," Millie says. "I won't have you talk that way."

"Well, maybe you'll get a chance to find out for sure," Zack says, scuffing the toe of his boot on the hard ground. "You might wash a little out of this. Enough to get sick on, maybe."

"Thanks for all your help," I says, when I seen he was starting to back off and head for home. He'd come out in his shirtsleeves and was looking shivery in the pale light that was fading out quick now.

"There's some of us still do a little of that," he says. "A

stranger used to be near as good as a pardner till proved otherwise."

We watched him hunch off, one leg swinging kind of bowlegged like it had been busted once or twice, and I got to work with the ax and whipsaw and laid in a little firewood while I could still see what I was aiming at. Millie unpacked Mr. Blue and give him some oats and turned him loose, and he come up and watched me sawing through a six-inch dead tree trunk like he was studying whether to get hold of the other handle or not. But he finally set off at an angle uphill through the trees, nosing at the thin brush here and there and taking a nibble, and disappeared.

I built the fire where Zack had showed me: just outside the crosspole so's we could set in shelter and it could burn out in the open. And after we'd et slow and quiet, and it had turned dark and the stars come out sharp and strong, I felt tireder than any other night on the whole journey and maybe in my whole life and had to keep jerking my head up so's it wouldn't fall off and roll down into the crick.

After a bit, Millie says, "Mr. Bender, you brought us safely all the way."

"If it wasn't for you, I'd be back at Fort Kearny or someplace welldigging," I says.

"And we're here, and we've actually begun building our castle," she says. "We don't have our battlements up yet or our men-at-arms or our drawbridge, but we've made a start."

I'd read some of them books like that too, so I says, "Well, the throne room's as big as all outdoors, and we got the moat running right in front, and the treasure's all spread out underfoot. I hope."

"It doesn't really matter, does it?"

"I'd just as leave find it as not, wouldn't you?" I says, but she didn't say nothing, just begun getting our blankets ready, spreading our canvas over the bed of boughs first, and we slept sound through that cold night in a cloud of evergreen perfume, with me hanging on to one of the whipsaw handles and her nursing the crock of quicksilver at her bosom, which just goes to show you how good it was at locating gold.

Chapter Sixteen ★ ★ ★ ★ ★ ★ ★ ★ ★ ★ ★ ★

☞ There was so many things I wanted to do in the morning, I didn't know which ten of them to start off on. When I had shook the sleep out of my head and washed it out of my eyes in the icy crick, I seen everything fresh and strange: a hundred foot of crickbank and fifty foot up from shore and all claimed as ours and every square inch of it a wonder, even the parts I couldn't climb up to or didn't want to get wet admiring close. It may not of looked too good to Zack, but to me that humped-up, washed-out, rock-hard slice of gulch was the grandest in all Creation, and first off, I reckoned I'd get us a hearthstone, sort of to prove we'd chose the right name.

I took my pickax out to the crickbank where it begun to turn steepest yet still give me a foothold and spent ten minutes learning why Zack and the boys wasn't panning gold or using rockers or long toms yet. I settled on a slab of rock stuck into the bank edgewise and looked to be about the size of the petit-point cushion Miss Wilkerson used to keep on her horsehair sofa. But by the time I got it loose from the stuck-together dirt and gravel I had chipped and cracked it down to no bigger than a roast platter and half as thick as it started out, and my elbows was buzzing and I was scairt of breaking the pick handle. So I left it go at that and hauled it back to the lean-to, where Millie was arranging things here and there under shelter, fussy and happy and whistling, which she could do near as good as a bird.

And I says, "Well, the Hearthstone Mining Company's got itself a hearthstone. Now all it needs is some mining and some company."

She laughed and admired it more'n it deserved, and I commenced hollowing out a shallow place for it where our fire had thawed the dirt some, and when I'd got it laid in level, I stood up and done some admiring myself and held hands and felt married and pardners and in love, and then I went loco.

I seen that dirt and gravel I'd scraped loose to fit the stone in, and it dawned on me clearer than the real dawn that was looking brighter and bluer by the minute, *There's no reason a pan of that wouldn't wash.*

And I dug into my wheelborrow and come out with my big pie pan, which I hadn't used since way back on the Platte, and I scraped it full of that wet, cold dirt and all-sized gravel and run down to the crick with it, lucky not to fall down on my face and send it flying. I hunkered the way I seen the old-timers doing it downstream, dipped it full, and begun swirling and spilling it little by little, trying to go slow and be in dead earnest but all the time feeling fuller than the pie pan, and Millie came down half-way to watch and the clear water skimming along next to me, leaving thin slivers of ice along the edge and me panning for gold on my own claim (though I hadn't wrote nothing down yet nor drove a stake nor been to the Land Office) and everything seeming like a joy, even the hardest chores which I probably hadn't even thought up yet.

First nothing but muddy water come over the sides (and

oh! my fingers commenced getting cold), but then little gritty pieces of crushed rock that wasn't quite sand come along and the water got lower and I could pluck out some bigger chunks, making sure each one wasn't no nugget in disguise, and then I could spill some more and pick out some more gravel and add a little more water and spill it, and pretty soon I could tell I wasn't going to have much of nothing left in the bottom except what Pa left when he got hold of a real pie in a pan like that. Finally there was just a quarter inch of scummy brown-and-black sand for me to poke at. I rubbed it between my thumb and finger, and I seen gold specks in it.

I reared up and says to Millie, "I think I struck it," and my mouth wouldn't go shut, and next thing I knew I was running along the edge of the crick, holding that pan with both hands like it was the last drop of water in the desert, and heading for the hut, yelling, "Zack! Zack!"

He come out of the door and gawked at me, wearing an old long sheepskin jacket with the wool inside like he'd been set to go out, and first he just stood there waiting, but finally did some hoppity-skip running hisself to meet me with his eyes popped wide but puzzled-looking, the wrinkles in his forehead going up in the middle.

I didn't say nothing but slowed down without knocking him over and give him the pan and watched him squint down in it and rub it and hand it back, smiling now.

"It's gold, ain't it?" I says, feeling even more certain with that look on his face.

"Well, you might call it that," he says.

I let out a whoop and a yip and almost dropped the pan, but Zack got hold of me before I could commence running back to Millie.

"It needs some more separating, and if you feel inclined, you can scrape it off into something like a spare pan till you get enough to be worth working on with some of that quicksilver," he says.

He was so calm and offhand, I felt some of my blood go back where it belonged, and I says, "This isn't no good?"

"Well, you got a little color there, son, maybe about average for the worst places along here," he says. "One cent, maybe two."

I had worked ten or fifteen minutes and froze my hands numb and used up most of what little the fire had thawed, and I was one cent the richer. Yet somehow I didn't feel bad about it. "Oh," I says. "I reckoned it was more'n that."

He give me a dark smile through his beard and says, "So I noticed."

"But it sure is fun, ain't it?" I says. "Maybe I better hunt some more," and I turned to start back.

He come along, strolling slow like he didn't have nothing better to do, and out of the corner of my eye I seen Staggs stick his head out the door to watch.

"Bedrock's down four or five feet," Zack says. "Deeper some places. If there's good paydirt here—and I think the signs show it—it'll probably be down there. Gold likes to go deep and lay low."

Well, I'd known that, or thought I had, but sometimes forgetting is too much of a pleasure to pass by, and besides, now I knew what I'd act like if I ever did strike it.

Zack must of known pretty much what I was thinking. "You find out something about yourself, boy?" he says.

"Yes, sir."

"Bound to do lots of that in a gold field, and some of it's a caution and a revelation, and some's dreadful, and some's just plain tiresome," he says. "What was yours?"

"A caution, I expect."

"We can all do with some of that," he says.

I thought for a little ways, then says, "What do you reckon Kit's learnt so far?"

"Can't say for sure, but he most likely has a pretty good idea how hungry he is by now. Is and was." Zack give me a glance to see if I was listening, which I was. "And I don't mean just belly hungry."

I walked some more and thought it over and says, "Why'd he go up in the mountains by hisself?"

"Hard to say. I think he was scairt he'd kill Staggs or Badger or both or get kilt trying and figured he might's well risk his life doing something'd make him rich instead, such as prospecting in snow. I've done it myself, boy, and for my druthers, I'll take hunting grizzly with a spoon."

"Do you think he's froze?"

"Probably not," Zack says. "But sick maybe and sure enough sorry."

"Think I should go look for him?"

"Not unless you can swim upstream like a trout," he says. "This crick don't amount to much, but it's going to rise and so's every other trickle out of them mountains, and if you think you seen slow country before, you just try springtime in the Rockies. Ever been in the mountains?"

"No, sir."

"*Any* mountains?"

"No, sir."

He stopped and spit in the crick, then looked along it both ways like he was expecting a stagecoach to come along, and says, "You been used to the kind of country that just lays down and minds its manners. Well, I know prairies too. You can say what you like about prairies—"

"I wish you could hear my pa when the wind and rain gets up," I says.

"But at least a prairie don't raise all this commotion of boulders and smashed-up-looking heaps of Nature bigger than the biggest thunderhead you ever seen." He leant forward with his toes almost in the crick and looked upstream and motioned me to do the same.

I looked, and by leaning way out and peeking between the sides of the gully I could see the top of a mountain, white and jagged and gleaming in the sun. And I knew right off I was never going up anything like that. Kit was welcome to it. If that's where they wanted to put gold, then somebody else could have it.

Zack says, "There's something *wrong* about a mountain. It looks like somebody went and made a mistake, and they *did*, all that heaving and jumbling and snow laying slantwise instead of nice and flat so's you know where to put your foot down. And you can see what's coming on a prairie. You may not be smart enough or strong enough to do nothing about it, but at least you can see it ahead of time and get set or get moving."

"Well, you don't get no mirages up here anyways," I says.

"You get worse," he says. "You get surprises. Now, you take that grizzly I mentioned. He wouldn't be nothing much on a prairie. He'd be *ashamed* of hisself out in the open like that, and you and him'd take one good look at each other and say, *Well, there's some trouble I don't happen to need.* But on a dang slope on a narrow trail or with a bunch of pine trees getting in your road, you and him has got to figure out the do's and don'ts and whys and wherefores right there on the spot up close right now. And I'll tell you a little secret: he can do it better than you because if you don't like what he decides, he don't *care*."

"Reckon I'll stay down here," I says.

He looked back toward his hut, and I did too: Staggs and Badger was both out watching him now, and he says, "They don't much like you being here."

"I figured that out already," I says.

"We been keeping this place quiet, and so far, nobody much has come sniffing around. There's another sweet little stretch upstream about a mile and a half. Might be better than this, but I don't think so. Hope not. Anyway, if we was to start washing enough color out of here, they'd know it down along Cherry Crick, even if we kept still about it and didn't take none down for assay or minting. Don't ask me how. Gold don't just talk, it hollers and whistles. And if enough people started sluicing and long-tomming upstream, no telling what kind of water we'd be getting down here, if any. So if you stake a claim down in town, don't go lying or bragging."

"I don't do much of that," I says.

"Your brother's pretty good at it. I've heard better, but he's pretty good."

Staggs and Badger was still watching, and Millie too, and I says, "Did them two tell you to get my mouth shut down?"

"Now right there you sounded like a Bender, all right," he says. "Did I say anything that didn't sound like good advice?"

"No, sir."

His forehead had started going deep red like his nose, but it lightened up when he seen I was still friendly. "Then don't bite the hand that's feeding you a little up-country wisdom, boy." He tipped his old flat-topped felt hat toward Millie, who was a hundred foot off, waiting. "My respecks to Miz Bender, and if I can lighten the load of your youthful ignorance any further, just come a-running."

"It don't shame me to ask questions," I says.

"Glad to hear it," he says, and he started to back off, scuffing the side of one boot at the ground. "Don't mind me. Been a long time since I seen a young man in love, and it keeps me from thinking straight."

"Me too," I says.

He give me one of his gray-colored smiles then and squinted around and snuffed the air and says, "We're in for a thaw." He went bowlegging back to the hut, where the other two was still waiting.

When I got near enough to Millie with the pan, before I could say a word, she says, "Don't be too disappointed." And her smile was a different color altogether.

"I don't expect nothing but the best," I says. "Makes the worst more interesting when it shows up."

Millie put our two cents' worth of grit (I exaggerated a bit) in a tin can she'd picked up on the road and been saving for something or other, but instead of panning any more right away, I took it into my head to expand our lean-to so's it was more like a house. There was two more pine trees pretty close behind us, and I figured I could run crosspoles back and another pole across and get a slant roof on it, and we'd be right comfortable if I could find something to wall it up with. It was going to be lob-sided because the trees wasn't the same distance apart, but she liked the idea and helped strip the aspen poles as fast as I cut them.

While we was working, Mr. Blue come back, weaving downhill among the trees like he'd been living in the neighborhood for years. He must of found plenty to eat because he wouldn't take no more'n a handful of oats from Millie, and then he hung around watching us work for a spell, probably thinking we'd slap that pack on his back again any minute and get in our customary day of hauling and wheelborrowing. But in a half-hour he seen something new was going on, and in forty-five minutes he begun to get restless about it.

"Do you think I should tie him to a tree so he can figure out this is his home?" Millie says.

But I didn't want to wreck his disposition, and he wasn't rightly ours (nor nobody else's neither), so I says, "Let's leave him make up his own mind," which we done, and by the time an hour was up, he seemed to get it all straight in his head and went back zigzagging up the slope the way he come.

I run out of nails about the same time I got tired of chopping and sawing, but we had the framework up anyway, leaving the lean-to kind of inside it so's we'd have a dry place if it snowed before we was done. But by midday it was halfway warm and felt about like it had back on our farm, and I seen Zack and Badger and Staggs, sometimes separate, sometimes together, walking and scuffing along the crickbank and talking, and once Badger brung out a pickax and tried to drive it into the ground and then stood there rubbing his hands and squinching over like he'd near broke his wrists. So it looked like the Collywobble Mining Company wasn't going to start doing business just yet.

But the sight of them give me the budge I needed, and after we'd et (the *sight* of beans all swole up from hours of soaking and then boiling was getting to be enough to fill me up without me going to the trouble of chewing and swallering) I got out my forty foot of welldigging rope and went down to the near stake of Kit's claim and commenced measuring off our claim, which I reckoned to be two and a half ropes, the hard part being I couldn't go more'n twenty foot without wading, clinging on to the sheer bank, or going gulch climbing thirty or forty foot up on the bare, steep, hard, slippery, red-and-brown-streaked dirt without no handholds, and since Millie wouldn't let me try the last one and I *couldn't* do the middle one, I decided to go wading.

"You'll ruin your boots," she says.

"Then I'll wade barefoot."

"You're going to freeze your feet off in that water," she says.

"Then I'll wear my socks," I says. "Both pair."

"You'll fall down on those slick stones and drown," she says. "Can't you just *estimate* a hundred feet?"

"No man alive can spit that far," I says. Women get funny notions when they take to worrying. "And I can't drown in a foot of water. Next week it might be *five* foot deep."

I seen her trying to be patient with me, which is a good idea when two stubborn people try to mend each other's ways. "If that's the case, where's your stake going to be then, Mr. Bender?" she says. "Who's going to see it or read it under water?"

"I just want to do it legal," I says, but I didn't have no good answer except to say, "I'll drive it in as high up as I can reach." I had fixed up a tough, skinny stick of pine with a sheet of Millie's letter paper stuck in one split end and already glued in tight by the resin and had the pencil stub already sharpened and licked and set to go, down on my knees, using our hearthstone like a desk.

But she says, "What exactly is a claim notice supposed to say?"

"I don't know," I says, kneeling there and feeling like a mortal jughead. "I forgot to ask."

So there wasn't nothing to do but go ask Zack. I stayed off from the hut and give him a holler, and all three of them stuck their head from around back where I'd seen the sluice boxes stacking up. They jawed at each other a minute, and then Zack come down to the crickbank and says, "What is it, boy?"

"What's sposed to be wrote on a claim notice?" I says.

He glanced back over his shoulder. "They don't like me helping you." He made a sound like spitting, but nothing come out. "Wisht I had some chaw so's I could spit proper. Your claim's Number Five Upstream of Collywobble Discovery. Sign it, date it, give it a fancy name if you feel like." Again, he glanced back at Staggs and Badger, who was standing, staring, too far off to hear. "I'd sooner be upstream of the likes of them myself, but you can't make nothing out of this kind of placer gold without a company. When we get the long tom set up and going and they start busting their backs over it and maybe only making a little money, they might ask you in as a pardner, boy, specially if you got a little dirt and some quicksilver to add on."

"I'll see what Kit wants me to do," I says.

"You don't act much like him." Zack give hisself a good scratch up under the sheepskin. "And that's a step in the right direction. Usually, if there's one mean one in a family, they're all mean."

"Maybe I'm mean too," I says, starting back, "and too dumb to know it."

He give a cough or a cackle at that, then all of a sudden commenced jumping up and down, pounding his boot heels on the hard ground, and I stopped still, thinking he was having a fit or had got roostered up with whiskey, and in a loud voice he says, "Thaw, damn you, thaw! I'm tired of waiting on a bunch of dirt that don't know enough to reckonize springtime." He swept his arms out and ran his eyes back and forth along the whole crickbank. "No use pretending you're solid rock, goddamn you! You're going to get dug and ditched and washed down and tailed off, and we're going to pull them gold teeth right out of you."

I seen Staggs coming, but Zack didn't and went right on: "And if you don't have no gold in you to speak of, why, we don't give a damn, do we, boy?"

Meaning me, so I says, "No, sir."

"We'll just go dig someplace else."

"Come on, cut out all this booming and help us put the riffle box together," Staggs says, giving me a tight-eyed look.

"I'm just giving this claim fair warning," Zack says.

"You're so full of bullshit, you should take to farming," Staggs says. "Never have to buy no manure."

"Keep on my good side, Staggs," Zack says. "Pretty soon somebody's going to have to know what he's doing around here and know what he's looking at and know what to look for next, and I don't see nobody like that but me in this neighborhood."

"Then come on, use that big old self-rising brain on this riffle box," Staggs says.

"You're a man after my own heart," Zack says. "And I'm after yours. And I'll have it too, someday, Staggs. I'll have it broiled on the end of a willow switch."

I seen Staggs trying to hold his temper down. He says, "Some folks would eat most anything. Why don't you eat this dirt and shit us some nuggets?"

Zack seemed like he was all churned up, and one eye had commenced wandering off sideways. "I've et things I can't believe now, and I've et things I can't even remember because I worked so hard to get them out of my head."

"Jesus B. Christ, don't start telling stories," Staggs says. "How the hell did we ever get through the winter without killing each other off?"

I drifted further away, and Zack started up the slope with Staggs. "We *did* kill each other off," Zack says. "We're just too ornery to fall down."

I went about fifty foot, and Zack commenced yelling again. "Boy! Boy!" He'd cupped his hands to make it carry good, and Staggs was standing by, watching him, looking worried. "What do you want with gold anyway, boy?" Zack yells, and didn't give me no time to think up an answer, but went right on, "What do they do with it? Make watches and knobs for canes and teeth and wedding rings and braid for admirals and generals. Want to risk your life for any of them things? For a rich man's toothpick?"

Staggs hauled on his arm, and they went behind the hut.

Millie wrote down what Zack had told me (she can do pretty curlicue printing most as good as a sign painter), and we both wrote our name at the bottom and called it Hearthstone Mining Company. And after arguing a bit more, I done what she suggested: put the stake in as far upstream as I could reach without getting wet, with an arrow along the top of the page, then below it—"This Sign Belongs 75 More Foot Upstream But We Can't Get There," which was sposed to keep everything fair and square, and I hoped so. I had to pickax a little hole for the stake and wedge some gravel in to hold it up, but finally it was all done, and we stood back proud and looked at it every which way and felt like we had at the christening of my wheelborrow, only better.

Then we went wandering up along the steep, bare gully-side above the crick, picking up little pieces of rock and staring around at the view and scaring me some because there wasn't no good footholds out there, but Millie was sure-footed as Mr. Blue and I was getting used to all this slipshoddy country, and while we was standing there, feeling like our own landlords, I seen Badger and Staggs come out of their hut and down near the crick, Badger flapping his deerskin around like a dog worrying a blanket, and then Zack come out and did a dance too, and I thought they'd all got drunk.

But then Millie and me felt it too: a warm wind coming up the draw from the bottom land. It must of had to take as many zigzags as my wheelborrow to get up here to us, but now it was blowing in our face, as warm as a stove almost, and you could feel the melt starting in every dead inch of this little crank turn of a gulch, even up at our end, as sure as morning.

Chapter Seventeen ★ ★ ★ ★ ★ ★ ★ ★ ★ ★ ★

☞ Mr. Blue showed up again soon after dawn to make sure he hadn't made no mistake, and he *had*, because Millie was waiting for him with a saddle she'd folded up out of a blanket, and after she'd tied it on and give it a try side-saddle to see if he'd buck or run and he didn't do neither, we was ready to head for town.

I had strung my pickax, shovel, and whipsaw together and lashed them halfway up a thick pine tree fifty yards up the slope from our house and tied the flour and bacon up there too and had packed my wheelborrow light, taking my ax along for kindling and comfort. We had figured to bring the wheelborrow to sleep under, since it would take us more'n half the day to get there and probably more time to file the claim and Millie wanted to shop if there was anything to shop and, besides, I didn't feel right walking very far without them handles pulling down on my arms. It sort of kept me balanced and springy-footed. And I didn't want Staggs or Badger wrecking it or stomping it for spite.

Millie left most of our kit behind but for a little food already cooked, so we both felt light as goosefeathers (though I brung the crock of quicksilver along to keep it from straying off), and we felt cheery and loose in our bones, and I give Staggs a smile and a howdy when we passed by the front of the hut.

He was splitting small logs into some rough kind of lumber, and he looked up, sweating and slope-shouldered and thick-set like he belonged inside the bearskin he was wearing. He says, "Well, now you're getting some sense. Tell the folks back home it's all a swindle."

"See you tomorrow," I says, which didn't seem like what he'd reckoned on hearing, because he scowled.

Zack come around the side of the house carrying the front end of a double-bottomed box like a coffin without no lid and Badger on the rear end, and I says, "Can we bring anything from town, Mr. Orfrey?"

"Don't bring back nothing," Staggs says. "And *nobody*. Keep your mouth shut about this crick. Tell them you're homesteaders."

"If there's such a thing as a plug of chaw laying around free, I'd sure admire it," Zack says.

Walking downhill beats walking up in just about every way you can name. It's mighty strange to get *help* walking, to find out your foot's going a little further each step than you thought it would and there's no such thing as a dead end or a blind draw. Mr. Blue didn't seem to mind being rode, and Millie took to riding like she done everything else (she hadn't complained none on the way, but many's the night back on the road I seen her holding a bare foot in her hands and rocking back and forth with it like it was a sick babydoll, and nothing I could do about it), and even though the day hadn't stayed as warm as that one patch of evening had been, everything was commencing to thaw.

She sang and whistled and learnt me a song about

"Green grow the rashes O," which sounded kind of ugly till she explained it was some kind of grass instead of the itch, and we had a grand time, making more commotion in that crooked, steep little Slab Crick valley than it had ever heard before unless the Injuns had warpathed it there sometime. I don't know what made us so happy: we hadn't washed but two cents' worth of gold, if that, and there was no telling how long Millie's money would keep us in supplies (I still hadn't had the courage to ask her how much she had), and we didn't have nothing to depend on in this world but us, which seemed like enough.

There was a few more tents sprung up on the lower stretches and men out panning or using rockers about the size of washtubs, but they must not of been finding much to crow about because nobody was crowing but us. Millie had learnt me another song which you was sposed to sing separate, one trailing along behind the other and singing what the other had just sang, and I got mixed up at first but finally got the hang of it, and we done that one for about eight miles through them glum-looking sand scratchers. They'd stop panning or rocking and just stare at us going by, and it went like this (it don't look like much wrote down but makes you feel sad and happy both at once):

Heigh-ho, nobody home.
Food and drink and money have we none.
Still we will be merry.
Heigh-ho, nobody home.

And then you just started in all over again like you never meant to stop, and I didn't. I even sung it while we crossed on the ferry over the South Platte (another dollar and a half, which left me only two dollars and the Major's fifty cents and two cents' worth of muck), but my voice had got raw by then, so I had to quit.

We was back in the thick of things now, wagons coming and going, and people looking poorly, and the ones leaving yelling and mocking at the ones just now making it to Cherry Crick, and we took our share of it, mostly keeping beside the road where it hadn't been mudholed and rutted, but after you've been hollered at to turn back and called every kind of fool enough times, you get mule-headed about being yourself and answering curses with a smile, and we even sung some more along the road, which like to drove some people purple, seeing us enjoying ourselves when we should of been played out and dragging.

When we come to the town in late afternoon, it didn't look like a whole lot to be aiming for: Denver City and Auraria was pretty much like one place with Cherry Crick separating two bunches of tents, tepees, log cabins, and sod-roof huts, some only half built—maybe a hundred fifty in all, and wagons camped hither and skelter, but Millie got all excited over it, admiring this and that kind of house and saying we could do it this way and that way our own selfs. There was lots of Injuns in town, mostly Arapahoes somebody told me, and lots of Mexicans, which I hadn't seen none of before but looked tough and lean and fierce-eyed, and men wearing pieces of soldier uniforms and animal fur and only a few women here and there. Horses, mules, and oxen—even a few skinny cattle—was strewn out all over, trying to graze on grass that hadn't come up yet, and they had laid out crisscrossed streets with names on them, but people seemed to walk straight to where they was going, even if it meant cutting through yards.

Cherry Crick was three times as big as Slab Crick, and I seen men panning and rocking and long-tomming it for miles, but nobody seemed het up about it, more like slow-as-summer ditch digging, and the whole place smelt of manure and whiskey and wood smoke.

Millie says, "Isn't this wonderful? This is going to be a wonderful city."

We was stopped in front of a place called Mountain Boys Saloon, a low shack with a lot of shouting coming out the front door and two men arguing and pawing over a heap of green buckskins out front, each with a big navy revolver stuck in his belt. I heard some shots fired a hundred yards off, but nobody even turned around that way to look, and I begun to get the idea this might be a mighty rough place come sundown, so I says, "Let's find the general store before it shuts."

Passing by a couple of wagon auctions right in the middle of town, like the sad, angry ones we seen back in Julesburg, we come to a low building with a glass window called Wootton's Outfitters with a clutch of people shoving around the front, grim-looking and mad but not making much noise, and there was a big man with garter sleeves and a leather eyeshade blocking the door and shaking his head No at everybody. "No grubstaking," he says. "No grubstaking, boys. The answer is No. No," and on and on like that.

I had been about to wheelborrow right on by, but Millie slid down off of Mr. Blue, tied his rope to one of my handles, and started at the outer edge of the bunch as dainty as you please, saying, "Excuse me, gentlemen, excuse me."

They made a passage for her, shuffling back kind of awkward, and one fat-faced man even took off his wool cap to her, and she kept smiling and saying, "Excuse me," till she was right up to the door.

The big man looked flustered but kept his arm across in front of her and says, "Cash, trade, or lies, miss?"

"Cash, of course," she says. "I don't know you well enough to permit you to give me credit, sir. That will depend on the nature of your goods. *And* your prices."

He let her through, giving a little hunch like a bow, and some of the lunkheads tried to gawk through the window at her and the rest turned to gawk at me. I tipped my hat and held my ground, and the big man stayed in the doorway, and in about two minutes somebody come from inside and whispered something at him, and he says, "Mr. Bender?" peering around over the heads to find me. "Mr. Bender, would you mind stepping inside, please?"

They all turned and give me a going over, head to toe, and I just stood there and says, "No, thanks. I'll wait," not wanting to leave my wheelborrow and Mr. Blue among men looking for prospectoring outfits.

The big man done some more whispering inside, then says, "Your wife would like your opinion about some French gingham, Mr. Bender. She says it's most important, and she says to bring the crock too."

"I don't have no opinion about French gingham," I says. "I never seen any."

After some more muttering and conferring inside, the big man says, "The stockboy will be glad to watch your burro and—ah, your wagon, Mr. Bender. It won't take but a minute."

I felt like a prize hog at a fair with all them men searching me over, and when a boy wearing gray homespun and knickers come galloping out to take hold of Mr. Blue's rope, I was glad to get inside, and I dug under my oilskin and brung the crock of quicksilver, glad enough to do what she told me, since it kept the back of my mind at ease while I was using the front.

The store was all cramped up with stacks of picks and shovels and harness and wagon parts and rope and packs and windlasses and rocker boxes and pans and skillets and barrels, and when I had finally wove my way over to a side counter with two heaps of candle boxes next to it, Millie was draping herself in a long swatch of striped blue cloth and looking happy as pie, and there was a second man in garter sleeves and a leather eyeshade—this one small and jumpy and a face like an ax blade—and he says, "My missus'll be right along. She knows all about styles and that.

Sews a mighty fine stitch." Then he says to me, "Gets the newspaper all the way from St. Louie," like that explained it all.

"Mr. Bender, do you fancy this material?" Millie says, smiling so big and sweet I couldn't say nothing but what I was sposed to.

"Yes," I says.

"Isn't it heavenly?" she says. "I think I'll need a party dress for when we go to California. I hear the ladies in California are very smart."

"Well, they was sure smart when I was there nine years ago," the storekeep says. "Don't expect they've forgot much yet."

"I mean they are distressingly fashionable, and when one has become accustomed to the laxities of hard travel and the mining camp, one must be extra careful to keep up one's standards."

"Exactly," the storekeep says like he understood, and maybe he did.

But I wasn't any too sure *I* did, and I shuffled around on the canvas floor a little where the sawdust was leaking through, trying to catch Millie's eye and calculate what she was up to.

The storekeep's missus come bustling in from the back, squinting behind little round spectacles and moving like a bird picking up seeds, and her and Millie commenced talking about ruffles and pleats and bodices and shirtwaists and boleros, and the storekeep looked relieved to get out of it.

He says to me, "Been up in the mountains a ways, I understand."

"Yes, sir," I says.

"Still pretty cold up there?"

"Well, I wouldn't plant no wheat yet," I says.

"Some are lucky and some aren't," he says. "Wish you all the luck in the world. Or maybe I don't need to."

"So far I've had every bit I could need or expect," I says. "How much do these here tents fetch?" I tugged at a heap of folded-up canvas to get him off the subject.

Millie laughed her soft coming-down-the-scale laugh and says, "It will be a comfort to keep my hands out of ice-cold creek water now. It does parch them so. I can hardly wait to see what the hotels in San Francisco offer in the way of suites."

"Have your own mining company, do you?" the storekeep says to me.

"Yes, sir. How much does a small tent weigh, counting the poles?"

"Name of—?"

"Ike Bender," I says. I set my crock down on the counter so's I could heft one of them tents myself, and it weighed too much extra for Mr. Blue unless we dumped off some of our pack. Millie had me so confused, I reckoned we was going on the road again right away.

"I meant the name of the company," the storekeep says.

"There's only nine other women in town," the storekeep's wife says. "And only four what you'd call respectable, and we'd sure admire to have you come on Thursday nights. It's a Sewing Circle, but you wouldn't have to sew none. We mostly talk."

"Hearthstone," I says, since that didn't tell him nothing.

"Why, I'd be delighted," Millie says. "We won't be leaving for a few weeks, and I suppose I'll need two fittings for the dress if you wouldn't mind combining business with society."

"No, ma'am, it would be a pleasure," the storekeep's wife says, her eyes hopping around behind her specs.

"Mr. Bender, would you mind getting us five pounds of dried apples and five pounds of rice while you're waiting?" Millie says. Then to the storekeep's wife, "Mr. Bender is very indulgent of me. He caters to all my whims, and I feel so spoiled and wonderful and fortunate, especially among all the *less* fortunate we saw along the road and here in town. Can you direct us to the assayer's office?"

"Just up Larimer Street," the storekeep's wife says kind of hollow.

"Oh, and don't forget some chewing tobacco for Mr. Orfrey," Millie says.

"Zack Orfrey?" the storekeep says, his mouth going open a notch, and I seen he was getting too interested in us and ours.

So I says, "Five pound of rice, five pound of dried apples, and a plug of chaw."

But the storekeep says, "Zack Orfrey, old-timer with long gray hair and a gray beard, and his left leg kind of sprung out?"

"How much'll that be?" I says.

While he got behind his scale pans and commenced parceling out the rice and apples, the storekeep give me two or three nervous looks, then smiled when I caught him doing it, and he says, "Old Zack's a smart customer. He don't waste his time unless there's something to it. How's his health?"

"Seems fine," I says, feeling uncomfortable and wishing we was back outside. "Whereabouts is the Land Office?"

"The Mining District Recorder's Office is right across the street and down a ways," he says, and then like it was the most natural thing a storekeep could do, he picked up the crock of quicksilver and set it on the scale pan where the rice and apples had just been, and it sank down with a clunk before I could snatch it back.

"Would you like me to pack that up with the rest?" the storekeep says, flicking his nervous smile at me again. "That's some mighty heavy—ah, *jam* you got there."

"No, thanks," I says. "I can handle it."

Millie says, "Then it's all settled?"

"Yes, ma'am," the storekeep's wife says, doing a curtsy about one inch deep.

"I can't tell you what a joy it will be to feel like a frilly and fluttery lady again," Millie says. "With a sweet bolt of cloth like that, I don't care *what* it costs."

"You don't?" the storekeep's wife says, like she'd been waiting all her life to hear or say them magic words.

Glancing back and forth between us, the storekeep says, "Will this be cash or—ah, dust? Common form of payment around here. Least till the ground froze."

Millie looked at me bright, sparkling, and innocent, and says, "Oh, I expect it had better be cash, don't you, Mr. Bender?"

"Yes, I expect it better had," I says.

"We'll settle the price of the dress when I see it being pinned on me, is that all right?" Millie says.

"Yes, ma'am," the wife says.

"That'll be eight dollars even," the storekeep says.

While Millie was dipping into her reticule, I started to say I never heard of no dress costing that much, but it turned out that was for the rice, apples, and a plug of chaw, and I seen why Staggs and Badger was out shooting deer and grouse.

Millie paid the bill, looking happy and careless like she was playing with buttons instead of coins, and while she was at it, she spilled out Blue Bird's little pouchful of gray stones on the counter in front of the storekeep and scooped them all back in her reticule kind of hasty and laughed and says, "I thought I had more coins in there," while he gawked.

I tried to get us outside, but the storekeep come zipping around and got hold of my elbow and says, "You tell Zack he better not forget Amos Wootton grubstaked him."

"All right," I says, aiming Millie for the door, where the big man was still barring the way.

"Listen, young man," the storekeep says. "My cousin Bert's president of the only bank in town worth calling a bank. If I was you, I'd go see him right away and not go carrying anything too valuable around on me. There's a lot of hungry men in town, and some snorty ones, and for instance, if you was to show up in the Assay Office with that much gold, you'd start a riot."

"I'm not looking for no Assay Office," I says.

"Be discreet," he says, commencing to whisper. "And for God's sake, put that crock away someplace and register your claim like you was already disgusted with it. Look, you can trust me. I'm kind of a pardner of Zack's, see, being his grubstaker. Whereabouts is he at?" He was sweating out from under his eyeshade and had to tip it up to make room for his shirtsleeve to wipe.

"I don't believe Mr. Orfrey is interested in having any visitors just now," Millie says. "Isn't that what he said, Mr. Bender?"

I only got about half a word out when the storekeep says, "Is it a mountain or gulch claim? How much is left?"

Millie started to say something, but I says, "Now you hush up," which I had never told her to before, but she didn't seem to mind. She smiled as sweet as you please and let me get her under the big man's arm and out through the knot of men that spread apart for us. Mr. Blue and the wheelborrow was still there, being watched after, and Millie give the boy a penny, and at the rate our money was going, I'd have to start panning night and day.

"What was all that talk in there?" I says. "We'll have Slab Crick so full of people, we won't be able to—"

"Let's get busy at that Land Office," she says.

Behind us I heard the door of Wootton's Outfitters slam shut, and through the glass I seen the storekeep talking to the big man and pointing, and I got us moving before we done anything else wrong.

We only had about a hundred foot to travel, but we managed to pick up three loyal followers from amongst the lunkheads outside Wootton's, acting sort of curious or suspicious or both, partly because Millie sang and laughed all the way, and in a town as full of low-spirited, colicky, mean-mad people as this one, you didn't hear too much in the line of happy noises like that. I think she done it a-purpose, though she acted that way most times, and I couldn't help catching it too, even when I seen the big man from the store come scooting out the back and beat us to the Mining District Recorder's Office, Office Hours When the Door's Open (like it said on a plank out front), and stand leaning on the counter with a calm, blank look on his moon face when we got there, just like he didn't have nothing better to do than listen to people file claims.

The chunky man with black hair and a thick black mustache behind the counter come away from his iron stove, where he'd been baking his hands, and I says, "I'd like to file a claim."

He shoved a stack of ledgers over my way and says, "Lode, placer, water, millsite, timber, patch, cabin, or tunnel?"

"Placer," I says.

"And lode, please," Millie says.

"You together or separate?" the recorder says.

"Can we do this in private?" I says, looking at the big man, who didn't even blink.

"Public place," the recorder says.

"Is it legal to have both a lode and a placer claim on the same property?" Millie says.

"Well, they're different sizes," the recorder says.

"It doesn't matter if they overlap, does it?" she says.

The recorder worked on his mustache with the butt of a steel pen and says, "That problem don't generally arise. Two different kinds of gold. As a matter of fact, I don't recollect—"

One of the lunkheads from outside tried to come in, and the big man planted the flat of his hand on his shirtfront and showed him how to get out the door backwards, then shut it and stood listening again.

"Who done the survey?" the recorder says.

"Zack Orfrey," Millie says quick as a snap.

I felt like things was getting away from me, so keeping my voice low, I says, "Slab Crick, Number Five Upstream of Orfrey's Collywobble, and where do I sign because we got to get—"

"Just a minute, just a minute," the recorder says, hauling out a bunch of rolled-up maps and peeking at three before he laid one out on the counter. The big man come up to watch over my shoulder, and I didn't know what to do but let him since I wasn't much for shoving people his size out of doors.

Millie pointed and says, "That's it right there. Now, how wide is a lode claim?"

"You mean there's a quartz lead there?" the recorder says, like she'd told him she'd seen a dragon with fire coming out of both ends.

"That's what I wish to claim," she says. "How wide?"

"Fifty foot each side."

"Well, that should work out very nicely, Mr. Bender, shouldn't it?" she says. "And how long?"

"Three hundred foot."

"That's fine," she says. "Then our property will just be two hundred and fifty feet further up the hill than before."

The big man was drinking it all in, and me too, since it seemed like I should keep track of what I was getting into. The recorder filled out two forms, using numbers off of the map, and Millie and me both signed and called us Hearthstone again, and she paid the fee and folded up our copies, and the big man was gone before she could stuff them in her reticule.

"Have to work both of them, you know," the recorder says. "Otherwise the claim lapses."

"Excuse me," I says, and went outside to chase a lunkhead away from my wheelborrow. And when Millie come out, I says, "I know you're a willful woman, but I got a suggestion to make."

"What's that, Mr. Bender?"

"If you're going to get me acting out lies for you, you'd best give me a little more time to practice up."

"I haven't told any lies I know of," she says, looking gentle and barefaced.

"You said there was a quartz lead on our claim."

"I *claimed* there was," she says. "It's a very important distinction. And there may very well be for all we know. Meanwhile our property's six times as big."

"And you said we was going to California."

"Wouldn't you like to go to California someday?" she says. "I hear it's very lively and interesting and instructive."

"Right now I'd like to get back over the river before the ferry stops running," I says. "I got a feeling we're going to have a little company up the Slab Crick valley, and we might's well get back home before they beat us there."

"Whatever you say, Mr. Bender," she says, very meek and sweet, which just goes to show you something or other. "Do you want to heat up the beans and bacon or just eat them cold while we walk?"

Two of the lunkheads was following us, kind of hesitating like they hadn't quite made up their mind yet, so I says, "Let's get out of town first, then decide. You made that storekeep think we struck it rich."

"I did?" she says. "Well, we *are* rich."

Which I had to admit felt like it was true, and no lie, so I tried to shrug off the worry and perk up, in spite of the mud and all the arguing going on around us. We seen four men having a fist fight in front of a tepee and two Injuns sitting by, watching the ceremony, and further on, a Mexican down on his knees vomiting blood and shaking his head sort of casual in between and smiling at the wonder of it, and two old men having a shoving match, too feeble to hurt each other much but one weeping all the while and moaning about his wagon, which had gone bust or something. And Millie seen every bit of it, and more, including men doing calls of Nature out in the open, and she took it without flinching, even singing a little song in her quiet, clear voice, which I couldn't hear the words of for all the commotion.

And then outside a shacky-looking place with no windows and a handwrote sign on it—"Hotel"—setting on a crate with a pair of homemade crutches propped beside him and a pair of boots slit up both sides and along the uppers so's to make room for bandages, was my brother Kit. He didn't have no hat on, and his head was hanging down while he stared at his hands, which, to judge from the way the dirty bandages fit around and over, didn't have no fingers on them.

Chapter Eighteen ★ ★ ★ ★ ★ ★ ★ ★ ★ ★ ★ ★

☞ I stopped dead, and Millie seen him and stopped too, but he didn't see us. He kept looking at the bandages on his hands like he was reading them and didn't have but two pages to turn, then had to go back and start over. His face was creasier and more weathered-looking and older than I remembered, though he wasn't but five years ahead of me, and I says, "Kit."

He looked up and give me a long, slit-eyed look, then done the same with Millie, staying still and not getting up and not even acting much surprised. He nodded a couple times like he was saying, "Well, here's two more."

I couldn't shake hands with him, so I says, "I come like you said." I seen his eyes moving back and forth between us. "Millie and me got married."

I hadn't reckoned on it being like this but more like whooping and chi-yukking and throwing our hat around, and I tried to smile at him, but my face wasn't working right. "They been waiting for you up on the crick," I says. "What happened?"

"Froze," he says. "Just a little friendly frostbite. You been up there already? Have they started washing yet?" He seemed to of woke up a bit now. It was like his voice needed exercise. "Are they long-tomming?"

"No, but they're fixing to," I says.

"Have you seen a doctor?" Millie says.

He smiled at that and set up straighter on the box, easing his boots back slow and painful. "There's a dentist fixed me up." He seen me looking at his boots and says, "Lost all but my big toes too, while I was at it. Still got most of my thumbs, though." He smiled hard and bleak, not meaning to smile. "They turn blue when they get froze, case you're interested."

"I'm right sorry," I says.

"Well, that just makes me feel a whole lot better," he says, and I didn't like the sound of it.

"Can we be of any assistance, Mr. Bender?" Millie says. Her and him had never been too friendly because she done all Miss Wilkerson's lessons faster than him, which didn't bother me none since I like smart people. "Are you getting enough to eat?" she says.

"Why, yes," Kit says. "I can hold a fork pretty good with my thumb, and a bottle's no trouble at all with both hands."

He made it sound like she was the one went and froze off his fingers and toes, and I seen she didn't like it no more'n me.

"I wasn't referring to your unfortunate disability," she says. "I meant, is good food and care available here, and do you have sufficient funds?"

"I brung back one hundred and eighty-five dollars in shot gold, most of which I still got. And aim to keep," he says, turning kind of loud.

"I wasn't asking to borrow any," Millie says.

"Why'd you bring a girl way out here to this goddamn place?" he says to me. "You're dumber than Pa."

"Well, I may be dumb, but I ain't been selling off my fingers and toes for ten dollars each yet," I says.

"I'll heal up," he says. "I'm healing fast." He glanced around at nothing, kind of jittery. "I got to get up there and help work the Collywobble or them bastards will squeeze me out. Is it thawed yet?"

"On its way," I says, feeling edgy and helpless and mad and gut-shrunk and sorry and dizzy, realizing I hadn't had Kit lined up proper in my head so's I could keep clear what was his life and what was mine. And now seeing him crippled up so bad, I felt worse off than if I'd stayed home and let Pa run me. "Are you living in there?" I says, meaning the hotel.

He nodded, looking at my wheelborrow and Mr. Blue. "Where you aiming for?"

"We was heading up Slab Crick again," I says. "Just come down to get supplies and—" I trailed off, not knowing if I should tell him about our claim for fear he'd get mad or start mocking at us. I don't know how come brothers can make you feel so worthless when they've a mind to, but they can. Millie says it's the same with sisters though she never had none but had daydreamed out how it would be.

Kit says, "All right," kind of slow like he was thinking the idea over. "That's all right. You go on up there." He paused, still thinking it out. "You go tell them you're working for me, and I'll be up soon as I get healed up better. Only be a couple days more, maybe. And I'll—I'll *pay* you something. We'll work it out. If we strike it pretty good, I'll pay you two dollars a day." He glanced at Millie sort of impatient, like she was a problem he shouldn't need to fuss with. "Or two and a half, maybe."

"Well, I'll be glad to help out," I says, figuring I could work our claims on my own time if it come to that.

"Perhaps you'd like to work for *us*," Millie says.

But I didn't like the sound of that, with Kit setting there

dirty and hurt and not knowing we was both grown up, so I smiled like it was half a joke and says, "We formed us a mining company too." And I couldn't figure out why the next was so hard to get out but I finally done it. "We staked a claim right next to yours."

"There's nothing there to claim," he says very quiet.

"Well, we done it anyway," I says, trying to keep that smile where it belonged but probably looking like I'd caught a fishbone in my back teeth.

Kit decided he thought it was funny. He let out a short grunt of a laugh and says, "How you aiming to wash a high bank like that?"

"I have read several books on modern California mining methods," Millie says, which was news to me. "And I believe that particular property is subject to development."

Kit stared at her like she'd just tried to render a minuet on a jew's-harp. "So little Millie Slaughter's still got all the answers for the teacher. Well, you won't find no sweet old Miss Wilkersons up in the mountains. They don't have no teacher's pets up there, just goddamn hard knocks and bad news."

"My name is Mrs. Isaac Bender," she says. "And you're my poor, suffering brother-in-law."

"I ain't poor and I ain't suffering!" Kit says, hitting one hand by accident against the hotel wall and having to clench it between his knees and wince down over it and squeeze his eyes shut.

"I think we need a little time to figure each other out here," I says. "I don't think we know each other any too well. We changed. Or we forgot. Come on now, let's—"

"I think that's a very sensible and reasonable idea, Mr. Bender," Millie says, meaning me.

"Some things don't change much, such as smarty-ass little girls and dumb kid brothers," Kit says, straightening up and looking flushed and fidgety, and just then a plump, stringy-haired squaw in a buckskin dress fringed down to her ankles come waddling out of the hotel, scuffing her torn boots in the mud and carrying a tin cup which smelled like corn whiskey when it passed by three foot in front of me, and she held it for Kit and giggled while he got the flat of his palms adjusted on each side and could tip it up by hisself.

The squaw said something in Injun, and Kit says, "Get the hell out of here," scowling at her and still scowling when he looked from me to Millie, taking two deep swigs at the cup like he was daring us to tell him not to.

The squaw mumbled something else, and Kit says, "Get away before I bust you one," and she backed off, looking sorry, and went inside.

"You sure there's nothing we can do for you?" I says.

"I told you what you can do," Kit says. "Tell those bastards up there they better not try to skin me, or I'll come up and fix them good. Tell them I'm down here holding on to my share, and I mean to have it."

"Would you like some cold beans and bacon?" Millie says.

"Go on, eat your own mess," Kit says, swigging at the cup again.

"You should be polite to my wife," I says.

He give me another long, slit look. "I'm doing what I please, brother. Ain't that what you're doing?"

"I reckon so," I says, reaching down for my wheelborrow handles and getting set to move, though it seemed like I was partly doing what *he* wanted me to do.

"If you'll accept some sister-in-lawly advice," Millie says, "one of the first things you'd best learn how to do is hold a knife or a gun." She clumb up on Mr. Blue sidesaddle.

"Now you're talking sense for a change, little girl," Kit says, setting there with the empty cup in his short, stubby palms.

We got out on the road before dark, me feeling heartsick

and confused and Millie keeping quiet and three lunk-heads following us now, two with packs and one with nothing, and nobody was singing or whistling or enjoying theirselves. The three kept about fifty yards back, seeming like they'd thrown in together, because I seen them talking, and they hiked along like they was set to dog us.

And we made the ferry while there was still some light left, and the whole bunch of us got on, kind of embarrassed and looking the other way and pretending we didn't know what was going on. The one who didn't have no pack had to argue a little cash out of his new pardners, and for a second I thought he was coming over to borrow it off of me, but they finally give him enough, and we all wound up on the west bank of the South Platte with the sun dropping quick and being smudged out by clouds, and then it commenced to rain.

I got my yellow slicker on, and Millie got hers on too (which had belonged to Sam or Frank or Hotchkiss once upon a time, back in the days of my youth), and we kept moving, and I had a picture in my mind what this hard rain was going to look like if it happened to be snow up on our claim. But it felt warm enough so far, and maybe it was just what we needed for a full thaw.

We went on a ways till I couldn't see to haul or push my wheelborrow no more, then camped without a fire, et some beans, turned Mr. Blue loose, and got snugged in under our canvas like we done our first night together. And as soon as we was all quieted down, I commenced crying, thinking how I wasn't going to be able to shake hands with Kit no more.

Millie says, "Hush now, Mr. Bender. Don't cry."

I went on for a bit, then says, "You told me it was all right for a grown man to cry over a chest of drawers or a soaked mailsack. How's come I can't do it over my own brother?"

She kept still a minute, holding me. "Very well then," she says, patting my back while I done it some more, and after a bit I must of fell asleep.

I don't know what them other three done to while away the hours, but at first light they looked like they wished they'd gone in for some other line of work besides following us. Mr. Blue hadn't wandered off, so we got a good start without waiting for him, and the three men come plodding after.

When we passed some of the same solitary old-timers with their pans and rocker boxes and pup tents we'd give a treat to yesterday by singing and cutting up foolish, some of them scrambled around quick, broke camp, and fell in behind, and by the time we come to the steeper foothills in the rain, which had slowed way down to a drizzle, and I looked back along the crick a half-mile, I counted eleven altogether, all afoot. We had the makings of a rush, and there wasn't nothing I could do about it.

"You think I should go back and tell them there's nothing much up ahead and they should stay where they're at?" I says.

Millie was looking pleased and fresh-faced. "I don't think they'd listen to you, Mr. Bender."

"No, I spose not. What's Staggs going to say?"

"Whatever it is, I doubt it will be very interesting or original," she says. "And if a gentleman as large as the assistant at Wootton's Outfitters shows up, as I suspect he will, I don't believe there will be very much Mr. Staggs *can* say."

I mulled that over for a half-mile while the going got steeper, and then I says, "When did you read them books about mining?"

"I thought it was the least I could do to prepare myself to be your helpmeet," she says. "I read one in Nebraska

City and another in St. Joe. They were too heavy to bring along, so I just had to memorize their contents."

"Do you really think we staked us some paydirt?"

"Well, if we didn't, at least we'll have plenty of people to sell our claim to, so we can afford to move on somewhere else," she says.

"That don't exactly seem honest," I says.

"Mr. Bender, didn't you tell me you were different from everybody else in the world and born to rise and lucky-starred?"

"I didn't say nothing about lucky stars," I says, feeling prickly-faced and worried and looking back at this straggly parade we had commenced leading.

"Be that as it may, the first thing you learn when you read about gold discoveries and prospecting and mining methods is that you can only be sure of one thing: once you have *found* gold, there will be a way to extract it from whatever mess it's in, but that *nobody* knows for sure how to find it. Not even the most distinguished experts. And since nobody knows, you might as well look where nobody else is looking. Someplace where it's not supposed to be. Because that's where it almost always is."

That made sense for about a hundred yards, but then I says, "If that's so, why don't we go climbing trees and hunting for it in birds' nests?"

"I think that's a very good idea," she says.

Which is the kind of talk you have to swaller with a smile if you want to get the good out of being married, and I done so.

Chapter Nineteen ★ ★ ★ ★ ★ ★ ★ ★ ★ ★ ★ ★

☞ About noon we come to our stretch of crick, and we seen Zack, Staggs, and Badger struggling to get a long tom going in the slow, easy rain. They had rigged up about forty foot of sluice boxes along the edge with short, cross-legged trestles to bring water into the long tom itself, which was about twelve foot long and a foot deep and widened out to a riffle box under the end of it. They was getting too much water and trying to slow it down by arranging the slope of the sluice different, and it looked like a good time for us to get by. Staggs grabbed his rifle when we first come into sight, but put it back when he seen it was us, then snatched it up again just as we was even with them and says, "Who the hell is that?"

I looked back and seen two of the lunkheads from outside Wootton's had just hove into view (the third was either straggling or had quit), and I says, "They're no friends of mine till next Sunday," which is what Pa used to say to make Ma mad about church, and I wished I hadn't said it.

Staggs says, "Goddamn it, I thought I told you—"

"Get that sluice box back in line, you whey-bellied youn-ker, you," Zack says.

And I took the opportunity, while they was sloshing around up to their ankles in the crick, to get us further past toward our claim, where I wanted to get a fire going and dry out and make sure nobody mistook our house for kindling.

Hollering after us, Staggs says, "You got no more brains than—"

But I guess he was too dumb to think up something brainless enough fast enough, so we kept on past Kit's claim and up to our hearthstone, which had been pried out of its hole, and our house, which hadn't exactly been wrecked but had been ransacked every which way and not put back together much.

Millie didn't get mad but just nodded like she was seeing what she'd expected, and I says, "Maybe a bear done it." But nothing had been busted and the pack hadn't been clawed open but untied and no chaw marks, so I didn't bother believing no bear stories yet and she didn't neither.

While Millie put our bough bed back together, I clumb up the tree to get my tools and the flour and bacon and had a grand view of the gold rush down at the other end of the gully. The two lunkheads didn't seem to like the looks of Staggs and his rifle, and they stood on a brushy hump for a while and talked things over. Now and then Staggs would yell something at them, but I couldn't hear what. Finally they got their courage up and come edging along, keeping well away from the crickbank and trying to circle the long tom by going up behind the hut. But Staggs wasn't having none of that. He marched up the slope with his rifle aimed their way, and they had a palaver there for a spell, while Zack done the yelling for a change, motioning for Staggs to come on back to work.

Then three of the old loners from down on the flats come to the butt end of our stretch of gully at once (maybe they'd all been forming mining companies in the night) and stood looking things over, and Staggs switched his head from the lunkheads to the loners and back like he was trying to calculate who'd be best to shoot first. But when the three loners, all carrying big heavy packs, come trudging toward Zack, who was trying to run the long tom at both ends and the middle and pointing here and there for Badger to do things he wasn't doing, Staggs come striding down to bar the way, and the two lunkheads hurried on toward me and Millie.

I clumb down, still watching, and the three loners didn't seem ready to listen to much in the way of nonsense from Staggs, and I seen one had a revolver out in his hand. They paused for a while to talk, but nobody loosed off a shot, and just about the time they started coming our way too, the lunkheads come to the foot of our bank.

They looked pretty well wore out, both around thirty, sunk-faced and wiry, and one of them tipped his hat at Millie and says to me, "This your claim?"

"Hundred foot along and three hundred foot upslope," I says. "Hearthstone Mining Company, Watch Us Grow."

"What's up ahead?" the second one says, like we was trying to sell him homemade stock in a brass-spittoon factory.

"The Rocky Mountains," I says.

Still acting polite, the first one says, "Mind if we cross through?"

"Just wipe your boots first, boys, and don't spit on the floor," I says. I don't know what was making me act so loose-headed. Maybe I was just tired out, setting there in front of the fire, which I hadn't finished making yet, and looking at all the near-thawed dirt around me, which I hadn't washed yet and didn't seem likely to for a while.

"We don't need no permission to pass through," the second one says, sounding like he'd just thought up what to say to Staggs.

The first one smiled at him, then at me, and says, "Sometimes what the law says you don't need turns out to be what you need most." He tipped his hat at Millie again. "Maybe we'll be seeing you." And they started up around our house, skirting the high bank through the start of the woods.

Before the three loners reached us, two more men come over the hump at the foot of the gully and stood gawking, and I seen Staggs throw down his shovel and give it a kick, but he didn't bother picking up his rifle or yelling no more, maybe seeing they had a land-office business going in newcomers and he didn't want to wear hisself out greeting one and all.

None of the loners was as old as Zack, but they had that look on them: that all-weather, many-a-year, many-a-hole-in-the-ground look, and when they stopped a respectful twenty foot short of our house, one of them rubbed the gray stubble on his jawbone and smiled and says, "Still feel like singing, folks? Be glad to sing along if we had something worth singing about."

Another one of them hunkered down and run some of our dirt through his hand, which I didn't know if it was polite or not but didn't mind.

"Do what you like, as long as it's a hundred foot upstream or three hundred foot upslope," I says.

"You got a lode claim here?" the first one says, frowning and looking puzzled. "What kind of quartz is it?"

Well, he had me there, since I'd never laid eyes on it. If there *was* any.

But Millie says, "Just as rotten as it can be and still stay together, gentlemen. No stamping mill required. My husband could crush it to dust with a potato masher."

Which we didn't happen to own, but I kept still, and all three of the loners looked doubtful.

The second one, who'd picked up the dirt, brushed his hand off on his jeans and shook his head. "Wish you lots of luck with it."

"We've had more than our share of luck already, thank you," Millie says.

"Reckon we'll look a ways upstream," the first one says, and they tromped up the slope and out of sight.

By the time I got the fire going, the rain had stopped, but I straightened up the boughs on the lean-to roof anyway, and the two newcomers hustled along the crick, being helped by Staggs yelling and shaking his fist at them. They hurried up past us without a word or a by-your-leave.

When Millie begun soaking some dried apples, I says, "You may not of been lying exactly, but you got to admit to a little stretching."

"Well, if I am, it's in a good cause," she says.

"What's that?"

"Us," she says. "Mr. Bender, I'd like to ask you a favor."

"Why, sure," I says.

"If you're not too tired, I'd like you to start digging us a well."

I looked down at the crick, which was going clear and fast and already two foot wider than two days ago.

"I know the creek is convenient," she says. "But those men will be camping upstream and probably washing for gold, and more will be coming along. Don't you think we should be prepared? This might be our home all summer."

I seen what she meant, and I also seen a lone old man come to the hump at the foot of the gully and stand there hunched under a big pack and Staggs running after him with a shovel and chasing him back. But Staggs couldn't do that with everybody, as seven men had already proved

—or nine if you wanted to add in me and Millie—so I says, "Where do you reckon I should dig?"

"Anywhere," she says. "It doesn't matter." She seemed pleased and excited, and I emptied out my wheelborrow and hauled it up the slope with my pickax and shovel, then turned onto the steep, bare gullyside where it washed down to the sheer crickbank. She followed me and begun moving slow to keep from slipping and sliding, while the dirt and gravel changed color underfoot from light brown to dark brown to gray and back again and all of it darker than before from being soaked by the rain.

"Wouldn't you prefer some easier place?" she says.

I had to be careful to keep my wheelborrow from tipping over, and I says, "I'm following that lesson you give me a while back. I asked myself, 'Where's the worst place to dig a well and where's the hardest, unlikeliest place to dig a mine? Someplace where nobody's been hunting water nor gold yet, and when I put the two together, I come up with this here."

She looked a little vexed with me, but didn't make no fuss and pretty soon went back down the hump and left me to it.

First off, I had to dig and scrape myself a level platform the size of my tripod so's it wouldn't tilt over later when I commenced using the tub and windlass to haul up the dirt. Then I scratched out a three-and-a-half-foot square and started limbering up my pickax muscles. Though I don't much like sodbusting, I like digging holes. Turning grass under seems mean-spirited, but with a hole you're actually looking for something and making something. It's like building a tower, only you're emptying it out instead of stacking it up.

After I got down a couple foot, I struck a layer still half-froze, but it was only a little over a foot thick, and I got through it when I was about chest-deep. I had filled up the tub of my wheelborrow along the way, since I didn't reckon nobody had tried panning any of this from up here, but I had to shovel most of the loose dirt onto the slope, where it begun sideslipping down and into the crick about forty foot below. I was just getting the hang of it and getting the rhythm going and enjoying the red streaks in the sky when I heard Millie calling me.

I clumb out and seen her halfway up from the house, and she says, "Some more men have come, and Mr. Staggs is yelling for you."

I packed up my gear and pushed the wheelborrow full of dirt real careful along the slope till I was past the danger of sliding and followed her back to the fire. "Maybe I should tell them I'm going to work Kit's share," I says.

"I don't wish to contradict you, Mr. Bender, but I don't think it would be a good idea to give Mr. Staggs too many things to be angry about at the same time. Perhaps you should wait a while."

The light was going bad, but I could see five people down by the long tom, two of them on horseback, and Staggs yelling, "Bender!" about every ten seconds, so I started off that way, just to keep the peace, though I didn't much like being hollered for like a dog, and Millie trailed along.

When I come close enough, I seen one of them on horseback was the big man from Wootton's wearing a floppy-brimmed black hat, and the other was a middle-sized paunchy man that looked like the storekeep, only fattened up some for auction, and he had on a dark wool cap with ear flaps. He glanced at the big man, who nodded, and then he says, "Mr. Bender?"

"Yes, sir," I says.

From over by the long tom, Staggs says, "What the hell did you do, Bender, walk up and down Cherry Crick with a sign and a bass drum? You got every old plow chaser in the Territory stomping through here."

"My name's Bert Wootton," the paunchy man says. "I

believe you already met my brother and Mr. Smith here."
Both of them had rifles in saddle scabbards and bedrolls
tied on behind.

Zack, who was shoveling tailings out of the perforated
iron end of the long tom, paused long enough to yell at
Badger leaning on his shovel halfway along the line of
sluice boxes, "Goddamn it, keep using that banjo, excuse
me, ma'am, we got about as much daylight left as you got
brains."

Badger scooped some gravel and dirt out of the start of
a trench and slung it into the sluice box, where the water
was running.

"This here's my wife," I says, since it was mostly Millie's
chickens coming home to roost, and maybe she'd know
what to feed them.

"How do you do, ma'am," Wootton says, giving his cap a
twitch.

"Why, I'm doing just fine, Mr. Wootton," she says. "I am
enjoying the wonders of mountain air, far away from the
noxious vapors of the town."

That seemed to set him back a bit, but he says, "Well, I
don't believe they're as noxious as all that. With proper
management, Denver City has a great future."

"I believe my husband and I have a great future too,"
she says, looking about as happy as a girl can look at sundown by a mountain crick.

"With proper management," Wootton says, leaning sideways and forward in the saddle and squinching his eyes
kind of eager.

"How was things down in town, Bender?" Staggs says.
He was pickaxing to loosen dirt for Badger but didn't
seem in no hurry about it. "We sort of thought you might
head on back to Nebraska and put us out of our misery."

"Why, we thought you must of been under that miscal-
culation," I says. "Because you went clawing through our
house to make sure we hadn't forgot nothing."

He grinned and sucked his front teeth. "House? What house? I seen a heap of brush up there, but no house."

"I wonder if I could have a word with you in private, Mr. Bender, Miz Bender?" Wootton says.

And I don't know why I done what I done right then. Maybe it was because I didn't know what to say to no president of a bank in public or private and I wanted to get another skillet on the stove, but I says, "Kit's back."

"What?" Staggs says. "Where?"

The long-tomming come to a halt except for the water running through, and Zack says, "Where's he at?"

"Why didn't you say nothing before?" Staggs says, coming toward me with the pickax like he meant to dig the news out of me.

"Mr. Bender," Millie says, coaxing. "Mr. Wootton wishes to—"

But I was too busy keeping track of that pickax, standing there barehanded, and I says, "He's down in Denver City with most of his fingers and toes froze off."

"Oh, Christ on a crutch," Zack says.

"What did I tell you?" Staggs says, his face lighting up and looking almost happy. "What did I say about that damn fool?"

"It's going to be dark pretty soon, Mr. Bender," Wootton says. "And I'd like to use what light there is."

"Please, Mr. Bender," Millie says.

But I felt like taking things one at a time. Aiming it mostly at Zack, I says, "Kit wants me to work his share of the claim so's he won't lose it, and I'm willing."

Zack says, "Well, I spose we—"

"I didn't see you out here on this long tom today," Staggs says. "I didn't see but three pardners out here busting their back."

"I had some chores to do like putting our house back together and doing some digging of my own, and I wanted to think it over," I says.

"I reckon we'll just think it over too," Staggs says.

Zack says, "Aw, come on, now. We can—"

"We'll think it over a couple days till we figure out what our shares is worth," Staggs says. "If Kit wants something special, he can crawl up here and ask for it. We vote our shares here, and Badger votes the way I do, don't you, Badger?"

"Yep," Badger says, looking big Mr. Smith over like they might of been built by the same carpenter and had ought to compare roofbeams and rafters.

"Toes *and* fingers?" Zack says, looking pained.

"I'm sure your time is valuable, Mr. Bender," Wootton says. "I know mine is. There are fortunes being made in real estate and trade goods and—"

"He said he got a hundred and eighty-five dollars in shot gold to keep him till he heals up," I says. "So if you'll just let me do some shoveling for—"

"The hell he did," Staggs says. "He couldn't find no gold if you set him down on a sack full of it and kicked it open."

"Mr. Bender, opportunity knocks but once," Millie says.

Wootton coughed and says, "Well, I don't mind knocking two or three times, but—"

"What are you good for besides keeping the wind off?" Badger says to Mr. Smith.

"Why, I make sinners see the light," Mr. Smith says, not looking extra worried.

"Now, Mr. Smith," Wootton says.

"Kit knows the rules," Staggs says. "How's he ever going to wash any of this without no fingers and toes I'd like to know. What's he going to do, stick a pick handle up his ass and plow his share loose? Who's going to hold his shovel for him?"

"I am," I says.

"Where's that light at?" Badger says. "I'd sure admire to see it."

"You ain't a big enough sinner yet," Mr. Smith says.

"Well, you won't work an inch of this company unless we say you can," Staggs says. "If Kit don't show up by the time we pan that first riffle box and cut shares, then I say Kit and his whole caboodle can just go to hell, and that goes for his baby brother too."

Zack tipped his hat back and leaned on his shovel. "Mind if I have a little say in this, being discoverer of this goddamn unexcavated gravel pit?"

"I hate to intrude in a domestic quarrel," Wootton says.

"Then why don't you put your nose back on your face?" Staggs says.

"Now, you don't want to qualify as a sinner, do you?" Mr. Smith says. "You keep a civil tongue in your head when you talk to President Wootton."

"What the hell is he president of?" Staggs says. "You starting up a new country down there so's you can skin everybody legal?"

"Mr. Bender, I won't take much of your time," Wootton says.

"Please," Millie says.

"I have been a square-dealer all my life, and I ain't about to change now," Zack says, looking hard and straight at Staggs. "If one of my pardners is crippled up, he don't stop being my pardner."

"You do anything you want with your share," Staggs says. "Just don't try doing nothing with mine."

"I asked you where that light was at," Badger says.

Mr. Smith leaned a little sideways in the saddle and says, "It's way deep down inside that thick skull of yours, but it wouldn't take but one crack to let it out."

"Now, now," Wootton says, like a Sunday-school teacher who just seen his first spitball.

Millie took my arm, smiling and happy-seeming but actually tugging at me pretty strong, and I says to Zack, "I wouldn't want my brother to get cheated."

"He won't," Zack says.

"He already done all the cheating hisself," Staggs says. "Why'd he go pirooting around up in the snow, in some of the roughest country God ever coughed up, when he was sposed to be down here knocking sluice boxes together?"

"Same reason you was off hunting mountain sheep," Zack says.

Millie finally hauled me off, and Wootton stayed on his little filly and walked her along the crick past the end of the sluice, and Mr. Smith followed sort of reluctant, turning to look back at Badger a couple times. My head felt full of two or three kinds of commotion, and it was getting so dim we could hardly make out our house from the trees.

Wootton says, "Let's see now, your claim—"

"Number Five Upstream," Mr. Smith says, standing up in his stirrups and peering ahead. "About where the bank starts sheering off."

"We'd be delighted to show you around our country seat," Millie says, "but I'm afraid we'd have to do it by torchlight."

"It can wait," Wootton says, glancing back toward Staggs, who was yelling something at Zack. "You've got a mighty loud neighbor."

"One can't have everything in the wilderness," Millie says. "Though Our Savior was made a very good offer in just such a territory, I understand."

Wootton grunted. "I'm not about to be Satan, Miz Bender. Nor am I prepared to offer anyone the Kingdoms of This World. On the other hand—"

"Why, we already have our kingdom," she says. "Don't we, Mr. Bender?"

I hadn't much liked the general goings-on in the last fifteen minutes, since arguing and confusion and yelling turns me shy till I feel like soaking my head in a tub of vinegar water and calling it a day. But I could tell Millie was setting us up for some kind of big moment, and I didn't want to disappoint her none. She'd come all this way afoot and been a mainstay and a blessing, and if she wanted to play pish-tosh and how-do-you-do, she was welcome to the pleasure. "That's what it feels like to me," I says.

"Well, it takes a little extra effort to run a kingdom," Wootton says. "There's always others wants to be king too. 'Uneasy lies the head that wears the crown,' I believe the saying goes."

"My crown feels just fine," Millie says, smiling and serene in the twilight. "Doesn't yours, Mr. Bender?"

"I reckon so," I says.

"I'll be brief and to the point," Wootton says, having to raise his voice over another stretch of yelling with Zack trying to top off Staggs. "The early stages of a gold strike are crucial to the future welfare of them that finds it. They need protection, physical and legal. There comes a time when the news can't be sat on any more, and then it's up to them to be quick enough and smart enough for management and development and investment."

"You are speaking to the co-owners of the Hearthstone Mining Company," Millie says.

"You can write something like that down on paper," Wootton says. "But somebody could just come along and scratch it off. It don't put anything in the bank for you."

"What's the name of your bank?" I says.

Wootton shuffled his rear end around in the saddle, and if he'd of been in a swivel chair, he'd of leant back and put his feet up on something. "The First Bank of Denver City," he says, rolling it around a little.

"Where's it at besides on paper?" I says.

"We have a temporary, purely temporary, building right in the heart of town, front made out of the finest kiln-dried pine and—"

"What's the back made out of?" I says.

His mouth flattened out. "We plan a two-story structure with hardwood floors, and as soon as the marble quarry gets going over in—"

"It sounds quite respectable," Millie says, locking her arm in mine and giving it a squeeze.

"It *is* respectable," Wootton says. "I was about to say it is extremely unwise to keep large amounts—even *fairly* large amounts—of negotiable currency, such as gold, for instance, on one's person, in town or out, during this unsettled period. Lynch law hasn't stopped the thieving that goes on."

I says, "If you're so short of business, you come all the way up here and—"

"We appreciate your advice, Mr. Wootton," Millie says, clamping my arm.

He leant our way, as solemn as a preacher getting ready to drop the first handful on the Dear Departed. "Buy real estate down in Denver City," he says. "Don't let your money sit idle and vulnerable. Get yourself an estate going. Why, if I was a young couple and had me two thousand dollars in gold—" He left off, and his eyes flicked back and forth from Millie's to mine, trying to read us. "Approximately. If I had that much, why, I'd be a very rich man next year."

"What would you be this year?" I says.

"I'd be a very lucky young couple," Wootton says.

"Well, soon's we find two thousand dollars' worth of anything, we may look you up," I says. "And then again—" But Millie clamped my arm, so I hushed.

"Mr. Bender, my brother saw your gold and even got its approximate weight," Wootton says. "Inadvertently. He's a shrewd and successful merchant, and not much gets past him."

"We don't have no gold," I says. "Least, not to speak of," remembering our two cents of muck in the tin can and at the same time remembering how the storekeep had put our crock on the scales.

Wootton twiddled his fingers. "Whatever you say. But this is what I propose. With your leave, Mr. Smith and I will camp here tonight, and tomorrow when the light's good we'll give your claim a look, and if the signs are as good as I suspicion they are, then I'll be prepared to offer an advantageous business arrangement through my bank."

I opened my mouth but never found out what would of come out of it, if anything, because Millie says, "We have heard every word you said, Mr. Wootton. We shall discuss those words in the privacy of our home, and meanwhile I agree with Mr. Bender, the less said the better."

So I stayed agreeable for the time being, and Wootton says, "Excellent," and when him and Mr. Smith had used the last light to tether their horses up behind our house and some of our kindling to get their own fire going and had bedded theirselves down near the crick, me and Millie et some supper and laid down under our blankets on the soft pine boughs, and I says, "We may not be telling no lies, but we're sure acting some out."

In a high, excited voice, Millie says, "Yes, and isn't it just wonderful and romantic and instructive?"

"Well, I hadn't noticed that part yet," I says. "What am I sposed to do in the morning? We can't sell him no quicksilver like it was gold at twenty dollars an ounce."

"Mr. Bender, my only love," she says, which is a sweet kind of music to go to sleep by, better than any song, "you are supposed to go right on doing exactly what you've been doing. Get up before dawn and dig some more on our well, as much as you can." Then after a long pause while I thought it over, she says, "Without endangering your health."

Chapter Twenty ★★★★★★★★★★★★★★

☞ Millie fixed me some bacon and bread and apples before first light, and we kept quiet so's not to stir up Wootton and Mr. Smith, and then she showed me where she wanted me to dump my wheelborrow load of dirt and gravel right below our hearthstone, and I started off up the slope.

But something made me hang back a little because I suspicioned she might be going to try some gold panning herself to see if she could do it better than me, but when I stopped among the pine trees and looked back through the greeny-blue light, I seen her take Blue Bird's pouch of rocks out of her reticule and sprinkle it over the heap of dirt like a salt shaker. And then I knew she had in mind fooling Wootton and Mr. Smith, and I felt embarrassed and uneasy and didn't know what to do right off.

While I was standing there doing nothing and trying to figure out the rights and wrongs of it and peering around at the cold morning, there was Mr. Blue looking mighty pleased with hisself, getting above his station by mounting up on Wootton's filly and violating her privacy as best he could without fetching something extra to stand on. I didn't think it was any too polite of him to catch her tethered like that while he was loose to rove, but truth to tell, she didn't seem to be minding too much, though this didn't look like it was starting out to be any too good a morning for Wootton. I left Mr. Blue at it and wove my way up the hump and along the slant, making sure I had enough purchase with each step, and stopped at the leveled-off rim around our well hole, spit on my hands, and got down to business to keep my mind from straying off.

There's no mystery about when you've got to switch from simple digging and heaving up and out by the shovelful to using the bucket and windlass: when you don't have enough room to swing the shovel high enough and hard enough to keep half of what was in it from landing on your head and shoulders and down your neck, you have come to the Great Divide. It took me an hour, while the sky turned raw blue and paled itself up, before I was in over my head and had to climb out and set up my tripod and thread the rope through the two holes I'd drilled in the sides of the tub with Mr. Slaughter's brace and bit far away and long ago and tie it on my crank and lower away.

Then I clumb down beside the tub (there wasn't but a foot and a half of room beside it, so after that I tied the rope off short so's the tub hung up off the bottom of the hole and I could dig under it too) and filled it up and clumb out and wound it up and dumped it and watched the load go sliding down the gullyside and over the bank and into the crick. It worked, and I felt proud. But after you've worked your tub like that nineteen or twenty times and a few to grow on, you don't feel so much proud as tired. So I took a rest with my feet hanging down in the hole, which had got deep enough now to be worth not falling into, and took a look at the day.

I could see Zack down at the foot of our gulch, doing

something or other to the long tom with a hammer and Staggs standing by, no doubt giving him important advice, and I also seen that Wootton and Mr. Smith wasn't sleeping no more, but our trees shut out the view and I couldn't tell where they'd went. Millie had something up her sleeve besides her funnybone, but I didn't see how nobody who had the least notion what he was looking at could mistake what I was digging for a gold mine. The dirt had changed color a couple times, but most dirt does that, as I had found out during my days of practice back home, so it didn't surprise me none when some of my tubfuls come up taffy-colored and some coffee-colored and some like crunched-up gray slate. Wootton had just had a long-distance joke played on him by his storekeep brother with Millie's help, and now he was going to come up here to my hole and take one sour look at it this morning and finish off the joke and go on back down to Denver City and try to get even.

And maybe Kit had played the same kind of joke on me, getting me to come all this way and snort after gold and wind up working for him for wages. But I couldn't say I wasn't happy. I *was*, except for having walked off and left him at that hotel the way he was feeling and acting and talking. Didn't seem brotherly, and I was going to have to help Zack change Staggs's mind. Or change his mouth, which was about the same thing.

I was just taking one last noseful of air and one last pull at the water in my canteen when Wootton and Mr. Smith come up over the hump and stood there teetery and gimp-legged like you have to do on a steep slope. They made me feel shy and sorry because I didn't know whether they'd seen Millie's salted dirt pile yet nor what I'd say if she'd got them believing in our mine.

They was about thirty foot off, and Wootton says, "Is *that* it?" looking over my rig and the mess of dirt and crushed rock that had spilled down the side into the crick, making half a dam and backing the water up in a pool.

He didn't seem too impressed nor sure-footed neither, taking hold of Mr. Smith's arm like an old lady getting down off of a boardwalk while he shifted his boots and squinted. "You been taking paydirt out of *that?*" he says.

"No, sir," I says. "I'm digging a well."

He'd had both his ear flaps pulled down, and now he lifted them up like he wanted to make sure he wasn't hearing things. "I didn't come up here to be made a fool of," he says, which showed he was a little behind the times. "Where's the real mine?"

"If you find another hole around here, it's none of mine," I says.

Mr. Smith whispered something to him and pointed partway down the gullyside where my dumpings had left a trail, each new one sliding down over the one before, and they stared and squinted, and Wootton took a couple of baby steps forward and stopped, throwing out one hand for balance. "What kind of rock you been hauling out of there?" he says.

"All kind," I says.

"Well, bring a handful of that gray stuff over here," he says.

I don't like being told to fetch and carry except by them I'm obliged to, but I felt kind of embarrassed about Wootton, who had goose-chased hisself a day's journey and wasn't going to get no more out of it than a blue-roan mule next winter, and between the two feelings I got stubborn. "If you want to look at it, either come on over yourself or fall down in the crick and have a look there, because that's where the rest of it went," I says.

"If we're going to be partners, I'll expect a little more cooperation than that," he says.

"I don't expect I'll belong to no bank for a while yet," I says.

"Bender, it isn't the first time a woman's had most of the brains in a family," he says. "No use being resentful about it."

"Maybe Mr. Bender needs to be shown the light," Mr. Smith says. "He's starting to sound like a sinner to me."

"Now, now," Wootton says.

"I already seen the light," I says, standing up and dumping out the tubful I'd hauled up before taking my rest and watching the gray crumbly stuff sort of like cinders go rolling down the gully.

Instead of sassing back, Mr. Smith says something low and fast to Wootton, and they both come slipshodding along toward me and my tripod, Wootton acting excited and holding both arms out like a kid walking a fence rail. "Jesus Christ, Bender, if you're doing what I think you're doing," he says, "if you're—" and his left boot slipped too far to catch up with except by tipping over sideways after it, which he naturally didn't feel like doing, so instead he swiveled and set down hard and commenced sliding downhill like one of my tub loads, yelling and gathering speed and raking his arms out and trying to dig his heels in, and when he hit the crickbank, he had a little landslide going with him and took a big chunk of the bank into the water with him just a bit downstream of my homemade dam and seemed to take a good jolt, though there wasn't no rocks big enough to hurt his head on.

Wootton laid there two thirds in the crick, except after a few seconds there wasn't no crick downstream of him but had drained off below the dirt and gravel he'd added to mine, which had turned into a dam that was going to take a little time to wash away.

"Don't try to climb back up, Mr. Wootton," I says. "You can walk out on dry land if you just go down the crick."

From about forty foot down below, he says, "I sprained my goddamn ankle."

"Don't move, Mr. Wootton," Mr. Smith says, balancing hisself backwards onto safer ground. "I'll come and fetch you." And he run off.

"Ow, ow, ow, ow, ow," Wootton says, clutching his ankle and trying to get his cap back on, the ear flaps sticking out, and the water pooling upstream and around a bend where I couldn't see.

In a few more seconds I heard Staggs commence yelling in the distance, which meant the Collywobble Mining Company was disenjoying trying to sluice without no water, and I couldn't blame him for a change. When I heard the yelling coming closer in a hurry, I lowered my tub back in the hole and got ready to go back to my digging because I didn't fancy dealing with Staggs when he had a genuine grievance to spur him.

And he come slopping right up the crickbed in and out of the pools that was left over, and he beat Mr. Smith to the scene of the commotion and says, "What the living hell is going on, you lard-assed sonofabunch, quit blocking this crick, ain't you never heard of riparian rights?"

"I sprained my ankle," Wootton says, still clutching on to it.

Holding his shovel like an ax, Staggs says, "I'll sprain your goddamn skullbone for you if you shut off our water one more minute."

I clumb partway down into the hole, but couldn't help keeping my head out to see the goings-on because Mr. Smith was coming along now behind Staggs.

And then Staggs seen my slide and the hump of dirt in the crick, which was mostly mine, and his eyes went back and forth from the rig to me, to the crick, and he says, "Bender," and he had time to shake his head once or twice before Mr. Smith spun him around and give him a clout on the side of the jaw that laid him down on the crick bottom next to Wootton and up against the heap of dirt that was starting to trickle over now as the water had rose far enough. He set there, still hanging on to the shovel, and looked like he was trying to think things out or maybe getting a good look at that light Mr. Smith kept talking about.

"Get me out of here," Wootton says, and Mr. Smith heisted him up on his shoulder, then stooped and used his free hand to go plucking among the gravel till he had a handful of them gray cinder chunks I'd dumped last, all about the size of marbles.

"Come on, ouch," Wootton says, and Mr. Smith straightened up and started down the crick just in time to turn Staggs's hefty swipe with his shovel into a glancing blow about knee-high instead of right on the side of the head, where it had been aimed at. Apparently Mr. Smith figured he'd ignore a little sin like that or maybe settle up later when he had something firmer to swing than Wootton, because he just kept on going.

Staggs got to his feet sort of wobbly and blinking and took a few steps after Mr. Smith, then recollected hisself and turned back and sank his shovel into the dirt blocking the narrow space between the cutbank and the clift on the other side, but before he took another shovelful out, he stood blinking some more, then stooped and grabbed up a couple of them chunks like Mr. Smith, and I didn't take to them doing all this prospectoring on my claim, so I yells, "We ain't hiring any help, so go work your own claim."

He looked up a second, his face blank, and that was about how long it took for the crick to breach the dirt, starting off with a wedge like water coming out of a pump and then whooshing the whole mess aside, and Staggs went staggering backwards in fast water over his knees and got turned around to head for home, using the shovel on the crick bottom to brace hisself.

And the water hit Mr. Smith from behind when he was on a stonier, slipperier patch near the end of the steep bank, but it didn't hurt him much when his boots went out from under him because he had Wootton for padding. Mr.

Smith scrambled up, both of them soaking, before Staggs could catch up and show him a little light with his shovel.

Since they was all so interested in that gray crumbly stone, I picked up a pocketful for myself from around the edge of the hole and took the loose prop out of the tripod so's nobody else could use it and left the rest of the gray layer where it was till I could find out what I'd struck, then started slow and careful back to our house, where it turned out me and Millie was likely to be rich, which wasn't no surprise to us because we'd been telling each other that for many a day.

Chapter Twenty-One ★ ★ ★ ★ ★ ★ ★ ★ ★

☞ First off, it didn't seem like being rich but being let out of church on a sunshiny day: everybody acted like they wanted to do all the talking after a dry spell of having to set up straight and keep still. When I got back to our house, Wootton was sprawled out by the fire, still hanging on to his ankle and trying not to listen to Mr. Smith, who was muttering low and fast in his ear, and Wootton was clutching Millie's skirt and talking a mile a minute at her when he could hear hisself think.

Millie tugged loose and kept inspecting a handful of them gray rocks which Mr. Smith didn't look any too happy to part with, but was asking for back when he could spare the time from telling Wootton all about it, which Wootton wasn't listening to. Millie was smiling, but not much more'n usual, and when she seen me coming, she waited nice and polite amongst all that gabble and says, "I understand you've made a discovery, Mr. Bender."

Wootton was saying, "—assuming of course the assay turns out as good as it looks and the lead don't taper off to nothing right off, the important thing is getting enough capital to set up the most efficient equipment, once we've got a good estimate of the—"

I handed her over my pieces of gray rock, and I says, "Don't seem like it should be that easy," but feeling mighty glad I'd spared her telling a lie.

"—just as soon as you can get it down in black and white, the coordinates of the claim checked by plumbline and transit, by God, and not just a hunk of rope, just in case there's any—ouch, Mr. Smith, damn it, watch what you're doing," Wootton says.

Millie took off her green wool cap and dropped some of the rocks in gently, like she was collecting little eggs, and says, "Let's go show Mr. Orfrey. I trust his judgment."

"Fine," I says, and we started off.

"Wait a minute," Wootton says, raising his voice. "We got to get this settled here, at least in a gentleman's agreement, before we can turn a lawyer loose on it."

"Just rest that ankle now," Millie says over her shoulder. "Go soak it in the creek."

"I already soaked it in the creek," Wootton says, commencing to yell as loud as Staggs. "Just hold your horses."

But we kept on going like as if it was a Sunday stroll and we was heading off to see if any of the cows had calved yet. Up ahead, I seen Staggs holding out both hands for Zack to look into. The crick was flowing full speed again, but Zack had took the riffle box out from under the end of the long tom and was down on his knees, panning what he'd scraped and swept out of it. I didn't feel much excited yet, just kind of vigorated and dirty from all that digging, and Staggs and Badger didn't look excited neither, but mad.

We heard horses behind us, and Mr. Smith and Wootton, with only one boot in his stirrups, caught up with us before we come to the long tom, and Wootton says, "You have to reckon on the mass of people that's going to be up here in a matter of days. Even with more melt-off, that creek's going to be drier than an Irishman's throat from all the sluicing bound to go on upstream, and you'll need *protection* and a friend in court, and now's the time to—"

Zack had took a good long look and a feel of what Staggs showed him (which I now seen was some more of our gray rocks), and he had stayed down on his hunkers, holding his pan half full of water and dark sand, without no change in his face, and when Millie stooped and held out her cap to him and says, "Would you kindly offer us an opinion of this rock or ore or whatever it is, Mr. Orfrey?" he took another good long look without showing nothing, and finally Millie says, "We would be glad to pay a professional assayer's fee for your opinion, however informal."

Wootton and Mr. Smith had both shut up for a change, and in a quiet, serious voice Zack says to me, "Where'd that float come from, boy?"

"Up on the steep part of the gullyside," I says.

"Just laying on the ground?"

"I was digging a hole," I says. "This was down about seven foot."

Zack looked from her cap to her palm and took a little feel and pinch at each, then run his finger through the pieces in the cap. "That right?" he says. "It's all together in a lead?"

"Yes, sir."

"How thick?"

"About two foot. I just now got through the bottom of it."

"Which way's it heading?"

"Northeast and southwest, I think." I tried to recollect for sure. "Yes."

"And it just come out like this with a pick and shovel?"

"Yes, sir."

He picked up a piece and pinched it and wetted it in the crick and licked it like a piece of candy and says slow and thoughtful, "Well, I would reckon it at between two hundred and fifty and three hundred dollars a ton."

"Well, I'll be an owl-headed, whittle-whanging, goddamn yannigan bag," Staggs says.

Wootton says to Mr. Smith, talking fast, "Move, right now, get Murphy on it, I want them papers ready and waiting, don't tell nobody else."

Mr. Smith nodded, reached down for a handful of the gray rocks, and trotted off toward the foot of the gully, looking too big for his horse.

Standing up slow and squirming a little to get the pinch out of his back, Zack says, "And do you know what you done, boy?"

"No," I says.

"He jumped my claim is what he done," Staggs says. "I had my stakes in down there long before he ever showed up, and I can point right to the very—"

"I don't believe you better try any of that with my partners," Wootton says. "Mr. and Miz Bender's interests and mine follow identical lines."

"You have struck it baggedy-ass rich," Zack says, getting a big goofy grin on his face that showed up through the hair. "A lead like that might go on for a hundred yards or it might go a mile, so you won't escape under twenty thousand dollars and maybe ten times that if you're unlucky. Or *worse*." He went into a stoop with his hands on his knees. "So let's hear you holler."

"You mean it's true?" I says, feeling uncomfortable.

"What am I telling you?" Zack says, watching like he was waiting for a show to commence.

"And I can just let it rip?" I says.

"Might's well whoop it up now so's it won't spoil your supper," Zack says.

"And that's really gold up there down that hole?" I says.

"It is unless you hauled a tubful in from someplace else, and if you did, I'd like to know where," Zack says.

"Is that what it looks like?" I says, still not feeling it yet.

"Sometimes," Zack says. "It looks like a whole lot of things."

They all stood there staring at me and waiting, and I says, "And I can just let her rip for sure?"

"Don't see why not," Zack says, turning to Millie. "Do you?"

"No, sir," she says.

"Yippee," I says, not making too good a show of it.

"Well, I'll be the busted end of a bull's pizzle," Staggs says, slamming his shovel down on the crickbank and busting it off short so's he had what looked like a piece of kindling left over.

"Well, now, you'd best size it up louder than that," Zack says.

"Yippee!" Millie says, not quite hitting high C but making a run at it from underneath.

"Let 'er buck!" Zack yells, swooping his hat around and jumping both feet off the ground.

Wootton's filly shied off and didn't look like she cared any too much for the commotion, and Wootton says, "Now let's be practical."

"Yippee!" I says, hitting it pretty good, through not up to Staggs for distance.

Zack done a little bowlegged buck and wing, and Millie clapped her hands for him and hopped, and I done a bit of the Chicken Reel but couldn't keep it up without no music, and Badger and Staggs stood there looking gray-faced and down in the mouth like they'd just heard the still broke down.

"Zack, you old fart-knocker, what're you getting fired up about?" Staggs says. "It ain't no lode of yours."

"Excuse me, ma'am, it's the principle of the thing," Zack says, flapping his long gray hair around and showing his gray teeth all the way back. "Got to celebrate while you can. I was damn *near* right, wasn't I?"

"Only missed it by a couple hundred foot," Staggs says. "And the wrong kind of gold."

Still going from heel to toe, Zack says, "How do you know we missed? Could be pockets all along here. We just have to go on digging unless we're all going to bust our shovels and head for the saloon."

"Hold it!" Wootton says, sounding like a bank president for the first time, and everybody kept still and watched two raggedy, stubble-faced men come hesitating over the hump at the foot of the gulch and start circling shyly to get by us, nodding and touching their hat and acting uneasy because we all stared quiet while they went on up the slope past our house and into the woods and out of sight upstream.

"There'll be more and more of that," Wootton says. "More every day whether the word leaks out or not. The weather's broke and there's a mob on the prowl through all these hills. Won't be an inch unclaimed by June. So let's sober up here and figure out what we're going to do."

"Mister, I'm so goddamn sober I can't see straight," Staggs says.

"Yippee!" I yells, getting it full blast this time.

"Hush now, hush up," Wootton says.

But it all begun to dawn on me: I had struck it, and if I felt like getting a new pair of boots and a shirt, why, all's I had to do was just march right in the store, if I could find one someplace, and say, "I want them boots and that shirt," and they'd have to give them to me. A fact like that turns a man's head. So I says to Millie, "What do you want to do first?"

"Now listen to me," Wootton says, getting his filly edged in close. "Slab Creek's going to be full of stampeders in no time at all, and we have to make plans."

"Go on, make your own plans," Staggs says. "What the hell do you know besides how to fall in a crick?"

Paying him no mind, Wootton leant over at Zack. "Mr. Orfrey, my brother tells me he grubstaked you."

"That's right," Zack says. "And damn poor stuff it was too."

"Well, anyway, perhaps you wouldn't mind telling me what the Collywobble Mining Company's prospects happen to be?"

Zack touched the riffle box with his boot and picked up his pan like he'd almost forgot about it and shrugged and says, "I don't have it all panned out yet, but with steady work and maybe the borry of a pound of quicksilver—" He give me a wink.

"I'd be proud to oblige," I says.

"—and the split going four ways and the water still coming like this and if we don't happen to hit no extra-rich pockets, which looks to be possible with that much float nearby but can't count on it, why, I'd say we could clear three or four dollars a day each all summer."

"Is that all?" Staggs says, looking sick.

"When'd you last scratch more'n that out of the ground?" Zack says.

"I didn't freeze my ass all winter just to make three dollars a day," Staggs says.

"What would you say to a guarantee of double that for six months?" Wootton says. "Subject to the approval of Mr. and Miz Bender."

"I believe I see the way your thoughts are tending, Mr. Wootton," Millie says. "And I believe Mr. Bender and I, if you'll give us a moment to confer, would be prepared to make that a bit more for each shareholder as long as he's working."

She walked me off a little ways and says, "Would eight be all right?"

And I says, "Make it twelve," which was our first official conference as rich folks, and we come back and nodded, and I says, "All right, make it twelve."

Wootton scowled, then shrugged, and says to Zack, "Twelve. And we're going to be bringing equipment in here and a stamp mill, probably, because Mr. Smith tells me no float can stay that soft for long."

"And he happens to be right," Zack says.

"And we need the good will of the Collywobble because we're probably going to crowd you out and wash you out and don't want to get sued. We'll share any and all facilities and take it on as a subsidiary of the Hearthstone Mining Company, with all placer gold going to Collywobble shareholders and all lode gold going to the Hearthstone. What do you say to that?"

"Done," Staggs says, looking a little happier. "For twelve dollars a day."

"Done," Badger says.

"Well, I spose it's got to be done," Zack says.

"And done again," Wootton says.

"What I'd like to know is how *you* come to figure so prominent in all this," I says to Wootton. "I didn't notice your name on the claim."

"Now, Mr. Bender," Millie says.

"Where's your capital?" Wootton says.

"Where's yours?" I says.

"Where's your legal and physical protection?" Wootton says.

Which was too many for me, so I says, "I don't know."

"Mr. Smith's on his way down to town right now to work with the only sober lawyer in fifty miles, and he'll have a limited partnership back up here for these three gents to sign by noon tomorrow," Wootton says. "He's a notary and he's my agent and he's nobody's fool."

"Well, around here, if he ain't nailed down, he must be somebody's," Zack says.

Wootton brushed the idea aside with one hand and says, "And he'll set up camp here to help oversee the proper expansion of our investment, and the fact these here adjacent claimholders will have a company interest in keeping off thieves and jumpers will let you lay your head down next to your sweet wife's and sleep like a baby."

"Well, it's none of your business, but I been doing that anyway," I says.

"Times have changed," Wootton says. "There may be a fortune at stake."

Millie says, "Now we need to know what your share will be in all this, Mr. Wootton. Precisely and in writing."

"All income is to be deposited in the First Bank of Denver City," Wootton says.

"You don't catch me putting no money of mine in no bank," Staggs says.

"Me neither," Badger says.

And the two of them stood there looking like a couple of critters excaped from an animal show, the bearskin and deerskin half-soaked and caked with dirt, and Wootton looked them over and says, "Your draw against your guarantee up to twelve dollars a day per man will be exempt, but placer money above that goes in."

Zack had come over close to me, still with a piece of smile coming through his beard, and says, "How do you like it, boy? The hard part's digging out from under the Woottons once you strike it."

"It don't sound like much fun," I says.

Zack give a high, laughing kind of snort. "For a country boy, you put your finger on the Queen of Spades in a hurry."

"What else?" Millie says to Wootton.

"My bank will be content with a ten percent agent's fee out of net profits and a commission to purchase all necessary equipment on credit against the company's account," Wootton says.

"At cost," Millie says.

"You can buy me a new shovel while you're at it," Staggs says.

Looking annoyed, Wootton says, "All right, at cost." Then his plump face brightened up a little. "But costs are running mighty high these days."

"And how much interest were you planning to pay these two companies for the deposit of their gold?" Millie says sweetly.

Wootton looked uncomfortable and squinched over sideways in his saddle so's he could rub his ankle. "Well, I hadn't figured on—I mean, I had figured on offering that gold a safe home, which by the way hasn't even had a chemical assay yet and might turn out to run a good deal under what an old prospector might say about it."

"I'd like to see a banker run a good deal under someday," Zack says. "You boys change your way of talking about as often as Badger does his long johns."

"I believe we'll have to have four percent on those deposits," Millie says, "which I am quite willing to regard as company profits subject to your agent's fee."

"I might see clear to two percent, just to sweeten it all," Wootton says.

"Do you think we might settle for three percent, Mr. Bender?" she says. "Seeing as how that lode looked so thick and rich and easy to get at?"

My mind had wandered off like Mr. Blue in a patch of brush, so when I called it back quick, it didn't come right away. I wasn't too sure what was going on and didn't care much. "Whatever seems right," I says.

"Exactly," she says, like I had put my finger on the Queen of Spades without even trying.

"All right, all right, *three*," Wootton says, reddening up a little.

Zack clapped me on the shoulder, still acting happy, and says, "You are the spit and image of a man I used to shave every morning. Why do you spose they have to drag all this kind of talk in when there's gold underfoot?"

"If there's so damn much gold underfoot, why don't we get at it 'stead of standing around like a bunch of crock-heads on the Fourth of July?" Staggs says.

"Well, that's settled," Millie says. "Mr. Bender and I will check it over when it's in print. You're welcome to spend the night, Mr. Wootton, and soak your ankle."

"No, thanks," he says. "I have a pint of whiskey, and I'll try soaking it from the other end and maybe catch up with Mr. Smith before dark. No time to waste."

"Mr. Bender and I will leave for Denver City first thing in the morning," Millie says, which was news to me.

"What for?" Wootton says, beating me to it. "Mr. Smith can bring up your papers with the others, and you can sign them right here."

Smiling as calm as a widow at her wedding, Millie says, "But we couldn't possibly enter into any agreement without first inspecting your bank and your books with our own lawyer along."

"A private word, please," Wootton says, turning his filly downstream a ways, and we followed, though I didn't see why, and he says, "Miz Bender, Mr. Bender, I have made a number of concessions in this affair, but I feel you ought to know I've about reached my limit."

"Well, when you reach it, quit," I says.

He give me a pinchy-lipped look and says, "We have a sheriff of sorts down in town, and he's no blamed good at his job of course, but he's not absolutely out of touch, now that mail wagons are getting through regular, and I think you ought to know you are wanted for questioning in a murder somewhere back between Nebraska City and Fort Kearny, and that you, Miz Bender—or am I addressing Miss Slaughter?—have been very accurately and angrily described in a circular issued by your father as a lost, strayed, or stolen minor."

I'd been half-expecting to hear something like this before long, and I hope I didn't look no more worried than Millie, which was not at all.

Wootton looked a little disappointed we hadn't broke and run, and he says, "These don't necessarily add up to serious drawbacks in a town as free and easy about people's past lives as Denver City, but I think they could fairly be called annoyances. And I wouldn't want to see either of you young folks annoyed."

"Did you kill a man, Mr. Bender?" Millie says.

"No, I didn't," I says.

"Are you fearful of prosecution or testifying or any other legal harassment?" she says.

"I am not," I says.

"And neither am I," she says. "Mr. Wootton, would you care to examine our marriage certificate? I have it right here in my reticule."

"No, thanks, Miz Bender," he says, looking flustered.

"Could you please give us the name of another bank in Denver City?" she says.

Smiling and giving up whatever he'd had in mind, Wootton says, "That won't be necessary. I respect spunk, and I know upstanding young folks when I see them. And of course *rich* young folks don't have to bother their heads about little matters like that the way poor folks do."

Millie stared at him a minute like she hadn't quite made up her mind to fire him or not, then seemed to relax and says, "Well, now that we've cleared that up, you may expect us at your bank tomorrow afternoon. With our lawyer."

"You'll have a hard time finding one sober enough to get up the front step," he says.

"I don't care whether it's an intoxicated lawyer or not," Millie says. "Surely there's some coffee in town, and I *know* there's plenty of cold water in Cherry Creek."

After a few seconds, Wootton shrugged and nodded

(which done more to make me believe he was halfway honest than anything he'd said so far), and he pulled down his ear flaps and says, "I'll be expecting you," and walked his filly off, wobbly in the saddle.

Staggs and Badger hung over Zack while he commenced panning out the rest of the scrapings from the riffle box, and I watched for a bit, then took a stroll up along the edge of the pine trees with Millie and kissed her a couple times to celebrate, feeling like them dreams where your feet move you along all right but you don't feel nothing under them. I had got myself all pried loose and ready to fling, and there didn't seem to be nothing to fling myself at.

"Mr. Bender, there's something you ought to know," she says, her nose looking pinched and her eyes not meeting mine.

"There's a hundred thousand things I ought to know," I says, but I could see she was serious, so I kept still.

"I've lost the contents of that pouch the Injun gave you."

"It don't matter," I says.

"It was gold ore—I recognized it from samples I was shown in St. Joe when I bought the quicksilver—and I was going to try to fool Mr. Wootton into buying our claim because I was greedy and anxious to help us both and wanted you to be a success and was afraid you wouldn't find any gold on your own, and I only had six dollars and fourteen cents of my mother's money left, and I was afraid you might fret and worry or even despair if we began to go hungry, and you might do something desperate or not permit me to stay."

"Well, how could you know I was going to be a fool for luck," I says, feeling all flushed up and full of gingersnaps because she'd told me.

"I hope you'll be able to put up with my character flaws," she says.

"You don't have none to speak of," I says, and if she

wasn't going to change the subject, I was. "Reckon I better start digging another well, with all them newcomers upstream."

"Do you really think so?" she says.

"And Mr. Smith coming and equipment and workers," I says. "It's going to look like a *mine*." I looked down at Zack and Staggs and Badger hunched over the riffle box. "And I hired them three at twelve dollars a day, and I haven't got but two and a half dollars to my name."

"You ought to realize we're going to lose our house, Mr. Bender," she says. "There will be a good deal of trenching and maybe even fluming and washing down, and I'm afraid we might find ourselves in the way."

We went back up to the house to have a look at it, and I knelt down and hunted through the heap of dirt below our hearthstone and managed to find about half the little rocks that had been in Blue Bird's pouch, which I now took back from Millie and dropped them in and drawed it tight and put it back around my neck to stay.

Then we enjoyed some Wedded Bliss, which is the surest way to put gold back where it come from, and when we strolled down toward the long tom later to see how our limited pardners was doing, we was just in time to see my brother Kit come up over the hump on muleback, holding the reins on his wrists and his bandages streaked rustylooking and his face drawn and wild and his brown felt hat as crooked on him as he was on the mule.

Chapter Twenty-Two ★★★★★★★★

☞ It wasn't hard to tell he'd had a steep, painful time getting this far and now wasn't even feeling too happy he'd made it: everybody was staring at him, and he was going to have to tell all about it again, one finger and one toe at a time, and get mad and work like the devil to get people to treat him like nothing was wrong, and it hurt me to look at him and try and figure out what he was going to say and how in the wide world I was going to tell him about the gold.

He had his crutches stuck in one scabbard and a short-barreled rifle with some kind of sawed-off stock in another, and he clicked his tongue at the mule and give the reins a shake and come at us slow.

Zack seen how awkward it all was and went forward like a welcome and says, "Kit, by God, it's good to see you."

Kit didn't say nothing, but looked all around careful at the long tom and riffle box and each of us, not giving me no more'n he give anybody else, like he had to be sure he'd got his voice gathered up.

"You left going uphill, and you come back uphill," Zack says. "So you must of went downhill somewheres else."

"In a hurry," Kit says.

"Your brother told us about the frostbite," Zack says.

"I bet he did," Kit says.

Sounding mad all of a sudden, Zack says, "What did I tell you? Didn't I tell you how to look out for it? I must of told you ten times how I—"

"You told me everything ten times," Kit says, seeming to get a bit stronger. "How much color's showing? How much you panning in a day?"

"Well, I—" Zack looked around like he expected me to horn in and get this settled straight off, but I couldn't get my mouth up to it yet.

"Didn't Ike tell you?" Kit says, snapping a look between me and Zack. "I told him to work my share till I healed up some, and if he ain't good enough, I'm here to help."

"He told us," Zack says.

Kit glared at Staggs. "Any objections?"

Smiling and giving hisself a good scratch inside the bearskin, Staggs says, "Far as I care, you can make yourself right at home, pardner. Long as you can figure out how to sign your name by tomorrow."

"I can do a lot of things might surprise you," Kit says, going red in the face and white along the mouth.

"Well, we had ourselves a couple surprises already," Zack says, looking at me again and sort of nudging me from ten foot off.

"Sign what tomorrow?" Kit says. "What was that Wootton doing up here? I passed him down at Whittle Fork, going so fast he had to shake hands with grandma."

"Far as I could tell, he split his time between falling in the crick and talking," Zack says.

Kit looked at the riffle box with the scrapings all down in one end and says, "Well, then, come on. What's happening? You done some panning—how much is a share worth?" And when Zack didn't answer right off, Kit says, "Don't matter if my brother knows. Our deal's between him and me, and if he wants to do the work, I'll do the paying out of my share, strictly mine."

"Look," Zack says, going to his side and starting to touch Kit's knee, then not doing it. "I don't want to presume or nothing, but would you like some help getting down so's you can set and rest a while?"

I could see Kit didn't want to do it, least not in front of everybody, but he must of been saddle-sore and arm-cramped and didn't look like he could put much weight on his stirrups, so he done it as fast and casual as he could, getting an arm around Zack's neck and throwing one leg over and sliding off the saddle and bracing one crutch down ahead of time to keep his boots from hitting the ground too hard. Then he used both crutches like he didn't really need them and set hisself on the edge of the long tom and leveled his breath off.

Staggs says, "Your brother says you panned a little shot gold someplace up in them fearful mountains."

"You are damn well told I did," Kit says, straightening his legs out so's only the heels touched and folding his arms so's the stubby bandages was hid under the sleeves of his dark-blue jacket.

"Whereabouts?" Staggs says, grinning slow and probably not expecting no answer.

"Think I'd tell you?" Kit says, one side of his lip sneering up. "I know where there's a pocket laying on bedrock, not more'n three foot down, and if there ain't a thousand dollars—or more—in there, I'll eat your winter blanket without no molasses on it."

I says, "Kit, I struck it rich today."

"What?" he says, scowling and looking like I'd interrupted a good one he'd been meaning to tell a long time, which I had, a-purpose, because I didn't want him to feel no worse about it than he was bound to, and if I let him commence puffing and bragging too much, he wouldn't have nothing to fall back on.

"Why ain't you and that girl making yourselves useful around here?" he says. "Earn your keep. Lots to do around a mining camp, case you hadn't noticed. If there's nothing else handy, you can always chop kindling."

"I struck it rich today," I says.

And this time he heard me, and it sunk in a little ways. "You?" he says, and I seen him putting the idea in the joke slot in his head, and he smiled around at his pardners but didn't see no jokes on their face. "Where?"

"On our claim, up on the steep gullyside," I says. "I was digging a well, and I—"

"That's just about where you'd *dig* a well, ain't it?" he says, but he begun going all pale and empty-looking.

"And I struck a lode," I says.

"A heap of that float must of washed into the crick over the years," Zack says. "We'll find our share once we dig down a ways. Must be pocketed all along here. All's we got to do is use a little elbow grease." He paused a second, but Kit didn't say nothing, so he went on. "And we're all going to get paid twelve dollars a day and be some kind of half-pardners with your brother when him and Wootton set up a flume and a stamping mill and probably a hydraulic telegraph or some such a thing. I seen it done in California."

"I don't want to be nobody's half-assed pardner," Kit says.

"You're already a half-assed pardner of me and Staggs and Badger," Zack says.

"Maybe he don't want no twelve dollars a day," Staggs says, sounding hopeful. "If he don't, we'll get Wootton up to sixteen each."

To help out and get that look off of Kit's face, I says, "You can be a pardner in the Hearthstone Mining Company too, Kit."

"What the hell is that?" he says.

"It's me and Millie's company," I says. "And we wouldn't of come all this way and found it but for you. And I reckon we'll need somebody to—to help out and help do something." Trouble was, I couldn't think of nothing he'd be able to do.

"We'll need somebody to watch over it when we're not here," Millie says.

"That's right," I says. "Like a watchman. Or—"

"Somebody that can keep on his toes," Staggs says. "Keep his fingers in the pie."

"Shut up," Zack says. "Fact is, you're going to have yourself a rich brother. That's the main point."

But Kit looked the way somebody's sposed to look when their family's been wiped out in a flood, and he says to Zack, "You mean there was a quartz lead _right next_ to my claim?"

"About two hundred and fifty dollars a ton," Staggs says, enjoying it. "Or maybe three hundred."

"No telling how long it is," Zack says kind of apologetic.

"And my goddamn kid _brother_ found it?" Kit says. "That couldn't find his own ass with both hands?"

Which didn't make me feel any too polite and helpful and generous and sweet-spirited and noble and all them other virtues, such as trustful and pure in heart and hopeful and being my brother's keeper and a friend to man or beast I had been hearing about since my ears was big enough to catch that kind of mess of pottage (and which I don't exactly disbelieve in), but I says, "The offer's still good, though I don't know how Wootton's going to have the papers wrote up. We'll have to—"

"Me work for you?" Kit says. "For you and her?" He glanced around, gaping at the comical wonder of it all. "Why, I wouldn't work for you if I—if I—"

"I didn't say you'd have to do no work," I says.

"This here's going to be some pardnership," Staggs says.

"I can see it now: every goddamn Bender in the Territory's going to be loafing around on his dead butt while us poor folks—"

"You keep busting shovels, and there won't be nothing for nobody to do," Zack says.

"I believe we'd best tend to our supper, Mr. Bender," Millie says. "Do you suppose your brother would care to join us for rice, apples, beans, bacon, and bread? He must be tired and hungry after his journey."

"Don't mind if I do," Staggs says.

"Me neither," Badger says.

Kit hove hisself forward and got his crutches shoved at the ground and sort of clumb up them till he could get the padded crosspieces under his armpits, and I come up close to give it one more try. "You wouldn't be working for me and Millie but yourself," I says. "You got to think of the future."

"What the hell do you think I'm thinking about?" Kit says, his voice sounding like a sheet being ripped down the middle to make rags, and he took a hobble forward on his crutches, aiming for the saddle on his mule. "I didn't come all this way and freeze myself up in them mountains just so's you could—" He made a grab with both stubs at the rifle butt, but Zack half-turned him and give him a little shove which wouldn't of bothered him more'n a couple inches if he'd had his toes on, but made him stagger off balance now, and while he was straightening out, he took a swing at me with one crutch, whizzing the end past my face and just nicking my nose, and it slipped out of his stubs and went end over end into the crick, and he crouched for balance but tipped over anyway and sprawled on the ground, finally just giving up and laying down sideways and commencing to bawl.

Zack led me off a ways and says, "You go on now. I'll talk some sense into him." He looked back at Kit, who had drawed his knees up into his belly and was holding his arms in close to his chest and his bandages under his chin and his eyes closed and his mouth open with crying sounds coming out of it I hadn't heard since Pa had first whipped us when we was both little.

"*Maybe* I will," Zack says.

And me and Millie went off, but when we come to our house, she says, "Mr. Bender, I believe we had better set off before dark and sleep somewhere on the trail and get those papers signed tomorrow, if the bank looks promising." She was talking quiet and soft and looking at me kind of sorry. "I believe it would be safer."

And I felt my head nodding at her all by itself.

I pulled the tub up out of our gold mine, which still didn't look like much though there was enough daylight so's I could see the dark-gray patch on two sides of the bottom, looking to be even thicker than the two foot I'd called it. And I put the wheelborrow back together and got back to our house without falling in the crick and helped load up Mr. Blue, who'd come wandering in early to get his suppertime oats and left-over beans. We didn't leave nothing behind we wanted to keep, and though neither of us said nothing about it, it seemed like we might not come back, and when we started off—with plenty of cherry-colored light left—Millie kept looking over her shoulder at the lean-to and the start of the house and biting her lips and frowning.

Zack was out panning at the riffle box when we come by, and Kit's mule was hitched to the side of the hut with the bedroll took off it. He stood up and nodded and says, "Probably a good idea to go."

"Is he all right?" I says.

"He will be, I spose," Zack says. "But I don't like to tell a man what his own brother's like. I figure he must know already, and if he don't, he won't believe it."

I untied the whipsaw and leant it up against one of the

sluice boxes. "Give him that whenever it won't make him mad," I says. "If he should happen to have somebody tie a rope from wrist to wrist, he could work one end of a whip-saw pretty good, couldn't he? And maybe feel better about earning his share?"

"Maybe so," Zack says. "We'll try him on it."

"I don't reckon Staggs can dig out too awful much of that ore before Mr. Smith gets back up here tomorrow, do you?" I says.

"I don't reckon so," Zack says. "Too much like work."

Millie and Mr. Blue waited patient while I scuffed around and tried to work out how to say it. "I expect we'll need some kind of a foreman or straw boss or something if this mine gets to going. Spose you wouldn't take no job like that, would you? For shares?"

"No thank you kindly," Zack says. "If this don't pan out here, I'll take what I got saved up and see if I can find me some other crick, maybe up a thousand foot or two. Even if it's like trying to find the long end of a square quilt, I enjoy the looking."

"Me too," I says. "But I didn't get much chance."

"Nothing to stop you from looking someplace else if you feel like it," Zack says.

Millie reached under the oilskin over my wheelborrow and done what I had been too shy to ask her for: she took out the crock of quicksilver and handed it to Zack and says, "We would like to present this five pounds of quick-silver to our partners in the Collywobble Mining Company who can make better use of it with their kind of gold than we can with ours, isn't that right, Mr. Bender?"

"It sure is," I says, feeling like smiling again for the first time in about two hours.

"With our compliments and best wishes for a royal show of color in every pan and riffle box," she says, handing him the plug of tobacco too. "Chew it in good health."

Zack took them both and give a little bow and says, "We

are deeply obliged, Mr. and Miz Bender, and will put both to good use, I do assure you, by God, and I hope you're both a whole lot happier rich than I was, because you sure as hell was a whole lot happier poor than me. You've been a sight for sore eyes."

"I hope you'll see many a more," I says.

"Well, if Staggs and that brother of yours don't kill each other by sunup—and me and Badger in the bargain—I expect to," he says.

"Bless you," Millie says.

"I been blessed before, Miz Bender, and so have you, I expect, and the more's the welcomer," he says. "Go on, think about something besides gold, soon as you can manage."

"We mean to," I says. I shook hands with Zack's cold, muddy claw, and we started off, and we could hear Staggs yelling up in the hut all the way till we got over the first hump.

Chapter Twenty-Three ★★★★★★★

☞ You can't be sad or sorry long by a crick—it's always being too cheery at you—nor you can't be any too extra proud of yourself sleeping outdoors in the dark with your unprotected lawful wedded wife, no matter how blissful you might happen to feel like under a wheelborrow, so between the two of them I felt happy and downhearted all night, even when I was asleep.

But after dawn, the further we got downhill, the more it seemed like we was going *towards* something instead of just away from it, and though I didn't know what it was, I sure enjoyed the company. Millie commenced singing again, off and on, and I did too, but we tried to keep it quiet so's we wouldn't start any more of a stampede than there already was. We passed six men in two bunches, all heading up toward the Collywobble and Hearthstone, which was going to give Staggs plenty of exercise chasing them off his territory, a dog's job not requiring no fingers nor toes nor brains but just a gift for making noise, so maybe Kit could learn a trade like that.

And the seventh man along just about noon was Mr. Smith, working his horse into a lather by just keeping it moving, and he tipped his big black hat real polite and says, "Mr. Bender, Miz Bender?" And the eighth man was behind him on a bay mare, a flinty-faced, narrow-between-the-eyes-looking man with a Wootton-the-store-keep cut to him, maybe a cousin. Mr. Smith fumbled in a saddlebag and says, "I have the limited partnership papers all made up, and if you'd care to sign, we could cut out one step of the process."

I started to say all right, but Millie says, "No thank you, Mr. Smith. When the other claimholders sign, you bring the papers down to the bank, and we'll try to do everything at once, tidily and leisurely and businesslike."

"Whatever you say, ma'am," Mr. Smith says. He tipped his head at the man behind him. "This is Si Wootton, who I took the liberty—with President Wootton's approval—of hiring on as a guard up at the mine. He'll see nothing gets mislaid or dug up."

Si didn't say nothing but just memorized us and then looked off at a clump of trees, waiting to get moving again, and I expected Staggs and Badger would find him a bit hard to talk to, but interesting.

Mr. Smith says, "I'll bring the papers down personally. Soon as possible. President Wootton's expecting you, and the preliminary assay averages two hundred and ninety dollars a ton!" His voice had commenced getting louder, but he hushed it up for the money, and they started up and rode around a boulder with Mr. Smith still grinning backwards at us.

We went on, keeping quiet and thinking about the money (least I was), and I says, "How many tons do you reckon'd be in a lode like that?"

"If Mr. Orfrey's right, perhaps a hundred or a thousand or more," she says, being good at arithmetic. "So we're going to have to decide what to do with thirty thousand dollars or even a great deal more, less expenses and commissions."

"Least, now I'll be able to pay you back your ma's money," I says.

She laughed and sang a piece of a song about where blossoms grow and winds are low and brooks run lightly by, but she had to leave off when we run into five stampeders in one cluster with that hurry-up, wide-eyed, searching look on their face, scanning us all over but scairt to ask right out if we knew something they didn't, and it looked like Mr. Smith might of stirred up a little interest (say about three percent) down in Denver City because they was pointing at the hoofprints here and there and telling each other to get a move on, some carrying small packs and some with none at all.

And by the time we got down on the flats we'd passed three more strung out by theirselves but with that bound-and-determined-to-bust look on their face, which meant there wouldn't be no shortage of entertainment up on the claims for a while to come—what with sixteen coming and only two on business—and then the seventeenth up ahead coming at us on a skinny mule was my pa.

He looked skinny too and smaller than I remembered and kind of dark in the eyes and cheeks like he'd been left out in foul weather. His felt hat was streaked and stained, and his left pants leg was tore halfway up to the knee, and he was hunched forward over his saddlehorn like he wished he could set on something besides his own behind. I seen him and knew him before he knew me, and Millie'd only seen him a couple times before in her life and wasn't expecting him to be nothing but another stampeder, so I had a while longer than them to figure out what to think, but it didn't do no good. I never could think much around my old man, which was his opinion too.

I stopped and set down the handles, and Millie stopped singing and give me a curious look, and when he was about fifteen foot away, he seemed to snap awake and reined in and stared at the both of us and says, "Well, well, well, if it ain't my own flesh and blood."

"Hello, Pa," I says. "Where's Ma?"

He pulled out a crinkled, thin, dirty sheet of paper from inside his jacket and unfolded what I reckonized as Kit's map and says, "Is this Slab Crick?"

"Yes," I says.

"Can't get nobody to tell you nothing in this damn country. Is Kit up there?"

"Yes," I says. "Where's Ma?"

"I don't spose there's any of that gold left up there," he says, talking faster now and giving a twitch with one side of his face. "Kit didn't find none, did he?"

"Yes, he found some," I says.

"How much?" His mouth hung open a little while he waited.

"Hard to say. *Where's Ma?*"

He give an impatient shake like Ma wasn't no proper kind of subject. "She didn't want to go no further. She's way the hell back at Fort Kearny, far as I know. Got herself a job as a maid, which is just about what she's good for." He glanced Millie over and nodded like she was about what he expected, and he says to her, "And you'll find out what *you're* good for when your pa catches up with you."

"We're married," I says.

He started to laugh, then just let it sigh out instead and shook his head like it was all too ripe for him, and he says, "Where the hell are you going with that contraption?"

"We're going down to Denver City for a while," I says. "Haven't quite made up our mind what we're going to do."

"I'd ought to skin your ass for running off," he says.

"Looks like I done just about what you been doing yourself, except I didn't desert my wife," I says.

He tasted that for a few seconds, then says, "If Kit's found gold, why the hell ain't you up there working it with him? Don't you have no family sense?"

"Millie's my family, and Kit didn't want to work with me," I says.

"Him?" he says, scowling and at the same time looking eager and lip-licking. "Well, I'll learn *him* a little family sense then. He better want to work with *me*." He looked me up and down. "You filled out and toughened up, didn't you. Well, you just turn right around and show me where that claim is because we can probably use every able-bodied man or boy we can get. They tell me it's hard work, but if we all pull together we can probably swing it."

"I don't feel like hunting for gold no more," I says.

It cost him a good bit to swaller being counterdicted like that, and he made half a motion to get off of his mule, but he didn't. "Same as always," he says, shortening his upper lip. "If you wasn't a fool, you was a quitter. And now you're going to be both."

"You just follow that crick, Pa, and good luck," I says.

"Don't wish me none of your kind of luck," he says. "You don't even know what it is."

"I surely don't," I says, picking up my wheelborrow handles and starting off. "I'd ask you to kiss my bride, but I got too much respeck for her."

"So you learnt how to backtalk, did you?" he says after me. "Will wonders never cease?"

"I hope not," I says, not looking back.

"Good thing you got that ax along, boy," he says, raising his voice.

I set them handles down and turned and give him a good looking over. He had his mule walking again but was slunched around in the saddle, ready for more sass if I was offering any, and I says, "If you ask Mr. Smith up there nice and polite and mention my name, you might get took on for twelve dollars a day."

"Why should I mention your goddamn name?" he says. "Same as mine, ain't it?"

I turned and started wheelborrowing again, and he hollered something I couldn't understand, not having the carrying power of Staggs, and when I glanced back after a bit, he was just a mule-colored speck on the crickbank, heading for the foothills, and for a long spell I imagined what a fine time he was going to have up there on the claims, getting it all figured out and argued out and maybe screamed and rassled out, and at least it would give Kit something new to fret over. The only one I felt sorry for was Zack, who'd probably have to listen to all of it, unless Mr. Smith decided to make Pa see the light early on.

Millie kept quiet a long time, letting me think it out, and then she says, "We can send your mother some money by mail wagon. Mr. Wootton will know how."

"All right," I says. "Let her make up her own mind if she wants to come this way or go back the other. And I want to send some money to your pa for grubstaking me."

"That's very nice of you, Mr. Bender," she says.

"And if I knew where that Sam was at, I'd send him some money to buy Mr. Blue."

And we went along some more, and Millie begun humming not much louder than the crick, and I hummed along after, Heigh-ho, nobody home, Food and drink and money have we none, which didn't seem to fit too good no more, but my spirits got up out of my boots and clumb my backbone and tipped my hat crooked, and I was feeling light in the heels and light in the head, and I says, "Pa's bound to be galloping down here to town before long and telling me how to do everything, and I don't think I can stand the noise."

"Maybe you won't have to listen," she says. "Maybe we

can make some kind of arrangement with Mr. Wootton. Have you ever sobered up a lawyer?"

"No, but I learn quick," I says.

She was quiet for a spell, then says, "Mr. Bender, which would you prefer to do: buy up half the lots in Denver City when the men desert them to run up Slab Creek to look for what we've already found, or build us a house somewhere with a bathtub in it?"

"Well, if it come to a choice, I'd as soon do both," I says.

"You don't want to dig for gold any more, do you?"

"Why should I?" I says. "I already know where it's at. I'd just as soon go someplace and dig for water."

We dried out an old lawyer who had about give up the idea of doing anything but creating empty corn-whiskey jugs, and he turned out to be near as smart as Millie when he could see straight, and he fixed up a set of papers that Wootton finally agreed to, and they made it so we didn't have to go back up there to Slab Crick if we didn't want to watch the dirt being washed and the rock pounded to smithers (which we didn't), but could go off and let the money pile up for us all by itself, which don't seem right but I hated to complain.

And Wootton talked me into putting the *Millicent Slaughter* on display in his bank with a brass plate on it with my name and its (which took care of Millie automatic) scratched on as discoverers of the "Fabulous Hearthstone Lode," which means people told fables about it such as two or three times the amount of gold actually dug out in the next year and a half (before it run short), which was $379,943, only part of it getting stole here and there by bankers and other kind of thieves.

We offered Pa a good-paying job which consisted of keeping away from us, and he done it gladly after getting in his share of yelling. We paid Kit to pretend like he was supervising up at the mine, though he only lasted two months, then rode off prospectoring in the mountains. And we only bought up about a quarter of Denver City instead of half because we didn't feel like living in it for fear they'd make me Mayor, so we had ourselves a place built right up against the foothills with me doing my best not to interfere with nothing important while the carpenters whacked away, and I took my wheelborrow back then, plate and all, and used it to dig us a sweet well, finding no gold on the way down and just as glad. We put Mr. Blue to pasture and resolved we was going to keep our troth just as plighted as it could be.

Ma never showed up after we sent her the money, and I didn't blame her none. Maybe she hired the Major's wife with it or done something just as foolish.

The Collywobble paid off pretty good till the Hearthstone begun fluming water in from a crick over in the next gulch and flooded them out, and after that Zack, Staggs, and Badger had the pleasure of drawing down twelve dollars a day for doing nothing but watch, but Zack got tired of that right off and headed up into steep country, saying (when he come down for supplies) he'd let me know if he run into Kit and that he was probably all right, but I doubt it and ain't heard nothing yet.

We're getting sort of restless now, and the ladies have begun bothering Millie to dress up all the time and learn them to talk fancy, so I been thinking of pushing on to California, just to keep Millie from being a liar about it, and she wants to too, but we haven't made up our mind for sure yet, not feeling no shortage of pleasure where we're at, though we mean to keep our eye on Ever After.

And like you might expect, there wasn't all that much different to being rich. You just got more money than before, but the same number of hours a day and the same mealtimes, and you stand on the same feet and do your walking on the same legs and do your worrying with the same head and your singing out of the same mouth.

But it does seem a fearful pity that all them people come and went and some stayed, dead or even less comfortable, and out of the whole straggling shivaree of high-hopers and firm-believers, there wasn't but eight or ten like me and Millie who chanced on to enough paydirt to turn their fellow mortals green for miles around, like we was as powerful as the sun on leaves. And the mystery of it has stuck with me strong as any wonder: now that I went and found gold, I feel like I ought to be able to go back and do my journey all over and *not* find gold and feel just as good and grand and full of spring and summer sweetness. But there don't seem to be no way to manage but how Zack done it: spend the whole mess and work out some way to feel as rich as I done when I used to sleep under that wheelborrow with my first and only love.